基礎文法寶典 ❺
Essential English Usage & Grammar

編著／J. B. Alter
審訂／劉美皇　呂香瑩

三民書局

國家圖書館出版品預行編目資料

Essential English Usage & Grammar 基礎文法寶典
／J. B. Alter編著;劉美皇,呂香瑩審訂.－－初版
一刷.－－臺北市: 三民，2008
　　冊；　公分

　　ISBN 978–957–14–5105–3　（平裝）

　　1.英語 2.語法

805.16　　　　　　　　　　　　　　　97018552

© Essential English Usage & Grammar
基礎文法寶典 5

編 著 者	J. B. Alter
審　　訂	劉美皇　呂香瑩
企 劃 編 輯	王伊平
責 任 編 輯	彭彥哲
美 術 設 計	郭雅萍
發 行 人	劉振強
著 作 財 產 權 人	三民書局股份有限公司
發 行 所	三民書局股份有限公司
	地址　臺北市復興北路386號
	電話　(02)25006600
	郵撥帳號　0009998–5
門 市 部	(復北店) 臺北市復興北路386號
	(重南店) 臺北市重慶南路一段61號
出 版 日 期	初版一刷　2008年11月
編　　號	S 807540

行政院新聞局登記證局版臺業字第○二○○號

有著作權‧不准侵害

ISBN　978–957–14–5105–3　（平裝）

http://www.sanmin.com.tw　三民網路書店
※本書如有缺頁、破損或裝訂錯誤，請寄回本公司更換。

Essential English Usage & Grammar by J. B. ALTER
Copyright © 1979 by Times Educational Co., Ltd., Hong Kong
Chinese translation copyright © 2008 by San Min Book Co., Ltd.

序

　　如果說，單字是英文的血肉，文法就是英文的骨架。想要打好英文基礎，兩者實應相輔相成，缺一不可。

　　只是，單字可以死背，文法卻不然。

　　學習文法，如果沒有良師諄諄善誘，沒有好書細細剖析，只落得個見樹不見林，徒然勞心費力，實在可惜。

　　Guru 原義指的是精通於某領域的「達人」，因此，這一套「文法 Guru」系列叢書，本著 Guru「導師」的精神，要告訴您：親愛的，我把英文文法變簡單了！

　　「文法 Guru」系列，適用對象廣泛，從初習英文的超級新鮮人、被文法糾纏得寢食難安的中學生，到鎮日把玩英文的專業行家，都能在這一套系列叢書中找到最適合自己的夥伴。

　　深願「文法 Guru」系列，能成為您最好的學習夥伴，伴您一同輕鬆悠遊英文學習的美妙世界。

　　有了「文法 Guru」，文法輕鬆上路！

前言

「**基礎文法寶典**」一套五冊，是專為中學生與一般社會大眾所設計，作為基礎課程教材或是課外自學之用。

英語教師往往對結構、句型、語法等為主的教學模式再熟悉不過。然而，現在學界普遍意識到**文法在語言學習的過程中亦佔有一席之地**，少了文法這一環，英語教學便顯得空洞。有鑑於此，市場上漸漸興起一股「**功能性文法**」的風潮。功能性文法旨在列舉用法並協助讀者熟悉文法專有名詞，而後者便是用以解釋及界定一語言各種功能的利器。

本套書各冊內容編排詳盡，涵蓋所有用法及文法要點；除此之外，本套書最強調的便是從不斷的練習中學好英文。每章所附的練習題皆經特別設計，提供讀者豐富多元的演練題型，舉凡**完成** (completion)、**修正** (modification)、**轉換** (conversion)、**合併** (integration)、**重述** (restatement)、**改寫** (alteration)、**變形** (transformation) 及**代換** (transposition)，應有盡有。

熟讀此書，將可幫助您完全理解各種文法及正確的表達方式，讓您在課業學習或日常生活上的英文程度突飛猛進。

給讀者的話

本書一套共五本，共分為二十一章，從最基礎的各式詞類介紹，一直到動詞的進階應用、基本書寫概念等，涵蓋所有的基本文法要義，為您建立一個完整的自修體系，並以豐富多樣的練習題為最大特色。

本書的主要細部單元包括：

USAGE PRACTICE →每個文法條目說明之下，皆有大量的例句或用法實例，讓您充分了解該文法規則之實際應用方式。

注意→很多文法規則皆有特殊的應用，或者是因應不同情境而產生相關變化，這些我們都以較小字的提示，列在本單元中。

但是我們會用→文法規則的例外情況也不少，我們在這單元直接以舉例的方式，說明這些不依循規則的情況。

小練習→每節介紹後，會有針對該節內容所設計的一段習題，可讓您即時驗證前面所學的內容。

應用練習→每章的內容結束後，我們都提供了非常充分的應用練習，而且題型豐富，各有其學習功能。建議您不要急於在短時間內將練習做完，而是漸進式地逐步完成，這樣可達成更好的學習效果。

本書文法內容完善，習題亦兼具廣度與深度，是您自修學習之最佳選擇，也可作為文法疑難的查閱參考，值得您細細研讀，慢慢體會。

基礎文法寶典 ❺
Essential English Usage & Grammar

目次

Chapter 18 直接引句與間接引句

18-0 基本概念	2
18-1 直接引句	2
18-2 間接引句	4
18-3 直接引句改為間接引句	9
18-4 祈使句或感嘆句改為間接引句	16
Chapter 18 應用練習	21

Chapter 19 附加問句

19-0 基本概念	38
19-1 附加問句的功能及構成	38
19-2 附加問句的主詞	40
19-3 附加問句及答句的動詞	42
Chapter 19 應用練習	45

Chapter 20 三大子句

20-1 名詞子句	55
20-2 形容詞子句	59

20–3 副詞子句　64

Chapter 20 應用練習　71

習題解答　136

Chapter 21 基本書寫概念

21–1 大寫字母　81

21–2 句點　83

21–3 逗點　84

21–4 引號　89

21–5 問號　91

21–6 驚嘆號　93

21–7 省略號和所有格符號　94

21–8 連字號　95

21–9 破折號　97

21–10 冒號　99

21–11 分號　101

21–12 括弧　103

21–13 商業書信的基本格式　104

Chapter 21 應用練習　106

基礎文法寶典 ❺

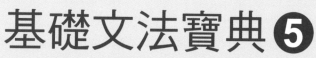

Essential English Usage & Grammar

Chapter 18 直接引句與間接引句

18-0 基本概念

直接引句是一字不改地引述某人所說的話，而間接引句則是用自己的陳述來表達別人所說的話。

18-1 直接引句

(a) 說話者所說的話和最後的標點符號要放在引號內。

> **USAGE PRACTICE**
>
> ▶ I said, "**Please take this to Mr. Stevens.**" 我說：「請把這個交給史蒂文森先生。」
>
> ▶ "**Shall we go now?**" she asked. 「我們現在要離開了嗎？」她問。
>
> ▶ I said, "**Please put the books on the table.**" 我說：「請把書放在桌上。」
>
> ▶ She exclaimed, "**What a beautiful day this is!**" 她大叫：「多麼美好的一天啊！」
>
> ▶ "**Let's go out for a walk,**" she said. 「我們出去散步吧。」她說。
>
> ▶ "**Did you do it?**" the inspector asked the man. 「這是你做的嗎？」督察員問這男人。

(b) 稱呼語在直接引句中要以逗號和其他的字隔開。

> **USAGE PRACTICE**
>
> ▶ He said, "**Angela, do your work quietly.**" 他說：「安琪拉，靜靜地做你的工作。」
>
> ▶ "**How many times do I have to tell you, Ricky, to behave yourself?**" she asked.
>
> 「瑞奇，我必須告訴你多少次要守規矩？」她問。
>
> ▶ The teacher said, "**John, will you come here?**" 老師說：「約翰，你會來這裡嗎？」
>
> ▶ "**I want to ask you something, Peter,**" the man said.
>
> 「彼得，我想問你一些事。」這男人說。
>
> ▶ "**Come here, Felix, and help me carry this load,**" his father said.
>
> 「菲利克斯，來這裡幫我搬東西。」他爸爸說。

(c) 當句中有別的引句時，必須使用另一組引號（通常為單引號）。

▶ He remarked, **"Mary said 'How do you do?' when she saw Tom."**

　他說：「當瑪麗看到湯姆時，她說『你好嗎？』」

▶ **"She replied 'I don't know' when I asked her about it,"** he said.

　「當我問她時，她回答『我不知道』。」他說。

(d) 有些直接引句聽起來像是疑問句，但切記，這類句子並不使用問號。

▶ **"Will you kindly keep quiet,"** the teacher said.　「請你保持安靜。」老師說。

▶ **"I wonder where he is now,"** I mused.　「我想知道他現在在那裡。」我若有所思地說。

(e) 直接引句有時候會被分開，請注意標點符號的使用。

▶ **"If she finishes her work,"** Colin said, **"she will help me."**

　「如果她做完工作，」柯林說，「她會幫我。」

▶ **"It's getting late,"** I said. **"We had better go now."**

　「天色逐漸變暗了。」我說，「我們最好現在就走。」

請將下列直接引句加上正確的標點符號，並注意大小寫。

1. Where are you going he asked me.

　→ _____

2. Please show me the way to the post office she said.

　→ _____

3. I would like to know what Mary is doing now said the man.

　→ _____

4. Father the girl called there's someone here to see you.

　→ _____

5. Samuel the teacher said can you tell me where Brussels is?

　→ _____

6. I am a doctor he said I can help you.

→ _____

7. He said it is already eight o'clock.

→ _____

8. Do you want to go with us Liza I asked.

→ _____

9. Thank goodness that you are safe she exclaimed I have been so worried about you!

→ _____

10. Won't you give me a coin sir the beggar pleaded I am so hungry.

→ _____

11. He asked anxiously are you sure that you're all right you still look a bit shaken.

→ _____

12. Give me time to consider your proposition I said I'll give you my answer tomorrow.

→ _____

13. When are you going to France she asked me perhaps I'll go to the airport to see you off.

→ _____

14. My father said all right when I asked him for permission the little girl stated.

→ _____

15. He scolded his younger brother what a careless boy you are now you'll have to do your work all over again.

→ _____

16. Aren't you hungry she asked you haven't eaten anything all day!

→ _____

17. Cease fire the major ordered.

→ _____

18. Alex where have you been all this while his sister asked your friends have been here for almost an hour.

→ _____

☞ 更多相關習題請見本章應用練習 Part 1。

18-2 間接引句

(a) 間接引句之前會使用多種不同的引述詞語。

USAGE PRACTICE	
▶ Josh wondered... 喬許想知道…	▶ He wants to know... 他想要知道…
▶ She asked me... 她問我…	▶ They guessed... 他們猜…
▶ Tell me... 告訴我…	▶ Please let me know... 請讓我知道…
▶ They don't know... 他們不知道…	▶ Do you know...? 你知道…？

(b) 在間接引句中，主詞要置於動詞之前，就像一般直述句的結構。在間接引句中，不使用引號、逗號或問號。

USAGE PRACTICE	
直接引句	間接引句
▶ "What is it?"	▶ Do you know what **it is**?
「這是什麼？」	你知道這是什麼嗎？
▶ "Where does Ben live?"	▶ She wants to know where **Ben lives**.
「班住在哪裡？」	她想知道班住在哪裡。
▶ "Why are they upset?"	▶ Tell me why **they are upset**.
「他們為什麼不高興？」	告訴我他們為什麼不高興。
▶ She asked me, "When did he leave?"	▶ She asked me when **he left**.
她問我：「他什麼時候離開的？」	她問我他什麼時候離開的。

(c) 疑問詞（如 what、where、how 等）可以直接放在引述動詞之後，引導間接引句。

USAGE PRACTICE	
直接引句	間接引句
▶ "What are you doing?"	▶ He asked me **what** I was doing.
「你在做什麼？」	他問我在做什麼。
▶ "Where does he live?"	▶ She wants to know **where** he lives.
「他住在哪裡？」	她想知道他住在哪裡。
▶ "Why did you stop?"	▶ He wanted to know **why** I had stopped.
「你為何停下來？」	他想知道我為何停下來。

▶ "When will she leave?"	▶ Tell me **when** she will leave.
「她何時會離開？」	告訴我，她何時會離開。
▶ "How do you feel?"	▶ I asked her **how** she felt.
「你感覺如何？」	我問她感覺如何。

(d) 當直接引句是敘述句而非疑問句時，可以用 that 引導間接引句。此時的 that 可以省略。

USAGE PRACTICE	
直接引句	間接引句
▶ I told him, "I'll do it."	▶ I told him **(that)** I would do it.
我告訴他：「我會做這件事。」	我告訴他説我會做這件事。
▶ He said, "She is sick."	▶ He said **(that)** she was sick.
他説：「她病了。」	他説她病了。

(e) 當直接引句是要用 yes 或 no 回答的問句時，就用 if 或 whether 引導間接引句。

USAGE PRACTICE	
直接引句	間接引句
▶ "Is he in good health?"	▶ I don't know **whether** he is in good health.
「他健康嗎？」	我不知道他是否健康。
▶ "Is he asleep?"	▶ She asked me **whether** he was asleep.
「他在睡覺嗎？」	她問我他是否在睡覺。
▶ "Will you come as soon as possible?"	▶ I asked her **if** she would come as soon as possible. 我問她是否會盡快來。
「你會儘快來嗎？」	
▶ "Will he be back soon?"	▶ I wanted to know **if** he would be back soon. 我想知道他是否會很快回來。
「他會很快回來嗎？」	
▶ "Has she changed a lot?"	▶ I asked him **if** she had changed a lot.
「她已經改變很多了嗎？」	我問他她是否已經改變很多了。
▶ "Has he gone out?"	▶ I asked her **if** he had gone out.
「他已經出去了嗎？」	我問她他是否已經出去了。
▶ "Has Mr. Jackson left yet?"	▶ We inquired **whether** Mr. Jackson had left

「傑克森先生已經離開了嗎？」	yet. 我們問傑克森先生是否已經離開了。
▶ The teacher asked us, "Is the lesson clear enough?"	▶ The teacher asked us **if** the lesson was clear enough.
老師問我們：「這課夠清楚了嗎？」	老師問我們這課是否夠清楚了。
▶ The man asked us, "Did you have a nice time?" 那人問我們：「你們玩得很愉快嗎？」	▶ The man asked us **whether** we had had a nice time. 那人問我們是否玩得很愉快。
▶ "Have you brought it with you?" he asked me. 他問我：「你有帶它來嗎？」	▶ He asked me **whether** I had brought it with me. 他問我是否有帶它來。

小練習

請以提示字為句首，將下列句子改寫為間接引句。

1. What do you have in the cupboard? (*Tell me...*)

    → _____

2. How did she do it? (*Do you know...*)

    → _____

3. What is the message? (*Does he know...*)

    → _____

4. How is he? (*Ask him...*)

    → _____

5. When is the concert going to begin? (*Does she know...*)

    → _____

6. Where are the envelopes? (*Ask John...*)

    → _____

7. What is the population of India? (*Please tell me...*)

    → _____

8. When does the train from Reno arrive in Sacramento? (*I don't know...*)

    → _____

9. How long does it usually take you to walk to school? (*Tell me...*)

    → _____

10. Why don't elephants eat meat? (*Do you know...*)

→ _____

11. What is the meaning of "euthanasia"? (*Ask Professor Howard...*)

→ _____

12. How long will it be before the mangoes ripen? (*Do you know...*)

→ _____

13. Why don't you get more sleep? (*Tell me...*)

→ _____

14. Where does he usually park his car? (*I don't know...*)

→ _____

15. Which color does she prefer, blue or green? (*Ask her...*)

→ _____

16. How many children does he have? (*Do you know...*)

→ _____

17. What is the matter with everyone in the house? (*Please tell me...*)

→ _____

18. What are the results of the experiment in the laboratory? (*Ask him...*)

→ _____

19. Who is that girl over there? (*Ask Danny...*)

→ _____

20. When are you going to visit your aunt? (*Do you know...*)

→ _____

21. How do you operate this machine? (*I want to know...*)

→ _____

22. Are there any letters for me? (*I'll ask the boys...*)

→ _____

23. When are they going home? (*He wants to know...*)

→ _____

24. Why do they always quarrel? (*I will ask them...*)

→ _____

☞ 更多相關習題請見本章應用練習 Part 2。

18-3 直接引句改為間接引句

(a) 當陳述某人在過去所說的話時，間接引句須改為過去式。

USAGE PRACTICE	
直接引句	間接引句
▶ She asked me, "Where is Desmond?" 她問我：「德斯蒙在哪裡？」（現在簡單式）	▶ She asked me where Desmond **was**. 她問我德斯蒙在哪裡。（過去簡單式）
▶ He asked, "Why is the door locked?" 他問：「門為什麼鎖著？」（現在簡單式）	▶ He asked why the door **was** locked. 他問門為什麼鎖著。（過去簡單式）
▶ I inquired, "Does Mr. Long live here?" 我問：「龍先生住在這裡嗎？」（現在簡單式）	▶ I inquired whether Mr. Long **lived** there. 我問龍先生是否住在這裡。（過去簡單式）
▶ She said, "He came home late." 她說：「他很晚才回家。」（過去簡單式）	▶ She said that he **had come** home late. 她說他很晚才回家。（過去完成式）
▶ He wondered, "What is going on here?" 他想知道：「這裡發生了什麼事？」 （現在進行式）	▶ He wondered what **was going** on here. 他想知道這裡發生了什麼事。 （過去進行式）
▶ I said, "They are watching television." 我說：「他們正在看電視。」（現在進行式）	▶ I said that they **were watching** television. 我說他們正在看電視。（過去進行式）
▶ She asked me, "Where have you been?" 她問我：「你去了哪裡？」（現在完成式）	▶ She asked me where I **had been**. 她問我去了哪裡。（過去完成式）
▶ He asked, "Have they gone hunting?" 他問：「他們去打獵了嗎？」（現在完成式）	▶ He asked if they **had gone** hunting. 他問他們是否去打獵了。（過去完成式）
▶ I asked, "Will she arrive on time?" 我問：「她會準時到達嗎？」（未來簡單式）	▶ I asked if she **would arrive** on time. 我問她是否會準時到達。（過去式助動詞）
▶ He said, "they sing." 　　　　"they are singing." 　　　　"they will sing." 　　　　"they will have sung." 　　　　"they were singing."	▶ He said that they **sang**. 　　　　they **were singing**. 　　　　they **would sing**. 　　　　they **would have sung**. 　　　　they **had been singing**.

| "they sang."/"they have sung." | they **had sung**. |

 直接引句如果用 shall 表示徵詢意見，間接引句要改為 should。但如果是用 shall 來當未來式的助動詞（現在多用 will 取代），間接引句則應該用 would。

▶ I asked him, "**Shall** I cook something special?" 我問他：「我應該煮些特別的菜餚嗎？」
  → I asked him if I **should** cook something special. 我問他說我是否應該煮些特別的菜餚。
  （表示「徵求意見」，改 should）
▶ He asked himself, "**Shall** I be on time?" 他自問：「我要準時嗎？」
  → He asked himself whether he **should** be on time. 他自問他是否應該準時。
  （表示「徵求意見」，改 should）
▶ "When **shall** I be able to pass it?" he asked himself. 「何時我才能夠通過考試？」他問自己。
  → He asked himself when he **would** be able to pass it. 他問自己何時才能夠通過考試。
  （表示「未來」，改 would）

(b) 直接引句變成間接引句時，如果敘述的是「普遍的真理或一般事實」，時態可以不做改變。

USAGE PRACTICE

直接引句	間接引句
▶ She said, "Man needs air in order to live." 她說：「人類需要空氣才能存活。」	▶ She said that man **needs** air in order to live. 她說人類需要空氣才能存活。
▶ He told the boys, "The earth is a sphere." 他告訴男孩們：「地球是一個球體。」	▶ He told the boys that the earth **is** a sphere. 他告訴男孩們，地球是一個球體。
▶ He said, "The earth revolves around the sun." 他說：「地球繞著太陽轉。」	▶ He said that the earth **revolves** around the sun. 他說地球繞著太陽轉。
▶ She said, "A spider has eight legs." 她說：「蜘蛛有八隻腳。」	▶ She said that a spider **has** eight legs. 她說蜘蛛有八隻腳。
▶ She said, "Greenland is the largest island in the world." 她說：「格陵蘭是世界上最大的島嶼。」	▶ She said that Greenland **is** the largest island in the world. 她說格陵蘭是世界上最大的島嶼。
▶ "Owls hoot," he stated. 「貓頭鷹梟叫。」他說。	▶ He stated that owls **hoot**. 他說貓頭鷹梟叫。

| ▶ The teacher said, "The sun rises in the east." 老師說：「太陽從東邊升起。」 | ▶ The teacher said that the sun **rises** in the east. 老師說太陽從東邊升起。 |
| ▶ He asked me, "Where is Singapore?" 他問我：「新加坡在哪裡？」 | ▶ He asked me where Singapore **is**. 他問我新加坡在哪裡。 |

(c) 直接引句變成間接引句時，如果引述動詞是「現在式」或「未來式」，時態也不做改變。

USAGE PRACTICE	
直接引句	間接引句
▶ He says, "It will probably rain tomorrow." 他說：「明天可能會下雨。」	▶ He says that it **will** probably rain tomorrow. 他說明天可能會下雨。
▶ She says, "John is coming here today." 她說：「約翰今天要來這裡。」	▶ She says that John **is coming** here today. 她說約翰今天要來這裡。
▶ I will say, "It is not my fault." 我會說：「這不是我的過錯。」	▶ I will say that it **is** not my fault. 我會說這不是我的過錯。

(d) 直接引句變成間接引句時，若強調「目前仍在進行中或將會發生的動作」時，可以視語意而不改變時態。

USAGE PRACTICE	
直接引句	間接引句
▶ She said, "My mother is cooking in the kitchen." 她說：「我媽媽正在廚房煮飯。」	▶ She said that her mother **is cooking** in the kitchen. 她說她媽媽正在廚房煮飯。（目前仍在進行中）
▶ I said, "I will go with you." 我說：「我將會和他一起去。」	▶ I said that I **will go with him**. 我說我將會和他一起去。（將會發生的動作）

(e) 為了使語意更清楚，直接引句改為間接引句時，代名詞和所有格形容詞的變化以轉述者為主，其後的動詞也要做相對應的變化。

USAGE PRACTICE

直接引句	間接引句
▶ She said, "I have to wash my clothes." 她説：「我得去洗衣服了。」	▶ She said that **she had** to wash **her** clothes. 她説她得去洗衣服了。
▶ He said, "I am sick." 他説：「我病了。」	▶ He said that **he was** sick. 他説他病了。
▶ He said, "I am in the hall." 他説：「我在大廳裡。」	▶ He said that **he was** in the hall. 他説他在大廳裡。
▶ He said, "I am waiting for Joseph." 他説：「我正在等待約瑟夫。」	▶ He said that **he is** waiting for Joseph. 他説他正在等待約瑟夫。（仍繼續在等）
▶ He will say, "I have work to do." 他會説：「我有工作要做。」	▶ He will say that **he has** work to do. 他會説他有工作要做。
▶ "What am I to do with this?" he asked me. 「我應該怎麼處理這件事情？」他問我。	▶ He asked me what **he was** to do with that. 他問我他應該怎麼處理那件事情。 （指示代名詞 this 要改為 that）
▶ He told me, "I am going to renew my identity card." 他告訴我：「我要去更換我的身份證。」	▶ He told me that **he was** going to renew **his** identity card. 他告訴我，他要去更換他的身份證。
▶ She says, "I will tell him the truth." 她説：「我會告訴他實話。」	▶ She says that **she will** tell him the truth. 她説她會告訴他實話。
▶ She asked, "Shall I make you a hot drink?" 她問：「我應該為你準備一杯熱飲嗎？」	▶ She asked if **she should** make **me** a hot drink. 她問她是否應該為我準備一杯熱飲。
▶ She says, "I'm sorry that I'm late." 她説：「我很抱歉，我遲到了。」	▶ She says that **she is** sorry that **she is** late. 她説她很抱歉，她遲到了。
▶ They said, "We are going home." 他們説：「我們正要回家。」	▶ They said that **they were** going home. 他們説他們正要回家。
▶ They said, "We will be playing in the field." 他們説：「我們會正在田裡玩。」	▶ They said that **they would** be playing in the field. 他們説他們會正在田裡玩。
▶ The boy said, "I am the captain of the	▶ The boy said that **he was** the captain of

team." 這男孩說：「我是隊長。」

the team. 這男孩說他是隊長。

▶ He said, "You may have it."

他說：「你可以擁有它。」

▶ He said that **I might** have it.

他說我可以擁有它。

▶ He asked me, "What are you doing here?" 他問我：「你在這裡做什麼？」

▶ He asked me what **I was** doing there.

他問我在那裡做什麼。

▶ He asked me, "Who are you?"

他問我：「你是誰？」

▶ He asked me who **I was**.

他問我是誰。

▶ He told me, "I borrowed your pencil when you weren't at home." 他告訴我：「當你不在家時，我借了你的鉛筆。」

▶ He told me that **he had borrowed my** pencil when **I was not** at home.

他告訴我，當我不在家時，他借了我的鉛筆。

▶ They asked me, "When will we see you again?"

他們問我：「我們何時會再見到你？」

▶ They asked me when **they would** see **me** again.

他們問我說他們何時會再見到我。

▶ She asked him, "Are you feeling all right?" 她問他：「你覺得還好嗎？」

▶ She asked him if **he was** feeling all right.

她問他是否覺得還好。

▶ She said, "I will bake a cake for you tonight."

她說：「今晚我會為你烤一個蛋糕。」

▶ She said that **she would** bake a cake for **me** tonight.

她說今晚她會為我烤一個蛋糕。

▶ She said, "I've forgotten to bring my books." 她說：「我忘記帶我的書。」

▶ She said that **she had forgotten** to bring **her** books. 她說她忘記帶她的書。

▶ Alice said, "I saw him take something from your desk." 愛麗絲說：「我看到他從你的桌上拿走某個東西。」

▶ Alice said that **she had seen him** take something from **my** desk. 愛麗絲說她看到他從我的桌上拿走某個東西。

▶ "I will do whatever I like with my money," he said. 他說：「我會用我的錢做任何我喜歡的事。」

▶ He said that **he would** do whatever **he liked** with **his** money.

他說他會用他的錢做任何他喜歡的事。

▶ I told my brother, "I will not go with you." 我告訴我弟弟：「我不會和你一起去。」

▶ I told my brother that **I would not** go with **him**. 我告訴我弟弟，我不會和他一起去。

▶ I asked her, "What is your name?"

我問她：「妳叫什麼名字？」

▶ I asked her what **her** name **is**.

我問她叫什麼名字。

(f) 直接引句變成間接引句時，表示「時間、地點」的副詞或副詞片語也會有所變化。

USAGE PRACTICE	
直接引句	間接引句
now 現在	then/at that time 那時；當時
today 今天	on that day 那天；當天
tomorrow 明天	the next day/the following day 隔天
next week 下週	the following week 隔週
here 這裡	there 那裡
yesterday 昨天	the previous day/the day before 前一天
last week 上週	the previous week/the week before 前一週
▶ He said, "I have to go now." 　他說：「我現在必須走了。」	▶ He said that he had to go **then**. 　他說他那時必須走了。
▶ He said, "John is coming today." 　他說：「約翰今天會來。」	▶ He said that John was coming **on that day**. 　他說約翰那天會來。
▶ I said, "I will meet him here." 　我說：「我將在這裡和他見面。」	▶ I said that I would meet him **there**. 　我說我將在那裡和他見面。
▶ I said, "He will be here today." 　我說：「他今天會在這裡。」	▶ I said that he would be **there on that day**. 　我說他那一天會在那裡。
▶ She said, "They went fishing yesterday." 　她說：「他們昨天去釣魚。」	▶ She said that they had gone fishing **the previous day**. 她說他們前一天去釣魚。
▶ She said, "I will come tomorrow." 　她說：「我明天會來。」	▶ She said that she would come **the next day**. 她說她隔天會來。
▶ He said, "I must finish my work by tomorrow." 　他說：「我必須在明天前完成我的工作。」	▶ He said that he would have to finish his work **by the next day**. 　他說他必須在第二天以前完成他的工作。
She said, "I have to go now." 　　"He is working here." 　　"I left last night." 　　"I will do this tomorrow."	She said that she had to go **then**. 　　　　he was working **there**. 　　　　she had left **the previous night**. 　　　　she would do that **the next day**.

但是，對說話者而言，相對位置並非一定，所以在地點的描述上很有可能不會改變。

▶ I said, "I will meet him here." 我說：「我將在這裡和他見面。」
  → I said that I would meet him **here**. 我說我將在這裡和他見面。
  （說話者仍在同一位置，所以還是用 here 表示）

(g) 根據語意或語氣，有時候可以改變引述動詞。

USAGE PRACTICE	
直接引句	間接引句
▶ "Hello! I didn't expect to see you here," he said. 「哈囉！我沒想到會在這裡遇見你。」他說。	▶ He **greeted** me and **added** that he had not expected to see me there. 他跟我打招呼，還說他沒想到會在那裡遇見我。

小練習

請用 "He says that..." 開頭，將下列直接引句改為間接引句。

1. I'm reading the newspapers.

   → _____

2. I will repair your bicycle for you.

   → _____

3. We are going to the fair on Saturday.

   → _____

4. Mary has lost the key to her room.

   → _____

5. I'll help you to pack your clothes.

   → _____

6. My parents are going on a trip next month.

   → _____

7. She knows my uncle very well.

   → _____

8. I'm cutting a slice of cake for you.

   → _____

9. I don't understand what you are talking about.

→ _____

10. Those fruit trees belong to us.

→ _____

11. I'm looking for my watch.

→ _____

12. The meeting will start at four o'clock this afternoon.

→ _____

13. I will be looking forward to your next visit here.

→ _____

☞ 更多相關習題請見本章應用練習 Part 3～Part 8。

18-4 祈使句或感嘆句改為間接引句

(a) 直接引句是祈使句，在改為間接引句時，必須使用不定詞片語。

USAGE PRACTICE	
直接引句	間接引句
▶ " Stand in that corner! " the teacher ordered them. 「站在那個角落！」老師命令他們說。	▶ The teacher ordered them **to stand** in that corner. 老師命令他們站在那個角落。
▶ "Be quiet!" he told us. 「安靜！」他跟我們說。	▶ He told us **to be** quiet. 他叫我們安靜。
▶ She told me, "Don't wait for me." 她告訴我：「不必等我。」	▶ She told me **not to wait** for her. 她告訴我不必等她。
▶ "Stand against the wall," he told us. 「靠牆站。」他告訴我們。	▶ He told us **to stand** against the wall. 他告訴我們靠牆站。
▶ "Don't be afraid," she told me. 「不要害怕。」她告訴我。	▶ She told me **not to be** afraid. 她告訴我不要害怕。
▶ He told to the boy, "Go away!" 他對男孩說：「走開！」	▶ He told the boy **to go** away. 他叫男孩走開。

▶ He told us, "Don't make so much noise."	▶ He told us **not to make** so much noise.
他告訴我們：「不要製造這麼多噪音。」	他告訴我們不要製造這麼多噪音。

(b) 將祈使句改為間接引句時，常常會根據語意或語氣而改變引述動詞。

USAGE PRACTICE	
直接引句	間接引句
▶ He said, "Hand me that book."	▶ He **asked** me to hand him that book.
他說：「把那本書遞給我。」	他要我把那本書遞給他。
▶ He said, "Please pass me the salt."	▶ He **asked** me to pass him the salt.
他說：「請把鹽遞給我。」	他要我把鹽遞給他。
▶ I said, "Bring the file to me, John."	▶ I **asked** John to bring the file to me.
我說：「約翰，把檔案帶來給我。」	我要求約翰把檔案帶給我。
▶ She pleaded, "Please come with me."	▶ She **begged** me to go with her.
她懇求：「請和我一起來。」	她懇求我和她一起去。
▶ "Stop!" the captain said to them.	▶ The captain **commanded** them to stop.
「停！」隊長對他們說。	隊長命令他們停止。
▶ "Forward, march!" the sergeant said to the soldiers. 「前進！」中士對士兵們說。	▶ The sergeant **commanded** the soldiers to march forward. 中士命令士兵們前進。
▶ The teacher requested, "Come over here, Francis."	▶ The teacher **asked** Francis to go over there.
老師要求：「法蘭西斯，過來這裡。」	老師要求法蘭西斯過去那裡。
▶ "Don't go near the snake," I said to him.	▶ I **warned** him not to go near the snake.
「別靠近那條蛇。」我對他說。	我警告他不要靠近那條蛇。
▶ "Come here!" he said to me.	▶ He **ordered** me to go there.
「過來！」他對我說。	他命令我過去。
▶ "Please give me some money," he said to me. 「請給我一些錢。」他對我說。	▶ He **requested** me to give him some money. 他請求我給他一些錢。

(c) 直接引句若是感嘆句，在改為間接引句時，可以使用語意適合的引述動詞，如 greet、exclaim 或 remark，並省略感嘆詞。

直接引句	間接引句
▶ She said, "No! We are ruined." 她說：「糟糕！我們完了。」	▶ She **exclaimed** that they were ruined. 她驚呼說他們完了。
▶ The doctor told the child, "Bravo! You've done very well." 醫生告訴小孩：「太棒了！你做得很好。」	▶ The doctor **applauded** the child, **saying** that she had done very well. 醫生稱讚小孩說她做得很好。
▶ "What a beautiful design!" she said. 她說：「這是多麼美的設計啊！」	▶ She **remarked** that it was a beautiful design. 她說這是很美的設計。
▶ "My God!" he said. "I have gambled and lost." 「天啊！」他說，「我賭輸了。」	▶ He **said with regret** that he had gambled and lost. 他遺憾地說他賭輸了。
▶ "Oh, what a beautiful sunset!" she said. 「噢，多美的夕陽！」她說。	▶ She **exclaimed** that it was a beautiful sunset. 她驚呼說夕陽很美。
▶ He said, "What a beautiful day!" 他說：「多麼美好的一天！」	▶ He **remarked** that it was a beautiful day. 他說那是美好的一天。
▶ "What a surprise to see you!" he said. 「遇見你多麼令人驚訝啊！」他說。	▶ He **exclaimed** that it was a surprise to see me. 他驚呼說遇見我是件令人驚訝的事。

(d) 敘述句、祈使句、感嘆句和疑問句常常一同出現在直接引句中，要改為間接引句時，必須使用適當的引述動詞。

直接引句	間接引句
▶ "Mother!" Benjy yelled. "Come out quickly! See what I have brought home." 班吉大聲叫：「媽！快出來！看我帶了什麼回家。」	▶ Benjy **called out** loudly to his mother to come out quickly and see what he had brought home. 班吉大聲叫他媽媽快出來看他帶了什麼回家。
▶ "Oh no! Nobody types in this way," she said. "Have you ever typed before?"	▶ She **made an exclamation of annoyance and said** that nobody typed

她說：「噢，不！沒人這樣打字的。你以前有打字過嗎？」

▶ "What's the matter?" the doctor asked. "I've got a terrible headache," I said. "Can you please give me something for it?"
醫生問我：「怎麼了？」我說：「我頭痛得很厲害。你能開一些藥給我嗎？」

▶ "Oh dear," the driver said staring at his van. "I wish that I had refilled the tank with gas before I left. How am I going to deliver these goods now?" 司機盯著他的貨車說：「噢，天啊，真希望我在出發前有把油箱加滿。我現在要怎麼送貨呢？」

in that way. She **asked** me whether I had ever typed before. 她苦惱地大叫說沒人那樣打字的。她問我以前是否有打字過。

▶ The doctor **asked** me what was the matter. I **told** him that I had a terrible headache and **asked** him to give me something for it.
醫生問我怎麼了。我告訴他我頭痛得很厲害，並要求他開一些藥給我。

▶ Staring at his van, the driver **sighed** and **wished** that he had refilled the tank with gas before he had left. He **asked** himself how he was going to deliver those goods then. 一面盯著他的貨車，司機嘆氣地說他真希望在出發前有把油箱加滿。他自問他該如何送貨。

 小練習

請把下列句子改為間接引句，注意必要的改變。

1. My father told us, "Don't open the can. Let me do it for you."
   →_____

2. The doctor told him, "Try to get out in the sun as often as possible."
   →_____

3. She ordered the girl, "Leave the books alone!"
   →_____

4. He told me, "Don't cause so much trouble on my account."
   →_____

5. The customer ordered the waitress, "Bring me a glass of water."
   →_____

6. "Don't be too confident of yourself," I advised her.

$\rightarrow$ _____

7. He told them, "Look after yourselves while I am away."

$\rightarrow$ _____

8. "Don't throw the trash on the road, or you may get fined," she told them.

$\rightarrow$ _____

9. "Bring me that jar from the shelf," she told him.

$\rightarrow$ _____

10. "Be early, or you won't be able to get a place to sit," he told us.

$\rightarrow$ _____

11. "Karen, explain the meaning of this word to me," I said.

$\rightarrow$ _____

12. They told us, "Wait here while we park the car at the end of the road."

$\rightarrow$ _____

13. "Look where you are going!" the motorist told us.

$\rightarrow$ _____

14. She told them, "Please help yourself to the food."

$\rightarrow$ _____

15. "Don't wake me up before seven o'clock," he said.

$\rightarrow$ _____

16. "Don't run along the hallways," the teacher told us.

$\rightarrow$ _____

17. She told us, "Hurry up, or you'll miss the bus."

$\rightarrow$ _____

18. "Make sure the gate is shut properly, Julia," she said.

$\rightarrow$ _____

19. He said to her, "Don't show the letter to anyone."

$\rightarrow$ _____

20. "Don't spend all your money on clothes," they warned her.

$\rightarrow$ _____

21. "Drop that stick at once!" he ordered the little boy.

$\rightarrow$ _____

22. "Oh!" exclaimed my sister. "I've forgotten to bring my books!"

→ _____

☞ 更多相關習題請見本章應用練習 Part 9～Part 10。

Chapter 18　應用練習

PART 1

請將下列直接引句加上正確的標點符號，並注意大小寫。

1. He remarked I heard her say to Harry what a lazy boy you are!

→ _____

2. Tell me young man the woman said is your mother at home?

→ _____

3. Tony run down to the shop and get me some groceries his mother said.

→ _____

4. Are you feeling all right he asked let me get you a drink.

→ _____

5. Molly asked have you seen the movie *Star Wars*?

→ _____

6. The military officer shouted to his men halt!

→ _____

7. If you see Paul she said send him to me.

→ _____

8. I exclaimed you have lived here all your life and you don't even know your neighbors!

→ _____

9. Do you have anything else to tell me Raymond I asked.

→ _____

10. Look here boys this is the way to set up a tent the young man said.

→ _____

11. Say thank you Shirley her mother told her.

→ _____

12. He scolded his younger brother I have often told you not to play with fire!

→ _____

13. Hurry up he shouted the ship Marianne is going to sail soon!

→ _____

14. Oh dear I am ruined the businessman cried.

→ _____

15. What time is it Robert asked I want to watch Mystery Movie on television.

→ _____

16. Mother the boy called where are you?

→ _____

17. May I have the book *Detective Stories* for today I want to read it my little brother asked.

→ _____

18. Of the two poems The Rain and Snow which one appeals more to you the teacher asked.

→ _____

PART 2

請以提示字為句首，將下列句子改寫為間接引句。

1. Why are they absent? (*I asked him...*)

→ _____

2. When did they leave the city? (*I don't know...*)

→ _____

3. What time is it? (*I want to know...*)

→ _____

4. How many people are there in the room? (*Tell me...*)

→ _____

5. What is the price of that shirt? (*I asked her...*)

→ _____

6. Where is the railroad station? (*He wants to know...*)

→ _____

7. What were they arguing about? (*Tell us...*)

→ _____

8. How do they go to work every day? (*I want to know...*)

→ _____

9. Where do you usually park your car at night? (*He asked me...*)

→ _____

10. What kind of house does he live in? (*We don't know...*)

→ _____

11. What is the date today? (*I'm not sure...*)

→ _____

12. Why is there a white line across the road? (*Nobody knows...*)

→ _____

13. How long does it take to go from your house to the school? (*Tell us...*)

→ _____

14. When will electricity be supplied to the new houses? (*I asked him...*)

→ _____

15. How much did the oranges cost? (*I want to know...*)

→ _____

16. What is she doing in that corner? (*Tell me...*)

→ _____

17. Are you going to the shop or to the market? (*Tell me...*)

→ _____

18. Whom are these strangers looking for? (*Do you know...*)

→ _____

19. Should I come back later to help you with your work? (*Ask your mother...*)

→ _____

20. Where is the bus stop? (*He'll ask them...*)

→ _____

21. Has she given you an answer yet? (*Tell me...*)

→ _____

22. When does the game start? (*They don't know...*)

→ _____

23. Is the car in good condition? (*I'll ask the mechanic...*)

→ _____

24. Are the boys coming along with us in this car? (*Ask Marina...*)

→ _____

PART 3

請以提示字為句首，將下列句子改寫為間接引句。

1. Do you know that girl? (*He asked me...*)

   → _____

2. Are you going to see "The Three Musketeers" tomorrow? (*He wanted to know...*)

   → _____

3. What are you doing with that piece of wood? (*They wanted to know...*)

   → _____

4. Are all of you going to the picnic on Saturday? (*They asked us...*)

   → _____

5. Why can't Uncle James and Aunt Alice come this week? (*I wanted to know...*)

   → _____

6. Did you see William or Alex when you went to the party? (*I asked her...*)

   → _____

7. Which one of you borrowed John's fountain pen during lunchtime? (*The teacher asked...*)

   → _____

8. Do the guards let you walk around the compound? (*The reporter asked the prisoners...*)

   → _____

9. Is it time for us to get up? (*Benny asked his mother...*)

   → _____

10. Why can't you tell us what the man looked like? (*The policeman asked the old lady...*)

    → _____

11. Where did you hide the money that I left on the dressing table? (*She wanted to know...*)

    → _____

12. Would you like to see some of the stamps I've collected? (*The boy asked me...*)

    → _____

13. Are you all right now? (*I asked her...*)

    → _____

14. What's the matter with you? (*My mother asked me...*)

    → _____

15. Where shall we meet? (*I asked the boys...*)

    → _____

16. What were you staring at? (*My sister asked me...*)

    → _____

17. How did you get this answer? (*The teacher wanted to know...*)

    → _____

18. When will you be free tomorrow? (*I asked her...*)

    → _____

19. Were they on holiday last month? (*Mr. Richards asked his colleague...*)

    → _____

20. Dare you go home alone? (*The boy asked the girl...*)

    → _____

PART 4

請以提示字為句首，將下列句子改寫為間接引句。

1. Are they listening to the radio? (*I asked him...*)

   → _____

2. Has your mother spoken to the shopkeeper yet? (*I don't know...*)

   → _____

3. Does he like to eat chocolate? (*We are not sure...*)

   → _____

4. Did the car skid on the road? (*He asked us...*)

   → _____

5. Is he a medical student? (*I'll find out...*)

   → _____

6. Are they making a clay model of the airplane? (*We are not sure...*)

   → _____

7. Does he plant orchids in his garden? (*He asked us...*)

   → _____

8. Has your writing improved since I last saw it? (*I want to know...*)

→ _____

9. Can we wade across the river? (*He'll find out...*)

→ _____

10. May I use the telephone? (*I ask him...*)

→ _____

11. Has he put the ointment on his feet? (*I want to know...*)

→ _____

12. Is there anybody practicing on the piano? (*She doesn't know...*)

→ _____

13. Can you look after my pet while I am away? (*I want to know...*)

→ _____

14. Have they been doing their homework lately? (*We are not sure...*)

→ _____

15. Have you looked through the history notes I gave you? (*He asked me...*)

→ _____

16. Shall we hold the meeting in the hall or in the classroom? (*I don't know...*)

→ _____

17. Is it possible for a person of my size to defeat a person twice my size? (*She asked me...*)

→ _____

18. Do you want to go swimming with us in the river after we have had tea? (*He asked me...*)

→ _____

19. Is there an empty room where I can stay for the night? (*He wondered...*)

→ _____

20. Shall I prepare a nice hot meal for you before you leave? (*She asked me...*)

→ _____

21. Will they help us solve this problem if we ask them to? (*I wondered...*)

→ _____

22. Are you angry with him for ignoring you in front of the others yesterday? (*He asked her...*)

→ _____

PART 5

請把下列句子改為間接引句，注意必要的改變。

1. I told them, "Exercise makes our muscles strong."

   → _____

2. She said, "Eggs contain a lot of protein."

   → _____

3. We reported, "She is painting a portrait."

   → _____

4. He says, "I'm grateful to you for your help."

   → _____

5. Mr. Brown said, "I'm trying to repair my watch."

   → _____

6. I will tell her, "You are making a terrible mistake!"

   → _____

7. "I have more endurance than you," he will say.

   → _____

8. They said, "We are polishing our shoes."

   → _____

9. Our Science teacher told us, "Light travels 300,000 kilometers in one second."

   → _____

10. He said, "I'm leaving for Sunway Park on the three o'clock train."

    → _____

11. My father said, "Success is the fruit of hard work."

    → _____

12. She is telling her friend, "My sister is absent today because she has sprained her ankle."

    → _____

13. The doctor says, "His condition is getting worse."

    → _____

14. "This road leads to Holly Avenue," he told us.

    → _____

15. Last week, his grandfather told him, "I'm making a will."

$\rightarrow$ _____

16. I thought, "The truck will hit the cow."

$\rightarrow$ _____

17. He said, "The boy hasn't had his anti-cholera injection yet."

$\rightarrow$ _____

PART 6

請把下列句子改為間接引句，注意必要的改變。

1. The shopkeeper said, "You can settle your account at the end of this month."

$\rightarrow$ _____

2. Peter told me, "I'm writing an article for the school magazine."

$\rightarrow$ _____

3. "He will arrive by train tonight," I said.

$\rightarrow$ _____

4. The radio announcer said, "The weather will be fine today."

$\rightarrow$ _____

5. "Everyone may leave the class now," the teacher said.

$\rightarrow$ _____

6. "You will be late for school if you don't hurry," my mother warned me.

$\rightarrow$ _____

7. The manager said, "You will have to complete the work by three o'clock this afternoon."

$\rightarrow$ _____

8. He said, "I have an appointment with the dentist at ten o'clock tomorrow."

$\rightarrow$ _____

9. She said, "I have read all the newspapers in the house."

$\rightarrow$ _____

10. He told me, "I was playing chess at my uncle's house last night."

$\rightarrow$ _____

11. "You may buy whatever you wish," his father told him.

$\rightarrow$ _____

12. The doctor explained, "Having an X-ray taken is not painful."

→ _____

13. The teacher told us, "A diamond is a very valuable stone."

→ _____

14. The teacher explained, "Intransitive verbs do not have objects."

→ _____

15. He said, "I will go there tomorrow."

→ _____

16. I said to him, "I will not take back what I have said."

→ _____

17. She says, "Examinations will never be abolished."

→ _____

18. "You are lying," they told her.

→ _____

PART 7

請把下列句子改為間接引句，注意必要的改變。

1. He said, "I have lived in India for many years."

→ _____

2. He will say, "We do not know where Polly has gone."

→ _____

3. "Her brother came here last week," I said.

→ _____

4. She told me, "I finished my work days ago."

→ _____

5. I said, "I must not be disrespectful to my elders."

→ _____

6. He told me, "My brother is not free now. He is writing letters."

→ _____

7. The man said to the girl, "I know your father very well."

→ _____

8. The gardener told her, "You can pick as many flowers as you like from this bed."

→ _____

9. He says, "I am not so foolish as to believe you."

→ _____

10. "We'd better start doing our work now as we have to hand it in next week," she said.

→ _____

11. "You mustn't be so slow with your work next time," the supervisor told the girl.

→ _____

12. I wondered, "Will I be able to beat them in the competition?"

→ _____

13. I asked the man, "Did you see the accident happen?"

→ _____

14. She asked her employee, "Have you done the marketing yet?"

→ _____

15. The stranger inquired, "Do you know where Mr. West has shifted to?"

→ _____

16. She asked her friend, "Were all your answers correct?"

→ _____

17. The children asked their mother, "When will Uncle come to visit us again?"

→ _____

18. "Where are you working now?" she asked.

→ _____

PART 8

請把下列句子改為間接引句，注意必要的改變。

1. "Why were you hiding behind the door?" the teacher questioned her.

→ _____

2. I wondered, "Do I have to apologize to her?"

→ _____

3. The doctor asked the mother, "Has the child been vaccinated against smallpox?"

→ _____

4. The landlady asked him, "Why haven't you paid me last month's rent?"

$\rightarrow$ _____

5. "Do you smell something burning?" she asked.

   $\rightarrow$ _____

6. "Were the lights still on when you came home last night?" she asked me.

   $\rightarrow$ _____

7. "Where have you put my gardening tools?" my father asked my sister.

   $\rightarrow$ _____

8. She said, "Aren't you feeling thirsty after the long walk?"

   $\rightarrow$ _____

9. They said, "We have our hair cut at the barber shop next door."

   $\rightarrow$ _____

10. He says, "I may be having a nap when you arrive at the house."

    $\rightarrow$ _____

11. I will tell him, "I am looking for my report card."

    $\rightarrow$ _____

12. The doctor told us, "He is out of danger now. You can probably take him home in a week."

    $\rightarrow$ _____

13. My grandfather always says, "The beaten road is the safest."

    $\rightarrow$ _____

14. The doctor said, "The soldiers donated blood to the hospital this morning."

    $\rightarrow$ _____

15. "Hydrogen explodes when it is lighted," she said.

    $\rightarrow$ _____

16. The farmer said, "The hens have laid some eggs. I will go to the market tomorrow to sell them."

    $\rightarrow$ _____

PART 9

請把下列句子改為間接引句，注意必要的改變及引述動詞的使用。

1. The teacher told them, "Sing louder!"

   $\rightarrow$ _____

2. "Take an aspirin, and go to bed," she advised him.

　→ _____

3. The teacher asked the students, "Pass in your books now."

　→ _____

4. "Be careful not to trespass while you are camping," he told us.

　→ _____

5. She advised him, "Sit down, and tell me the whole story."

　→ _____

6. My father told me, "Don't be too discouraged by your results."

　→ _____

7. "Don't strain yourself. Try to get more rest," the doctor advised him.

　→ _____

8. "Stand at ease!" the captain commanded them.

　→ _____

9. "Let us do it by ourselves," we said to them.

　→ _____

10. The teacher told his students, "Don't read the sentence so fast, or nobody will understand what you are reading."

　→ _____

11. "Don't play with fire," he warned me.

　→ _____

12. "Please sit down. The doctor will see you in a few minutes," the nurse said to them.

　→ _____

13. "Oh, what a fool you are!" my brother said to me.

　→ _____

14. He remarked angrily, "Your behavior is really stupid!"

　→ _____

15. "Help me carry this load. It's too heavy for my shoulders," the old man said to his son.

　→ _____

PART 10

請把下列句子改為間接引句，注意必要的改變及引述動詞的使用。

1. "Children, go out to play. Don't disturb me while I am cooking," she said.

   → _____

2. "Please come this way," the receptionist told him.

   → _____

3. "Good afternoon, sir. Here is a letter for you," she said.

   → _____

4. "Stop, thief!" the woman shouted.

   → _____

5. She said, "Please shut the door when you go out."

   → _____

6. "Please wait for me; I will be back in a few minutes," I said to my friend.

   → _____

7. "Be careful! The road here is very slippery," the lady advised the driver.

   → _____

8. "Please be quick!" I urged her. "I really can't hold on much longer."

   → _____

9. "Don't argue with your mother," Mr. Brown told Peter.

   → _____

10. She said, "Jane, please put the cake into the oven and turn the temperature to 150 degrees."

   → _____

11. He said to me, "Don't forget to lock all the windows and the door before you leave the house."

   → _____

12. "Go straight in, please. The manager is waiting for you," the secretary told me.

   → _____

13. "Good morning!" he said to us. "Open your books to Page 71, and start reading to yourselves."

   → _____

14. "Speak louder!" the teacher said. "No one can hear you if you murmur."

   → _____

15. He said to his secretary, "Don't open my mail while I am away. I will handle it when I return."

→ _____

16. "Please tell John to meet me at Mary's house in half an hour, Sally," Peter said.

   → _____

17. "It is the way to repair it," he told me. "Watch carefully while I'm repairing it."

   → _____

18. "What a beautiful painting!" she exclaimed. "Tell me who painted it."

   → _____

PART 11

請把下列句子改為間接引句，注意必要的改變及引述動詞的使用。

1. "I am sorry," she said to me, "but my brother won't be back until late tonight."

   → _____

2. The guard reported, "I heard some shots and ran out into the compound to investigate."

   → _____

3. "When will he be back?" Stella said. "I have something important to tell him."

   → _____

4. "Did you go to the circus that's performing here?" Jeffrey asked me. "It was a wonderful show."

   → _____

5. "Good morning!" she said when she saw me. "How are you today? I heard you had been quite sick."

   → _____

6. "Come here at once!" he ordered the frightened boy. "If you don't, I shall give you a beating."

   → _____

7. "Don't do too much heavy work," the doctor advised Mrs. Brown. "Get as much rest as possible."

   → _____

8. "Please come," he said. "I want to show you my new fish. My father bought it yesterday."

   → _____

9. "Are you going out now? If you are, see that you are back by ten," my mother said to me.

   → _____

10. "Yes, please do so," I answered her. "I will wait here until you return."

→ _____

11. "Where can I buy striped shirts like these?" he asked me. "They seem to be in fashion now."

→ _____

12. "Don't be afraid," she told the little boy. "The dog won't hurt you; it only wants to make friends with you."

→ _____

13. "Please shut the door properly as you go out, John," she said. "It keeps on banging away."

→ _____

14. "He is probably sleeping now," the maid said. "Shall I ask his sister to come down?"

→ _____

PART 12

請把下列句子還原為直接引句，注意必要的改變及引述動詞的使用。

1. He ordered him to leave the house at once.

→ _____

2. They told me that they had waited an hour for me.

→ _____

3. He said that he had come against his will.

→ _____

4. Peter asked Paul to go fishing with him.

→ _____

5. I said that I was not hungry and added that I did not want anything.

→ _____

6. My mother often tells me that if I am good, everything will be all right.

→ _____

7. She replied that she had seen the film before.

→ _____

8. He remarked that it was an interesting novel.

→ _____

9. He commanded them to stand at attention.

$\rightarrow$ _____

10. The teacher explained that temperature decreases with ascent.

$\rightarrow$ _____

11. He proposed that they should wait till the rain stopped.

$\rightarrow$ _____

12. He said that it gave him great pleasure to preside over the meeting.

$\rightarrow$ _____

13. She advised them not to quarrel among themselves.

$\rightarrow$ _____

14. Mrs. Lea shouted to her children to keep quiet.

$\rightarrow$ _____

15. I explained that the earth revolves around the sun.

$\rightarrow$ _____

16. I said that long ago, people had believed that the earth was the center of the universe.

$\rightarrow$ _____

17. The travelers said that he had come a long way.

$\rightarrow$ _____

18. She invited the visitors to sit down.

$\rightarrow$ _____

PART 13

請把下列句子還原為直接引句，注意必要的改變及引述動詞的使用。

1. The woman wondered anxiously whether her husband would get home safely.

$\rightarrow$ _____

2. The man asked them whether they should hang around in such a place.

$\rightarrow$ _____

3. I asked my brother whether he had collected the mail.

$\rightarrow$ _____

4. The policeman asked what had been going on in the casino.

$\rightarrow$ _____

5. She asked her husband if the weather was not too rough for fishing.

$\rightarrow$ _____

6. I asked Jane if she would lend me a pencil.

   $\rightarrow$ _____

7. The teacher wants to know where they have put the books.

   $\rightarrow$ _____

8. They asked us where we had gone during the interval.

   $\rightarrow$ _____

9. She asked herself whether she had done right.

   $\rightarrow$ _____

10. He wants to know if the road has been repaired yet.

    $\rightarrow$ _____

11. He demanded to know what they had done so far to remedy the situation.

    $\rightarrow$ _____

12. The lawyer asked him why he was snooping around the house.

    $\rightarrow$ _____

13. The child asked his mother where she had put the jam tarts.

    $\rightarrow$ _____

14. The little boy pestered his parents to buy him a toy train.

    $\rightarrow$ _____

15. She asked whether his name was Alfred.

    $\rightarrow$ _____

16. He wondered why nobody was at home.

    $\rightarrow$ _____

17. Miss Hillman asked the fortuneteller what her future would be like.

    $\rightarrow$ _____

18. The boys asked their teacher whether they should leave then.

    $\rightarrow$ _____

19. The students exclaimed how anyone could get distinctions for all the subjects in the examination.

    $\rightarrow$ _____

Chapter 19 附加問句

19-0 基本概念

英文口語中經常使用附加問句，用於當說話者期望得到聽話者的確認或肯定時。附加問句附加於敘述句或祈使句的後面，由簡短的疑問句構成。一般而言，回答含附加問句的句子時，多用簡答句。

19-1 附加問句的功能及構成

(a) 肯定的敘述句使用否定的附加問句，但通常期望獲得的回答是肯定的。

USAGE PRACTICE

肯定的敘述句	否定的附加問句	肯定的回答
"You were there,	**weren't** you?"	"**Yes**, I **was**."
「你當時在那裡，	不是嗎？」	「是的，我在。」
"He has finished,	**hasn't** he?"	"**Yes**, he **has**."
「他已經完成了，	不是嗎？」	「是的，他已經完成了。」
"She is young,	**isn't** she?"	"**Yes**, she **is**."
「她很年輕，	不是嗎？」	「是的，她很年輕。」

▶ "They must take the test, **mustn't** they?" "**Yes**, they **must**."

　「他們必須參加這個考試，不是嗎？」「是的，他們必須。」

▶ "You can read, **can't** you?" "**Yes**, I **can**." 「你識字，不是嗎？」「是的，我識字。」

▶ "I will get there on time, **won't** I?" "**Yes**, you **will**."

　「我會準時到達那裡，不會嗎？」「是的，你會。」

▶ "You have been sick, **haven't** you?" "**Yes**, I **have**." 「你病了，不是嗎？」「是的，我病了。」

▶ "She is here, **isn't** she?" "**Yes**, she **is**." 「她在這裡，不是嗎？」「是的，她在。」

▶ "He is the fastest runner in the team, **isn't** he?" "**Yes**, he **is**."

　「他是該隊跑最快的，不是嗎？」「是的，他是。」

▶ "The weather is fine, **isn't** it?" "**Yes**, it **is**." 「天氣很好，不是嗎？」「是的，天氣很好。」

▶ "The children are asleep, **aren't** they?" "**Yes**, they **are**."

「小孩們在睡覺，不是嗎？」「是的，他們是。」

▶ "He has eaten his dinner, **hasn't** he?" "**Yes**, he **has**."

「他吃過晚餐了，不是嗎？」「是的，他吃過了。」

▶ "She will conduct the choir, **won't** she?" "**Yes**, she **will**."

「她將會指揮合唱團，不是嗎？」「是的，她將會。」

 但是，「期望獲得肯定回答」跟對方是否給予肯定回答是完全無關的，也就是說，仍有很大可能對方回答是否定的。

▶ "I can get there just in time, **can't** I?" "No, you **can't**."

「我應該可以及時趕到那邊吧，不是嗎？」「不，你來不及。」

(b) 否定的敘述句使用肯定的附加問句，但通常期望獲得的回答是否定的。

USAGE PRACTICE		
否定的敘述句	肯定的附加問句	否定的回答
"You won't be late,	**will** you?"	"**No**, I **won't**."
「你不會遲到，	會嗎？」	「不，我不會。」
"I didn't hurt you,	**did** I?"	"**No**, you **didn't**."
「我沒有傷害你，	有嗎？」	「不，你沒有。」
"He isn't ready,	**is** he?"	"**No**, he **isn't**."
「他沒準備好，	是嗎？」	「不，他還沒。」
"She doesn't sing well,	**does** she?"	"**No**, she **doesn't**."
「她唱得不好，	是嗎？」	「不，她唱得不好。」

▶ "She didn't come to your house, **did** she?" "**No**, she **didn't**."

「她沒有來你家，是嗎？」「不，她沒有。」

▶ "I am not very late, **am** I?" "**No**, you **aren't**." 「我沒有遲到很久，是嗎？」「不，你沒有。」

▶ "We shouldn't tell them, **should** we?" "**No**, we **shouldn't**."

「我們不應該告訴他們，是嗎？」「不，我們不應該。」

▶ "He isn't here, **is** he?" "**No**, he **isn't**/he's **not**." 「他不在這裡，是嗎？」「不，他不在。」

▶ "It isn't true, **is** it?" "**No**, it **isn't**." 「這不是真的，是嗎？」「不，它不是。」

▶ "They can't leave now, **can** they?" "**No**, they **can't**."

「他們現在不能離開，是嗎？」「不，他們不能。」

▶ "She mustn't be absent, **must** she?" "**No**, she **mustn't**."

「她不能缺席，是嗎？」「不，她不能。」

▶ "You haven't seen it yet, **have** you?" "**No**, I **haven't**."

「你還沒看過它，是嗎？」「不，我還沒。」

 但是，「期望獲得否定回答」跟對方是否給予否定回答是完全無關的，也就是說，仍有很大可能對方回答是肯定的。

▶ "They didn't take away my book, **did** they?" "Yes, they **did**."

「他們沒有把我的書拿走，是嗎？」「有，他們拿走了。」

(c) 包含 never、rarely、seldom 或 hardly 等否定詞的敘述句在意義上是否定的，所以必須使用肯定的附加問句，期望得到否定的簡答。

USAGE PRACTICE

▶ "We never eat here, **do** we?" "**No,** we **don't**."

「我們從沒在這裡吃飯過，是嗎？」「不，我們沒有。」

▶ "They can hardly go home in the rain, **can** they?" "**No,** they **can't**."

「他們在下雨時幾乎無法回家，是嗎？」「不，他們不能。」

19-2 附加問句的主詞

(a) 附加問句的主詞必須與敘述句的主詞一致。

USAGE PRACTICE

▶ I am not included, am **I**? 我沒被算進去，是嗎？

▶ He stopped to talk to us, didn't **he**? 他停下來跟我們講話，不是嗎？

▶ They don't like to watch television, do **they**? 他們不喜歡看電視，是嗎？

▶ She doesn't want to eat, does **she**? 她不想吃，是嗎？

▶ There wasn't much food left, was **there**? 沒有剩下很多食物，是嗎？

(b) 當敘述的主詞為一般名詞（非代名詞）時，不管敘述句的主詞是指人或事物，其附加問句及簡答句中的主詞都要改為代名詞。

▶ "Peter and Paul are here, aren't **they**?" "Yes, **they** are."

「彼得和保羅都在這裡，不是嗎？」「是的，他們在。」

▶ "Some boys do want to come, don't **they**?" "Yes, **they** do."

「一些男孩的確想要來，不是嗎？」「是的，他們的確想。」

▶ "Those people saw you, didn't **they?**" "Yes, **they** did."

「那些人看見你了，不是嗎？」「是的，他們看到了。」

▶ "The cat broke the vase, didn't **it**?" "Yes, **it** did."

「貓打破花瓶了，不是嗎？」「是的，它打破花瓶了。」

▶ "The baby won't be in your way, will **it**?" "No, **it** won't."

「這嬰兒不會妨礙你，會嗎？」「不，它不會。」

▶ "That machine won't work, will **it**?" "No, **it** won't."

「那部機器不會動，是嗎？」「不，它不會。」

▶ "Alice must come too, mustn't **she**?" "Yes, **she** must."

「愛莉絲也必須來，不是嗎？」「是的，她必須來。」

(c) 當敘述句的主詞是 everyone、someone、anybody、nobody 等不定代名詞時，附加問句的主詞要用代名詞 they 並搭配複數動詞。

▶ "**Everybody** is to be here by noon, **aren't they**?" "Yes, **they are**."

「每個人在中午前都必須在這裡，不是嗎？」「是的，每個人都必須在。」

▶ "Everyone has done his work, **haven't they**?" "Yes, **they have**."

「每個人已經做好自己的工作了，不是嗎？」「是的，每個人都做好了。」

▶ "Everybody is anxious to go, **aren't they**?" "Yes, **they are**."

「每個人都急著要走，不是嗎？」「是的，每個人都是。」

▶ "Anyone can go to the picnic, **can't they**?" "Yes, **they can**."

「任何人都能去郊遊，不是嗎？」「是的，任何人都能。」

▶ "Someone can do this, **can't they**?" "Yes, **they can**."

「有人可以做這件事，不是嗎？」「是的，有人可以。」

▶ "Somebody helped in the search, **didn't they**?" "Yes, **they did**."

「有人幫忙搜尋，不是嗎？」「是的，有人幫忙。」

▶ "Nobody is allowed in here, **are they**?" "No, **they aren't**."

　　「沒有人獲准進來這裡，不是嗎？」「不，沒人獲准。」

▶ "Nobody wants to go, **do they**?" "No, **they don't**."

　　「沒人想要去，是嗎？」「不，沒人想。」

▶ "No one ever comes here, **do they**?" "No, **they don't**."

　　「沒有人來過這裡，是嗎？」「不，沒人來過。」

▶ "Nobody is waiting outside, **are they**?" "No, **they aren't**."

　　「沒有人在外面等，是嗎？」「不，沒有人。」

19-3 附加問句及答句的動詞

(a) 當敘述句的動詞是一般動詞時，附加問句及答句的動詞用助動詞 do、does 或 did。

USAGE PRACTICE

▶ "I walk very fast, **don't** I?" "Yes, you **do**." 「我走得很快，不是嗎？」「是的，你是。」

▶ "You want to go, too, **don't** you?" "Yes, I do." 「你也想去，不是嗎？」「是的，我想。」

▶ "They like candies, **don't** they?" "Yes, they **do**."

　　「他們喜歡糖果，不是嗎？」「是的，他們喜歡。」

▶ "They often come here, **don't** they?" "Yes, they **do**."

　　「他們經常到這裡來，不是嗎？」「是的，他們是。」

▶ "He plays hockey, **doesn't** he?" "Yes, he **does**."

　　「他打曲棍球，不是嗎？」「是的，他有打。」

▶ "He wants a share, too, **doesn't** he?" "Yes, he **does**."

　　「他也想要一份，不是嗎？」「是的，他想。」

▶ "She has her lunch at one o'clock, **doesn't** she?" "Yes, she **does**."

　　「她一點鐘時吃午餐，不是嗎？」「是的，她是。」

▶ "It runs very fast, **doesn't** it?" "Yes, it **does**." 「它跑得非常快，不是嗎？」「是的，它是。」

▶ "This metal melted easily, **didn't** it?" "Yes, it **did**."

　　「這金屬容易熔化，不是嗎？」「是的，它是。」

▶ "You answered the letter, **didn't** you?" "Yes, I **did**."

「你回信了，不是嗎？」「是的，我回了。」

▶ "They found it missing, **didn't** they?" "Yes, they **did**."

「他們發現它不見了，不是嗎？」「是的，他們發現了。」

▶ "She needs to come, **doesn't** she?" "Yes, she **does**."

「她必須來，不是嗎？」「是的，她必須。」

(b) 當敘述句使用 be 動詞或助動詞時，附加問句及答句的動詞也要用 be 動詞或助動詞。

USAGE PRACTICE

▶ "They are getting annoyed, **aren't** they?" "Yes, they **are**."

「他們在生氣，不是嗎？」「是的，他們是。」

▶ "They aren't going, **are** they?" "No, they **aren't**." 「他們不會去，是嗎？」「不，他們不會。」

▶ "You don't agree with us, **do** you?" "No, I **don't**."

「你不同意我們，是嗎？」「不，我不同意。」

▶ "She doesn't realize her mistake, **does she?**" "No, she **doesn't**."

「她不了解她的錯誤，是嗎？」「不，她不了解。」

▶ "We didn't talk to them, **did** we?" "No, we **didn't**."

「我們沒有跟他們說話，是嗎？」「不，我們沒有。」

▶ "He didn't lose it, **did** he?" "No, he **didn't**." 「他沒有弄丟它，是嗎？」「不，他沒有。」

▶ "They didn't see you, **did** they?" "No, they **didn't**."

「他們沒看見你，是嗎？」「不，他們沒有。」

▶ "We have seen him before, **haven't** we?" "Yes, we **have**."

「我們見過他，不是嗎？」「是的，我們見過。」

▶ "He has gone home, **hasn't** he?" "Yes, he **has**."

「他已經回家了，不是嗎？」「是的，他已經回家了。」

▶ "There hasn't been any change, **has** there?" "No, there **hasn't**."

「不曾有過任何改變，是嗎？」「不，沒有。」

▶ "The taxi hasn't come, **has** it?" "No, it **hasn't**." 「計程車還沒來，是嗎？」「不，它還沒來。」

▶ "He won't tell the truth, **will** he?" "No, he **won't**."

「他不會說出實情，是嗎？」「不，他不會。」

▶ "You will come early tomorrow, **won't** you?" "Yes, I **will**."

　「你明天會早到，不是嗎？」「是的，我會。」

▶ "We won't pass that way, **will** we?" "No, we **won't**."

　「我們不會經過那條路，是嗎？」「不，我們不會。」

▶ "They wouldn't let her in, **would** they?" "No, they **wouldn't**."

　「他們不會讓她進去，是嗎？」「不，他們不會。」

▶ "She can come to the picnic, **can't** she?" "Yes, she **can**."

　「她可以去郊遊，不是嗎？」「是的，她可以。」

▶ "They can help him, **can't** they?" "Yes, they **can**."

　「他們能幫助他，不是嗎？」「是的，他們能。」

▶ "It can't escape now, **can** it?" "No, it **can't**." 「它現在不能逃跑了，是嗎？」「不，它不能。」

▶ "He couldn't have seen us, **could** he?" "No, he **couldn't**."

　「他不可能見過我們，是嗎？」「不，他不可能。」

▶ "She should return it, **shouldn't** she?" "Yes, she **should**."

　「她應該歸還它，不是嗎？」「是的，她應該。」

▶ "We must leave now, **mustn't** we?" "Yes, we **must**."

　「現在我們必須離開，不是嗎？」「是的，我們必須。」

 敘述句若是 "I am..." 開頭時，附加問句用 "aren't I" 或 "am I not"。

▶ I am well qualified, **aren't I/am I not**? 我很有資格，不是嗎？

請在下列句子後加上正確的附加問句。

1. You can do the work by yourself, _____ ?

2. It hasn't been raining, _____ ?

3. He must take part in the swimming contest, _____ ?

4. You play tennis, _____ ?

5. The teachers are having a meeting, _____ ?

6. I can't believe everything that he says, _____ ?

7. She would be more comfortable staying with you, _____ ?

8. The electricity supply hasn't been cut off yet, _____ ?

9. Your father is very strict, _____ ?

10. The doctor will give her an injection, _____ ?

11. He doesn't know how to speak English, _____ ?

12. You go to bed early every night, _____ ?

13. He should inform the police of the theft, _____ ?

14. She visits her aunt twice a week, _____ ?

15. The children were playing in the garden, _____ ?

16. They haven't counted all the money yet, _____ ?

17. The car skidded while you were driving in the rain, _____ ?

18. Many women cried when they saw the film, _____ ?

19. He will come as soon as he hears the news, _____ ?

20. We won't let him bully the smaller children, _____ ?

21. Nobody saw him running away, _____ ?

22. You aren't to blame, _____ ?

23. Anything could have happened, _____ ?

Chapter 19　應用練習

PART 1

請在下列句子後加上正確的附加問句。

1. They will make it in time, _____ ?

2. The doctor should advise her to take a holiday, _____ ?

3. Anyone who wants to come can do so, _____ ?

4. You don't have to be a member of the society to attend its meetings, _____ ?

5. Peter and John are going to buy us some cold drinks, _____ ?

6. He had intended to come here as soon as he was able to, _____ ?

7. We didn't have much choice, _____ ?

8. You wouldn't want your children to behave like that, _____ ?

9. It looks quite easy to do, _____ ?

10. They had finished all their work before they started to watch television, _____ ?

11. We have nothing else to do, _____?

12. Everyone breaks down now and then, _____?

13. I should be given some compensation, _____?

14. She doesn't have much chance of winning, _____?

15. It rained very heavily last night, _____?

16. You slept very soundly last night, _____?

17. They know something about this incident, _____?

18. She has cleaned all the glasses, _____?

19. They took Billy and Johnny to the movies, _____?

20. Michael can drive the car, _____?

21. No one found the solution to the problem, _____?

22. The cold could have killed the animal, _____?

23. It may not happen, _____?

24. I am included in the trip, _____?

PART 2

請在下列句子後加上正確的附加問句。

1. Edward will come too, _____?

2. You could help me if you wanted to, _____?

3. Peter and Sally are quite late, _____?

4. There weren't many people at the stadium, _____?

5. He's making sure that everything is all right, _____?

6. It's rather too late to start hunting for the package, _____?

7. You should write a letter to him, _____?

8. Nobody was sure about the exact amount, _____?

9. We will be home in time for dinner, _____?

10. Somebody has to inform the police about the theft, _____?

11. Everybody is waiting for Irene and Lily to arrive, _____?

12. The doctor has decided to operate on his knee, _____?

13. You won't be angry with me, _____?

14. The boys daren't go to tell him, _____?

15. The news was startling, _____ ?

16. Everyone thinks that way, _____ ?

17. Somebody might have stolen it, _____ ?

18. The equipment looked new, _____ ?

19. Nobody needs a drink, _____ ?

20. The weather is fine most of the time, _____ ?

21. The price of pineapples didn't change much, _____ ?

22. Anybody could use the library, _____ ?

23. Something is stuck in the machine, _____ ?

24. The difference can hardly be noticed, _____ ?

PART 3

請在空格中填入適當的字彙以完成下列包含附加問句的句子。

1. No one _____ leave the room without permission, must they?

2. We _____ let sleeping dogs lie, shouldn't we?

3. They agreed to come to a compromise, _____ they?

4. Everybody _____ anxious to get started, aren't they?

5. These words don't mean anything, _____ they?

6. You didn't turn on the gas, _____ you?

7. She _____ have seen us, could she?

8. They had known each other for a long time, _____ they?

9. This meter measures the speed of the motor, _____ it?

10. No one found out the reason why they left, _____ they?

11. I've told you the story before, _____ I?

12. It's been raining since this morning, _____ it?

13. He seems a little upset today, _____ he?

14. Nobody _____ force you to do something you don't like, can they?

15. Everything is set for the show, _____ it?

16. Nobody heard him calling for help, _____ they?

17. Uncle usually blows the horn on his car when he arrives, _____ he?

18. Nobody likes to be cheated, _____ they?

19. Those boys shouldn't fight among themselves, _____ they?

20. Everyone here remembers the night of the incident, _____ they?

PART 4

請在空格中填入適當的字彙以完成下列包含附加問句及回答的句子。

1. "They wouldn't have seen us, _____?" "No, _____."

2. "No one _____ enter the room without permission, _____?" "No, they mustn't."

3. "Diana wasn't very rude to him, _____?" "No, _____."

4. "The goods arrived yesterday, _____?" "Yes, _____."

5. "You used to like coffee, _____?" "Yes, _____."

6. "All of us will help, _____?" "Yes, _____."

7. "The small boy _____ cry out, _____?" "No, he didn't."

8. "There isn't anybody who can do it, _____?" "No, _____."

9. "You'd rather go to the picnic, _____?" "Yes, _____."

10. "Everybody _____ left school, haven't they?" "Yes, _____."

11. "We _____ go to the haunted house, _____?" "Yes, we dare."

12. "She thinks carefully before she acts, _____?" "Yes, _____."

13. "Someone came when I was out, _____?" "Yes, _____."

14. "Everybody should be ready to go now, _____?" "Yes, _____."

15. "There must be a way out of this maze, _____?" "Yes, _____."

16. "They _____ have gone without us, could they?" "No, _____."

17. "Everything had been arranged, _____?" "Yes, _____."

18. "You have a tape recorder at home, _____?" "Yes, _____."

19. "It's made of genuine leather, _____ it?" "Yes, _____."

20. "The results of the competition _____ been announced, have they?" "No, _____."

21. "Anyone can come to the exhibition, _____?" "Yes, _____."

PART 5

請在空格中填入適當的字彙以完成下列包含附加問句及回答的句子。

基礎文法寶典 ❺
Essential English Usage & Grammar

1. "You shouldn't smoke, _____?" "No, _____."

2. "I'm a little late, _____?" "Yes, _____."

3. "She sang well, _____?" "Yes, _____."

4. "He might come, _____?" "Yes, _____."

5. "You don't know when he'll arrive, _____?" "No, _____."

6. "She might stop here on the way home, _____?" "Yes, _____."

7. "Sandy couldn't come with you, _____?" "No, _____."

8. "They mightn't be able to finish, _____?" "No, _____."

9. "He's got a car, _____?" "Yes, _____."

10. "She will be angry, _____?" "Yes, _____."

11. "You haven't been here before, _____?" "No, _____."

12. "You need to do this, _____?" "Yes, _____."

13. "Mary never used to be so nasty, _____?" "No, _____."

14. "He made you do it, _____?" "Yes, _____."

15. "They aren't happy with the results, _____?" "No, _____."

16. "He'll fall and break his neck someday, _____?" "Yes, _____."

17. "I haven't met you before, _____?" "No, _____."

18. "She loves to sew dresses for children, _____?" "Yes, _____."

19. "Everyone is going, _____?" "Yes, _____."

PART 6

請在空格中填入適當的字彙以完成下列包含附加問句及回答的句子。

1. "You didn't receive the money, _____?" "No, _____."

2. "He was very pleased with you, _____?" "Yes, _____."

3. "There are a lot of nails in the box, _____?" "Yes, _____."

4. "She fell down the stairs and broke her leg, _____?" "Yes, _____."

5. "She can't understand what they are saying, _____?" "No, _____."

6. "It is very windy outside, _____?" "Yes, _____."

7. "He hasn't mailed the letter yet, _____?" "No, _____."

8. "The boys will never agree to that suggestion, _____?" "No, _____."

9. "You have been to this art gallery before, _____?" "Yes, _____."

10. "He wants to borrow the ladder, _____?" "Yes, _____."

11. "She doesn't look very pleased to see us, _____?" "No, _____."

12. "He is the man who sold you the vegetables, _____?" "Yes, _____."

13. "Your uncle lives in Melody Street, _____?" "Yes, _____."

14. "They were playing hockey yesterday, _____?" "Yes, _____."

15. "The girls mustn't take things that don't belong to them, _____?" "No, _____."

16. "The river flows through the center of town, _____?" "Yes, _____."

17. "The lilies have been in bloom for a week, _____?" "Yes, _____."

18. "His father won't forbid him to go on the trip, _____?" "No, _____."

19. "He might have arrived by that time, _____?" "Yes, _____."

20. "We shouldn't have told her about it, _____?" "No, _____."

PART 7

請在空格中填入適當的字彙以完成下列包含附加問句及回答的句子。

1. "She can't have taken the car to the office, _____?" "No, _____."

2. "Many of these people have come to see the king, _____?" "Yes, _____."

3. "Anyone could have taken the test papers, _____?" "Yes, _____."

4. "I will have to get up as early as possible tomorrow, _____?" "Yes, _____."

5. "You will help me with all the arrangements, _____?" "Yes, _____."

6. "Alice does all the housework by herself, _____?" "Yes, _____."

7. "All of you promised to help me with the work, _____?" "Yes, _____."

8. "I am being rather silly, _____?" "Yes, _____."

9. "It starts getting dark very early these days, _____?" "Yes, _____."

10. "Everyone's got to come for the practice this afternoon, _____?" "Yes, _____."

11. "We won't obey him, _____?" "No, _____."

12. "There's no need to do all these exercises, _____?" "No, _____."

13. "All of us must do our work properly, _____?" "Yes, _____."

14. "Paul will be here soon, _____?" "Yes, _____."

15. "The office manager should attend to this matter, _____?" "Yes, _____."

16. "She mustn't be seen here, _____?" "No, _____."

17. "She hadn't been there long, _____?" "No, _____."

18. "There is a bus at six o'clock, _____?" "Yes, _____."

19. "Everyone has come, _____?" "Yes, _____."

20. "The police will send for reinforcements soon, _____?" "Yes, _____."

21. "I haven't been to their house for a long time, _____?" "No, _____."

22. "Climate affects the vegetation of a country, _____?" "Yes, _____."

PART 8

請在空格中填入適當的字彙以完成下列包含附加問句及回答的句子。

1. "The fire won't spread, _____?" "No, _____."

2. "May helped the old woman with her basket, _____?" "Yes, _____."

3. "I can borrow your car for the afternoon, _____?" "Yes, _____."

4. "Anyone can come and watch the rehearsals, _____?" "Yes, _____."

5. "Everybody has something to do, _____?" "Yes, _____."

6. "You knew the story before I did, _____?" "Yes, _____."

7. "Peter always works hard, _____?" "Yes, _____."

8. "He seldom goes to the office nowadays, _____?" "No, _____."

9. "The schoolchildren used to take that route, _____?" "Yes, _____."

10. "We rarely see him in town nowadays, _____?" "No, _____."

11. "She should have been there at that time, _____?" "Yes, _____."

12. "Her children used to visit her quite often, _____?" "Yes, _____."

13. "He never used to come home so late before, _____?" "No, _____."

14. "We must have a guide, _____?" "Yes, _____."

15. "I won't be a nuisance, _____?" "No, _____."

16. "Albert needs to have his dinner first, _____?" "Yes, _____."

PART 9

請在空格中填入適當的字彙以完成下列包含附加問句及回答的句子。

1. "That shirt needs to be washed, _____?" "Yes, _____."

2. "We always help one another, _____?" "Yes, _____."

3. "Jenny said that she would come to the picnic, _____?" "Yes, _____."

4. "I shouldn't have done anything about it, _____?" "No, _____."

5. "You let them do as they liked, _____?" "Yes, _____."

6. "It means that someone is after the money, _____?" "Yes, _____."

7. "The judge said that the prisoner deserved to be imprisoned for several years, _____?" "Yes, _____."

8. "Your grandfather won't like to hear about your failure, _____?" "No, _____."

9. "Everyone advised the lady to sell her house and to move to another district, _____?" "Yes, _____."

10. "We will not have much to talk about, _____?" "No, _____."

11. "There wasn't much that could be done to help those poor villagers, _____?" "No, _____."

12. "It isn't time to go to the office yet, _____?" "No, _____."

13. "Victor and Robert shouldn't have been so rude to their friends, _____?" "No, _____."

14. "You think there is simply no way to escape from this building, _____?" "Yes, _____."

15. "They could make up for the loss out of their own pockets, _____?" "Yes, _____."

16. "Everyone has to face the truth someday, _____?" "Yes, _____."

17. "He is waiting for you, _____?" "Yes, _____."

18. "Nick should enter the competition, _____?" "Yes, _____."

PART 10

請在空格中填入適當的字彙以完成下列包含附加問句及回答的句子。

1. "We must send for the doctor at once, _____?" "Yes, _____."

2. "I wouldn't have told them, _____?" "No, _____."

3. "Those animals can cross the river, _____?" "Yes, _____."

4. "She won't come here again, _____?" "No, _____."

5. "Peter wouldn't be afraid of the dog, _____?" "No, _____."

6. "They can leave any time they want, _____?" "Yes, _____."

7. "I should have sent a telegram home, _____?" "Yes, _____."

8. "He couldn't have been there, _____?" "No, _____."

9. "He might change his mind after all, _____?" "Yes, _____."

10. "I have to finish my work first, _____?" "Yes, _____."

11. "Children mustn't stay up late, _____?" "No, _____."

12. "We are willing to put in extra work, _____?" "Yes, _____."

13. "You will remember to bring it, _____?" "Yes, _____."

14. "I would have locked the door, _____?" "Yes, _____."

15. "The dog hasn't hurt its paw, _____?" "No, _____."

16. "You don't know the answer, _____?" "No, _____."

PART 11

請在空格中填入適當的字彙以完成下列包含附加問句及回答的句子。

1. "She seems quite nervous, _____?" "Yes, _____."

2. "The lady liked the pin you showed her, _____?" "Yes, _____."

3. "The swan looks very graceful, _____?" "Yes, _____."

4. "No one must leave the room, _____?" "No, _____."

5. "There aren't any letters for me, _____?" "No, _____."

6. "Those children shouldn't have played ball there, _____?" "No, _____."

7. "Everyone must attend the meeting, _____?" "Yes, _____."

8. "They understand each other quite well, _____?" "Yes, _____."

9. "We agreed to help each other, _____?" "Yes, _____."

10. "Somebody was hiding in the other room, _____?" "Yes, _____."

11. "The parrot is very amusing, _____?" "Yes, _____."

12. "Those questions were rather difficult, _____?" "Yes, _____."

13. "Anybody can go in, _____?" "Yes, _____."

14. "The news proved rather alarming, _____?" "Yes, _____."

15. "There is nothing more to be done, _____?" "No, _____."

16. "The bushes need trimming, _____?" "Yes, _____."

17. "Not everyone voted, _____?" "No, _____."

18. "Everything seems all right now, _____?" "Yes, _____."

19. "The furniture had to be dusted regularly, _____?" "Yes, _____."

20. "No one can climb over the wall now, _____?" "Yes, _____."

PART 12

請在空格中填入適當的字彙以完成下列包含附加問句及回答的句子。

1. You can bake an apple pie, _____?" "Yes, _____."

2. It can't live out of the water, _____?" "No, _____."

3. All of them have gone home, _____?" "Yes, _____."

4. I shouldn't have said that, _____?" "No, _____."

5. There is somebody waiting outside, _____?" "Yes, _____."

6. It might collapse under the weight, _____?" "Yes, _____."

7. I have to be alert, _____?" "Yes, _____."

8. You daren't answer him back, _____?" "No, _____."

9. They don't sell birthday cakes here, _____?" "No, _____."

10. She would have taken it with her, _____?" "Yes, _____."

11. The black dog can't come in here, _____?" "No, _____."

12. You won't leave us in the middle of nowhere, _____?" "No, _____."

13. These snakes are harmless, _____?" "Yes, _____."

14. Nobody offered him a lift, _____?" "No, _____."

15. Everything looks easy on the surface, _____?" "Yes, _____."

16. The news proved rather startling, _____?" "Yes, _____."

17. Everybody knows about the incident, _____?" "Yes, _____."

18. Someone saw him climb in through the window, _____?" "Yes, _____."

Chapter 20 三大子句

20-1 名詞子句

(a) 名詞子句在句子中具有形同名詞的功能，常由 that 或疑問詞（如 what、where、when、who、how、why）等引導。

> **USAGE PRACTICE**
>
> ▶ She asked me how **I was doing lately**. 她問我近況如何。
>
> ▶ What **I want to do** is not important. 我想要做什麼並不重要。
>
> ▶ I want you to find out where **he came from**. 我要你查出他從哪裡來。
>
> ▶ Tell me why **you did such a foolish thing**. 告訴我你為何做這樣的蠢事。

(b) 名詞子句可以當句子的主詞，後接單數動詞。注意此時若以 that 引導名詞子句，that 不可省略。

> **USAGE PRACTICE**
>
> ▶ **What they do** is not my concern. 他們的所做所為不關我的事。
>
> ▶ **What I said** was true. 我說的是真的。
>
> ▶ **What they had done wrong** is the question. 他們到底做錯什麼事是問題所在。
>
> ▶ **What she is doing now** seems very easy. 她現在正在做的事似乎很簡單。
>
> ▶ **How the lion escaped from its cage** is a mystery. 獅子如何從籠子逃出來是個謎。
>
> ▶ **How he can do that** puzzles me. 他如何做那件事令我困惑。
>
> ▶ **How he died** was a complete mystery to everybody. 他的死因對大家來說完全是個謎。
>
> ▶ **That he will reject the offer** seems unlikely. 他似乎不太可能會拒絕這項提議。
>
> ▶ **That she was not feeling well** was obvious. 很明顯地，她不舒服。
>
> ▶ **Why she did it** is her own concern. 她做這件事是她自己的考量。

 可以用虛主詞 it 代替 that 引導的名詞子句，置於句首。

> ▶ It is possible **that the train may be delayed**. 火車可能會誤點。
>
> ▶ It is possible **that the venture will not be a success**. 這個商業投資可能不會成功。
>
> ▶ It is certain **that he will come**. 他一定會來。

▶ It is true **that they have quarreled**. 他們爭吵過是事實。

▶ It is important **that you bring the letter with you**. 隨身帶這封信對你是很重要的。

▶ It was unfortunate **that you were not here at the time**. 很不幸你當時不在這裡。

▶ It seemed impossible **that he would do a thing like that!** 他會做那樣的事似乎是不可能的！

▶ It is uncertain **that he has really set a record**. 還不確定他真的已經創下紀錄。

(c) 名詞子句可以當動詞的受詞，此時子句中若有 that 通常可以省略。

USAGE PRACTICE

▶ I hoped **(that) he would come**. 我希望他會來。

▶ Maggie dreamed **(that) she was flying in a rocket**. 瑪姬夢見她乘火箭飛行。

▶ He denied **(that) he had committed the crime**. 他否認犯罪。

▶ I found **(that) he had been lying to me**. 我發現他一直對我撒謊。

▶ She heard **(that) I was very ill**. 她聽到我病重的消息。

▶ He said **(that) the car had broken down**. 他說車子已經故障了。

▶ Jill says **(that) she will not be back until ten**. 吉兒說她十點才會回來。

▶ They told me **(that) I should pay more attention to my work**.

他們告訴我說我應該更注意我的工作。

▶ He told me **(that) the prisoner had escaped**. 他告訴我犯人已經逃跑了。

▶ She does not know **when she will return**. 她不知道她何時會回來。

▶ I asked her **why she was crying**. 我問她為何在哭。

▶ She asked me **how I had managed to solve that tricky problem**.

她問我是如何設法解決那棘手的問題。

▶ Tell me **where you spent your vacation**. 告訴我你在哪裡渡假。

(d) 名詞子句可以當介系詞的受詞，此時名詞子句一般不能由 that 引導。

USAGE PRACTICE

▶ I am grateful for **what you have done for me**. 我很感激你曾經為我所做的一切。

▶ She is very grateful for **whatever she is given**. 她對被給予的一切感到很感激。

▶ My father laughed at **what we had told him**. 父親聽到我們告訴他的話後笑了出來。

▶ Is there any meaning in **wha t he says**? 他所講的話有任何意義嗎？

▶ They were amazed at **what they saw**. 他們對所看見的一切感到驚訝。

▶ No one is ever satisfied with **what one has**. 從來沒有人會滿意自己所擁有的東西。

▶ She is pleased with **what I have done so far**. 她對我目前所做的事感到滿意。

▶ Don't be too anxious about **what is going to happen**. 不要太擔心即將發生的事。

▶ We were worried about **what might have happened to him**.

我們擔心他可能發生了什麼事。

▶ She always listens to w**hat her parents say**. 她總是聽她父母的話。

(e) 名詞子句可以當主詞補語。

USAGE PRACTICE

▶ The fact is **that we don't know what to look for**. 事實是我們不知道要找什麼。

▶ Her prayer was **that her child might live**. 她祈禱小孩能存活。

▶ My wish is **that I may have the chance to travel**. 我的希望是能有機會去旅遊。

▶ Life is **what we make of it**. 人生端看我們的作為。

▶ This is not **what she wants you to do**. 這不是她要你做的事。

▶ My belief is **that he was too afraid to come**. 我相信他是太害怕而不敢來。

▶ What made me angry was **that he was rude to everyone**.

讓我生氣的是他對每個人都無禮。

(f) 名詞子句可以當名詞的同位語。

USAGE PRACTICE

▶ Your statement **that you were not near the scene of the crime** will not be believed.

你不在犯罪現場附近的聲明將不被採信。

▶ The idea **that he dislikes you** is totally wrong.

他不喜歡你的這個想法完全是錯的。

▶ Her answer **that she had a lot of work to do** was not convincing enough.

她有許多工作要做的這種答覆不夠令人信服。

▶ Your excuse **that you were ill** will not be accepted. 你生病的藉口是不會被接受的。

▶ The fact **that the man was guilty** was obvious to everyone.

這個人有罪的事實對大家來說顯而易見。

▶ The rumor **that war will break out soon** is untrue. 戰爭不久將爆發的謠言不是真的。

▶ There is fear **that the patient might not recover**. 病人恐怕無法復原。

(g) 有些形容詞（例如 sure、certain、afraid、glad、surprised 等）常接 that 引導的名詞子句，表示主詞對該子句的感覺；在此用法中，that 可以省略。

USAGE PRACTICE

▶ I am sure **(that) they will win the match**. 我確信他們將會贏得比賽。

▶ She is certain **(that) she saw a man lurking in the shadows**.
她確信看到一個男人潛伏在暗處。

▶ He was afraid **(that) he would be too late**. 他怕他會太晚。

▶ Are you glad **(that) the exams are over at last**? 你很高興考試終於要結束了嗎？

▶ He is very glad **(that) he is home again**. 他很高興再度回到家。

▶ You may be surprised **(that) one day we'll be able to spend our vacation on the moon**. 你可能會很驚訝有一天我們將能夠在月球上渡假。

▶ I'm sorry **(that) you have failed your exam**. 我很遺憾你沒有通過考試。

▶ We are sorry **(that) you were involved in the accident**. 我們很抱歉你被捲入這場意外。

▶ We are happy **(that) you have found a job to your liking**.
我們很高興你已經找到你喜歡的工作。

▶ She is sad **(that) she can't go on the picnic with them**.
她很傷心不能和他們一起去野餐。

▶ They are confident **(that) they will win the game**. 他們有信心能贏得這場比賽。

▶ I am quite confident **(that) our leader will not let us down**.
我相當有信心我們的隊長不會讓我們失望。

 小練習

請利用名詞子句將下列句子合併為一句。

1. I am very sure. He did not come to my house that evening.

   → _____

2. I agree. None of them should have approached the principal in such a manner.

   → _____

3. Please tell me. How did you manage to persuade that girl to come?

→ _____

4. People believe it. The treasure was hidden somewhere on the island.

→ _____

5. I am very confident. He will break the old record and set a new one for the high jump.

→ _____

6. It annoyed me. He kept on grumbling about it.

→ _____

7. His mother is worried. He may be too ill to go to school.

→ _____

8. I found it out. The man had been returning home very late every night.

→ _____

9. She was feeling homesick and longing to go home. That was apparent.

→ _____

10. The fact is this. No one except Mr. Smith will be able to solve such a difficult problem.

→ _____

11. What do I want to discuss with him? That is not important.

→ _____

12. It is certain. No one else could have had the chance to go into the room.

→ _____

13. I am afraid. He isn't going to like this at all.

→ _____

14. That is certainly incredible. Why did they do such a foolish thing?

→ _____

15. They told me something. I was going to be put in charge of the whole operation.

→ _____

16. Where else could they have gone in such stormy weather? That was the question.

→ _____

20-2 形容詞子句

(a) 形容詞子句經常由關係代名詞（如 who、whom、whose、which、that 等）引導，

用來修飾名詞或名詞片語。關係代名詞在子句中作動詞或介系詞的受詞時，可以
省略。

USAGE PRACTICE

▶ I was offered a lift by a man **who was passing by**. 一個過路人讓我搭他的便車。

▶ The person **who returned your wallet** was honest. 還你皮夾的那個人是誠實的。

▶ The boy **who broke the window** has been punished. 打破窗戶的男孩被處罰了。

▶ The students **who passed the exam** were happy. 通過考試的學生們很高興。

▶ That man, **who is standing near the table**, is my teacher.
那個正站在桌子旁的人是我的老師。

▶ My father, **who returned last night**, brought a present for me.
我的父親昨晚回來，帶了一個禮物給我。

▶ She is a girl **(whom) we all like**. 她是個我們都喜歡的女孩。

▶ The man **(whom) you saw yesterday** is the owner of the house.
你昨天看到的人是這間屋子的主人。

▶ The boy **(whom) she met yesterday** in town was my cousin.
她昨天在城裡遇到的男孩是我的堂哥。

▶ That was the boy **(whom) I was telling you about**. 那就是我向你提到的男孩。

▶ Mr. Rogers, **whom you met at my house**, has invited us to dinner.
羅傑斯先生就是你在我家遇見的那個人，他邀我們吃晚飯。

▶ The police have arrested the man **whose car bore a false license plate**.
警方已經逮捕那個在他汽車上掛假車牌的人。

▶ My best friend, **whose father has gone abroad**, will be here for the weekend.
我最好的朋友要在這裡度週末，他父親已經出國了。

▶ The story, **which is long**, has a sad ending. 這個長篇故事有個悲慘的結局。

▶ The furniture, **which was valuable**, was destroyed in the fire.
那個貴重的傢俱在大火中被燒毀。

▶ This poem, **which everybody likes**, was written by William Wordsworth.
大家都喜歡的這首詩是威廉‧華茲華斯寫的。

▶ The signature **which is at the top of the page** belongs to my father.
這頁上方的簽名是我爸爸的。

▶ The cat **(which) I was going to give Mary** has given birth to three kittens.

我本來要送給瑪麗的那隻貓已經生了三隻小貓。

▶ I lost the book **(which) I had borrowed from the library**. 我弄丟了從圖書館借來的書。

▶ Where's the book **(which) I left here a moment ago**? 我不久前放在這兒的書在哪裡？

▶ I turned to the page **which gave a description of Tom Sawyer**.

我翻到描寫湯姆・索耶的那一頁。

▶ This is the cat **that ate the fish**. 這就是那隻吃了魚的貓。

▶ He sold the dog **which had bitten his son**. 他把咬兒子的狗賣掉了。

▶ Those are the flowers **(that) she brought us**. 那些是她帶來給我們的花。

▶ He caught a fish **which was about one meter long**. 他抓到一條約一公尺長的魚。

▶ Bring me the book **(that) I left on the table**. 把我放在桌上的書拿給我。

▶ It was the most exciting story **(that) we had heard**. 那是我們聽過最刺激的故事。

▶ Eat all **(that) you can**. 吃你所能吃的。

▶ The movie **(that) we saw last night** was a most exciting one.

我們昨晚看的電影非常刺激。

▶ Who is the man **(that) you were talking to just now**? 剛才和你講話的人是誰？

 形容詞子句應該盡量靠近其修飾的名詞或名詞片語。

▶ The children **who were sitting on the swing** spotted the snake.
坐在鞦韆上的孩子們發現了蛇。（O）
　→ The children spotted the snake **who were sitting on the swing**. （×）
▶ The policeman **who was on duty** pursued the thief. 正在值勤的警察追捕竊賊。（O）
　→ The policeman pursued the thief **who was on duty**. （×）
▶ The tourists **that visited the zoo** admired the seals. 參觀動物園的遊客喜歡海豹。（O）
　→ The tourists admired the seals **that visited the zoo**. （×）

(b) 形容詞子句也可以用關係副詞（如 where、when、why 等）引導，修飾表示「地點、時間或原因」的名詞或名詞片語。

USAGE PRACTICE

▶ In the village **where he was born** lived an old fortune-teller.

在他出生的村莊裡住著一位老算命師。

▶ The place **where he used to live** is now deserted. 他過去居住的地方現在荒廢了。

▶ He showed me the place **where he had found the lump of gold**.

他給我看他發現金塊的地方。

▶ We saw the house **where Shakespeare lived long ago**.

我們看見莎士比亞很久前住的房子。

▶ I remembered the time **when she was a baby**. 我記得她還是嬰兒的時候。

▶ Does she know the time **when we are to meet**? 她知道我們要見面的時間嗎？

▶ Can you remember the day **when you first came here**? 你記得你初來此地的那一天嗎？

▶ On the day **when you pass your exam**, I will give you a present.

在你通過考試的那天，我會送你禮物。

▶ She told me the reason **why she had hesitated before making the decision**.

她告訴我她在做決定前猶豫不決的原因。

▶ The reason **why we have come** is to return your magazines.

我們來這裡的原因是要還你雜誌。

▶ She told me the reason **why her brother couldn't turn up**.

她告訴我她弟弟不能來的原因。

▶ The reason **why I did not bring my report** is that I have lost it.

我沒帶報來的原因是我把它弄丟了。

 由關係副詞引導的形容詞子句常會被誤認為副詞子句。記住，形容詞子句是用來修飾名詞的。

▶ I remember the time **when I was on vacation by the lakeside**.
我記得在湖邊渡假的時光。（形容詞子句）
▶ Lead me to the place **where you found it**. 帶我到你發現這東西的地方。（形容詞子句）
▶ I remember what happened **when I was on vacation by the lakeside**.
我記得當我在湖邊渡假時所發生的事情。（副詞子句）
▶ Just put the necklace **where you found it**. 就把項鍊放在你發現它的地方。（副詞子句）

請利用形容詞子句將下列句子合併為一句。請注意 that 僅限用於一定要使用的情況。

1. Did you watch the procession? It passed by here just now.

→ _____

2. There is a girl working in that shop. She looks like you.

→ _____

3. The insect is a cicada. You killed it just now.

→ _____

4. We spoke to the lady. You had rescued her cat from the tree last night.

→ _____

5. The roof needs repairing. A few tiles have been displaced from it.

→ _____

6. You should take the elevator. It goes to all the floors.

→ _____

7. Bring me the scissors. They are in the topmost drawer.

→ _____

8. He is the most conceited person. I have ever met.

→ _____

9. They postponed the match. It was supposed to take place tomorrow evening.

→ _____

10. The thief must have climbed in through that window. He left fingerprints on the window.

→ _____

11. Have you seen the movie? It was shown at the Grand Cinema last week.

→ _____

12. Did you tell the news to the man? You are very friendly with his daughter.

→ _____

13. One day he will meet someone. She means a lot to him.

→ _____

14. The article was printed in the school's newsletter. The article was written by Andrew.

→ _____

15. The person says that he is the former chief clerk here. He is waiting in the lounge.

→ _____

16. The boy broke both legs. He fell from the top of the tree.

→ _____

17. My mother told us an amusing story. She is a great story teller.

18. The friend is a real friend. He helps you in time of need.

→ _____

19. The child died from a disease. It was unknown to the doctors at that time.

→ _____

20. Did you read the notice? It was pinned onto the board two days ago.

→ _____

☞ 更多相關習題請見本章應用練習 Part 1～Part 4。

20-3 副詞子句

(a) 時間副詞子句表示 「一個動作在何時發生」，常用表示時間的從屬連接詞 （如 when、while、before、after、until、since、as、as soon as 等）來引導。

USAGE PRACTICE

▶ It was raining **when I woke up**. 當我醒來時，正在下雨。

▶ **When you see him**, please tell him about the message.

　當你見到他時，請告訴他這個訊息。

▶ They arrested the thief **while he was leaving the shop**.

　當小偷正要離開商店時，他們逮捕了他。

▶ She studied accounting **while she was in school**. 她之前唸書時修習會計。

▶ **While they were arguing with each other**, she slipped out.

　當他們正在爭論時，她溜了出去。

▶ They had seen it **before I did**. 他們在我看見它之前就已經看到了。

▶ I will come to your house **after the meeting is over**. 會議結束以後，我會到你家。

▶ The bus came **after we had waited for nearly an hour**.

　在我們等了將近一小時後，公車才來。

▶ He won't make any decision **until he has consulted his parents**.

　直到和父母親商量後他才會做決定。

▶ He will have to stay here **until the rain stops**. 他將必須留在這裡直到雨停。

▶ He did not go home **until he had finished his work**. 他直到完成工作才回家。

▶ **Since he was born**, his mother has never been well.

自從他出生後，他母親的身體就一直很不好。

▶ I have not seen her **since she left this place two years ago**.

自從她兩年前離開這個地方後，我就不曾見過她。

▶ He has been missing **since his mother was admitted to hospital**.

自從他的母親住院後，他就失蹤了。

▶ **As he walked home,** he kept thinking about the party. 走路回家時，他一直想著派對的事。

▶ The hotel is on the right **as you turn into the road**. 當你轉進那條路時，旅館就在右邊。

▶ I want to see him **as soon as he gets here**. 他一到達這裡，我就要見他。

▶ The child fell asleep **as soon as she was put to bed**.

這孩子一被放到床上，就立刻睡著。

(b) 狀態副詞子句表示「一個動作如何發生」，常用表示狀態的從屬連接詞（如 as、as though、as if 等）引導。

USAGE PRACTICE

▶ I will do **as I like**. 我喜歡怎麼做就怎麼做。

▶ I filed the documents **as he had taught me**. 我照他教我的方法來把這些文件歸檔。

▶ All of you must do **as you are told**. 你們所有的人都必須照著指示去做。

▶ You must do the work **as you think best**. 你必須照著你認為最好的方法去做這個工作。

▶ He ran **as if a tiger was after him**. 他跑得好像有老虎在追他。

▶ He behaves **as if he owns this place**. 他表現得好像他擁有這個地方一樣。

▶ He sounded **as if he knew the answer**. 他聽起來彷彿知道答案。

▶ They rushed around **as if they were crazy**. 他們彷彿瘋了似地衝來衝去。

(c) 地點副詞子句表示「一個動作在某地發生」，常用表示地方的從屬連接詞（如 where、wherever）來引導。

USAGE PRACTICE

▶ They always swim **where the river is the shallowest**. 他們總是在河流最淺的地方游泳。

▶ Please stay **where you are**. 請你留在原地。

▶ The accident occurred **where the road takes a sharp bend**.

車禍發生在道路急轉彎的地方。

▶ The children should play **where there is shade from the sun**.

孩子們應該在沒有陽光的蔭涼處玩耍。

▶ I will follow you **wherever you go**. 無論你去什麼地方，我都將跟隨你。

▶ You must find her **wherever she may be**. 無論她在哪裡，你一定要找到她。

▶ I am prepared to go **wherever they send me**. 我已經準備好要去任何他們派我去的地方。

▶ **Wherever I went**, she went, too. 無論我去哪裡，她也跟著去。

▶ Sleep **wherever you like**. 你想睡在哪就睡在哪。

(d) 原因副詞子句表示 「某一動作發生的原因」， 常用表示原因的從屬連接詞 （如 because、since、as、for 等）來引導。

USAGE PRACTICE

▶ He looks very pale **because he has just recovered from an illness**.

他看起來臉色蒼白，因為他才剛病癒。

▶ I can't go to see the football game **because I have no ticket**.

我不能去看美式足球賽，因為我沒有票。

▶ She doesn't feel like doing anything **because she is very tired**.

她不想做任何事，因為她非常疲倦。

▶ We brought her home with us **as she did not have any place to go**.

我們帶她一起回家，因為她沒有任何地方可以去。

▶ You'd better lead the way **as you have been here before**.

最好由你帶路，因為你以前曾來過這裡。

▶ **As my mother was away**, I had to do all the housework.

因為我媽媽不在家，我得做所有的家事。

▶ **As you have grown up**, you mustn't behave so childishly.

既然你已經長大了，你不能表現得如此孩子氣。

▶ You might stay at home **since it's raining**. 你不妨待在家裡，因為下雨了。

▶ I left early **since I had promised my mother to weed the garden**.

我早早離開，因為我已答應我媽媽要除院子裡的草。

▶ The children must go to sleep now **for it's their bedtime**.

孩子們現在必須上床睡覺了，因為他們的睡覺時間到了。

▶ I can't go to school today **for I have a high fever**. 我今天不能上學，因為我發高燒。

(e) 讓步副詞子句表示「即使、雖然、無論…」等意義，常用表示讓步的從屬連接詞
（如 although、though、even though、even if、whatever、however、no matter
how/what 等）來引導。

USAGE PRACTICE

▶ **Although/Though they were not well off**, they lived a happy life.

雖然他們家境不富裕，但他們過著快樂的生活。

▶ **Although/Though it was late**, they insisted on waiting for another hour.

雖然很晚了，但他們堅持再等一小時。

▶ She remained blind **although/though she had had a number of eye operations**.

雖然她已經動過好幾次眼部手術，但她仍看不見。

▶ She is a friendly girl **although/though she has a quick temper**.

雖然她性子很急，但她是個友善的女孩。

▶ **Even though they were frightened**, they did not show it.

雖然他們很害怕，但沒有表現出來。

▶ She scolded the little boy **even though it was not his fault**.

儘管那不是小男孩的過錯，她還是責罵他。

▶ I will go **even if he does not allow me to**. 即使他不准我去，我也要去。

▶ **Even if they threaten him**, he won't do it. 即使他們威脅他，他也不會做這件事。

▶ I will continue to stay there as before **whatever you may say**.

不論你說什麼，我都會繼續像以前一樣留在那裡。

▶ I will go there **whatever happens**. 不論發生什麼事，我都會去那裡。

▶ **However difficult the question may be**, you must try to answer it.

不論這個問題有多難，你都必須試著去回答。

▶ **However hard he tried**, he could not persuade her to change her mind.

不論他多麼努力地嘗試，他都無法說服她改變心意。

▶ The soldier remained in critical condition **however hard the doctors tried to save his
life**. 不論醫生們如何試著救他，這士兵仍然處於危險狀態。

▶ **No matter how fast I ran**, my pursuer seemed to run faster.

無論我跑得多快，追趕我的人好像跑得更快。

▶ **No matter how hard he tried**, he was always beaten.

無論他多麼努力地嘗試，他總是被擊敗。

(f) 條件副詞子句表示「某一動作發生的條件」，常用表示條件的從屬連接詞（如 if、
    unless、provided (that)、whether...(or not)、as long as、on condition (that)、
    supposing (that) 等）來引導。

USAGE PRACTICE

▶ **If you want to learn**, I will be pleased to teach you. 如果你想學，我會很樂意教你。

▶ **If you like it**, I will buy it for you. 如果你喜歡這東西，我會買給你。

▶ **If you see her**, tell her to return home at once. 如果你看見她，叫她立刻回家。

▶ We will go **if it doesn't rain**. 如果沒下雨，我們就會去。

▶ **If I were you**, I wouldn't do such a thing. 假如我是你，我就不會做這樣的事。

▶ **If he had seen her cheating**, he would have scolded her.

假如他看見她作弊，他早就罵她了。

▶ He would not come **unless you invited him personally**.

除非你親自邀請他，否則他不會來。

▶ I won't go **unless you go with me**. 除非你和我一起去，不然我不會去。

▶ You will fail **unless you work harder**. 除非你更努力工作，否則會失敗。

▶ **Unless you work hard**, you will not pass the exam.

除非你努力讀書，否則你不會通過考試。

▶ **Unless you answer me**, I won't let you go. 除非你回答我，不然我不會讓你走。

▶ She will sew it for you **provided (that) you help her with the housework**.

如果你幫她做家事，她就會替你縫製它。

▶ You may borrow those instruments **provided (that) you take good care of them**.

如果你好好照料這些儀器，你就可以借用它們。

▶ You must go **whether you hear from her or not**.

不論你有沒有收到她的消息，你都必須去。

▶ I will stay here **as long as you are with me**. 只要你和我在一起，我就會留在這裡。

▶ **On condition (that) we pay him well**, he will work for us.

基礎文法寶典❺
Essential English Usage & Grammar

如果我們給他高薪，他就會為我們工作。

▶ She will forgive you **on condition (that) you apologize to her**.

只要你向她道歉，她就會原諒你。

▶ **Supposing (that) she falls ill**, who will look after her? 如果她生病了，誰會照顧她呢？

(g) 目的副詞子句表示「做某一動作的目的」，常用表示目的的從屬連接詞（如 so that、in order that、in case (that)、for fear (that) 等）來引導。

USAGE PRACTICE

▶ I made a note of it **so that I might not forget**.

我做筆記，以便我不會忘記。

▶ He worked hard **so that he might pass the exam**.

他很用功以便通過考試。

▶ I've come early **so that I may help you with the preparations**.

我提早來了，以便能幫你準備。

▶ She switched on the light **so that she could see better**.

她把燈打開，為了要看得更清楚。

▶ He walked very slowly **so that I could catch up with him**.

他走得非常慢，以便讓我趕上他。

▶ She was talking loudly **so that everyone would be able to hear her**.

她大聲説話，以便大家都能夠聽到。

▶ They brought along some firewood **in order that they might make a fire**.

他們帶來薪柴，為了要生火。

▶ I'm reminding you **in order that you won't forget to bring it tomorrow**.

我正在提醒你，以便你明天不會忘記帶它來。

▶ **In order that it would not escape**, we tied a strong rope around its neck.

為了不讓牠逃跑，我們在牠的脖子上綁了一條結實的繩索。

▶ I took along a roll of bandages **in case (that) we needed it**.

我帶著一捲繃帶以防我們需要用到它。

▶ We rang the bell again **in case (that) they might not have heard it**.

我們再次按鈴，以免他們可能沒聽見。

▶ They evacuated to a safer place **for fear (that) the flood would reach them**.

他們撤退到安全的地方，以免洪水會淹沒他們。

(h) 結果副詞子句表示「做某一動作的結果」，常用表示結果的從屬連接詞（如 so、so...that、such...that 等）來引導。

USAGE PRACTICE

▶ The light was on, **so he could see what happened**.

電燈開著，所以他可以看見發生了什麼事。

▶ It was a fine day, **so we had a picnic by the river**.

天氣很好，因此我們在河邊野餐。

▶ It was raining, **so we had to use our umbrellas**. 下雨了，所以我們得撐傘。

▶ She talked **so** softly **that I could not hear her well**. 她說話如此輕柔，以至我無法聽清楚。

▶ She is **so** lazy **that she never passes any of the tests**.

她如此懶散，以至從來沒通過任何考試。

▶ We were **so** thirsty **that we drank from the river**. 我們如此口渴，以至我們喝河水。

▶ Is she **so** dumb **that she cannot answer any questions**?

她會笨到無法回答任何問題嗎？

▶ It was **such** a fantastic story **that nobody believed it**. 那故事如此古怪，以至於沒人相信。

▶ There was **such** a crowd **that there wasn't enough food for them**.

人群如此之多，以至於沒有足夠的食物供應他們。

(i) 比較副詞子句常用表示比較的從屬連接詞（如 as 和 than）來引導。

USAGE PRACTICE

▶ The question is not **as** difficult **as you think**. 這個問題不像你想的那麼難。

▶ He can run **as** fast **as a deer**. 他能跑得像鹿一樣快。

▶ The problem is not **so** easy **as you think**. 這問題不像你想的那麼容易。

▶ He seems better **than he was last week**. 他的狀況好像比上星期好些。

▶ The result was much better **than I had hoped for**. 這結果比我希望的好很多。

▶ She always works harder **than I do**. 她總是比我認真工作。

▶ The situation is more serious **than I thought**. 情況比我想的還嚴重。

請在空格中填入適當的連接詞（不限一字）以形成副詞子句。

1. He won't feel better _____ he has taken this medicine.

2. You must take off your shoes _____ you enter the house.

3. The children burned themselves badly _____ they were playing with the matches.

4. _____ you let her have the knife, she is sure to cut herself.

5. He carved the wooden figure _____ he was a professional.

6. They hid _____ they thought they would not be found.

7. _____ I were you, I would not let him cheat me out of my money.

8. _____ slow the child is in learning things, you must be patient with her.

9. He was seriously ill _____ he was bitten by a mad dog.

10. She will pay the grocer _____ she receives her money at the end of the month.

11. _____ they were rich, they were not happy.

12. The parcel will not be sent by air _____ she is willing to pay five dollars in postage fees.

13. "I'll meet you _____ I first met you," he said.

14. You must act _____ you don't know that anything has happened.

15. There won't be another world war _____ people make a strong effort to live in peace with one another.

16. Don't use the lawn mower _____ it belongs to you!

17. She had to do all the housework _____ her parents were away on vacation.

18. Why don't you get a lift from him _____ he is going to town, too?

19. I worked hard _____ I might win the scholarship.

20. It was _____ an interesting story _____ I read it again.

☞ 更多相關習題請見本章應用練習 Part 5～Part 8。

Chapter 20　應用練習

PART 1

請利用形容詞子句將下列句子合併為一句。請注意 that 僅限用於一定要使用的情況，同時也避免用非正式的 who 來取代正式的 whom。

1. The tree is beginning to die. It has lost all its leaves.

   → _____

2. Do you know the time? He came home at that time last night.

   → _____

3. The commander didn't know what to do. He gave the order himself.

   → _____

4. I can't remember the exact place. I have seen these books on display.

   → _____

5. His father gave him everything. He asked for them.

   → _____

6. The experiment proved that fish respond to light. It was tried on various kinds of fish.

   → _____

7. Success is the result of hard work. It does not come easily to people.

   → _____

8. The bridge is being repaired. It was destroyed during last night's storm.

   → _____

9. He put the straw near the fireplace. It was a dangerous thing to do.

   → _____

10. They planned to have the meeting on Sunday. It was the time when most of the adults were not at home.

    → _____

11. Their house has a big garden. It is surrounded by a tall hedge.

    → _____

12. The noise had been made merely by some mice scratching against a floorboard. It had disturbed him.

    → _____

13. The person has a unique style. He wrote that essay.

    → _____

14. He was given the Victoria Cross. Any person would feel honored to receive it.

→ _____

15. The plan is quite a sensible one. One of the boys proposed it.

→ _____

16. No one knew the reason. The reason was why he left so hurriedly.

→ _____

17. Shakespeare was buried in the place. He was born in that place.

→ _____

18. My father has invited you to stay with us during the holidays. You met him at the station once.

→ _____

19. I wonder if you still remember the day. We were discussing how farmers forecast the weather.

→ _____

20. In the cave was a huge lion. Andy had sheltered in the cave the previous night.

→ _____

PART 2

請利用形容詞子句將下列句子合併為一句。請注意 that 僅限用於一定要使用的情況，同時也避免用非正式的 who 來取代正式的 whom。

1. I have finished doing the homework. The teacher gave it to us this morning.

→ _____

2. He wants to go to the place. His grandmother had bought it a few years ago.

→ _____

3. The student will be severely punished. He was caught smoking in school.

→ _____

4. We saw the old lady. Her son had been seriously injured in an accident.

→ _____

5. The accident was a very serious one. It happened at the crossroads near the market.

→ _____

6. Can you describe the girl? You say that she was the one who stole your pen.

→ _____

7. Did you recognize the man? He was biking past us with a basket on the handlebars.

→ _____

8. I told her the time. He would be returning from the office.

→ _____

9. John is going off to South Africa this week. His cousin is your neighbor.

→ _____

10. Those children are my nieces and nephews. They are playing in the garden.

→ _____

11. The dog has already been tied up. It was chasing the neighbor's cat just now.

→ _____

12. Any person in the village can tell you the story. You ask them.

→ _____

13. The reason was unsatisfactory. She gave the reason for being late.

→ _____

14. The poem is a very beautiful one. It was written by Lord Byron.

→ _____

15. Stella has sent an invitation card to you. You met her in my house last week.

→ _____

16. This boy has been waiting to see me for half an hour. His brother is in my class.

→ _____

17. The students have applied for their identity cards. They are all twelve years old.

→ _____

18. We went to inspect the house. We wanted to buy the house.

→ _____

PART 3

請利用形容詞子句將下列句子合併為一句。請注意 that 僅限用於一定要使用的情況，同時也避免用非正式的 who 來取代正式的 whom。

1. The boy is sure to fall. He climbs too high up the tree.

→ _____

2. Where is the book? He left it there for me.

→ _____

3. Any person will show you the place. You ask him.

→ _____

4. I have received the message. You sent it to me.

→ _____

5. No one stopped at the grave. A wartime hero was buried there.

→ _____

6. He remembers the days of his childhood. He used to fish in the river. It is near his home.

→ _____

7. He cannot reach the encyclopedia. It is on the topmost shelf.

→ _____

8. The new manager called a staff meeting. He was appointed by the board of directors.

→ _____

9. The children have no need for a doctor. They are strong and healthy.

→ _____

10. The CD has a few scratches on it. You bought the CD recently.

→ _____

11. You proposed a plan. I think it is an excellent plan.

→ _____

12. He can't wear any shoes on his foot. It has swollen to twice its size.

→ _____

13. His father gave him ten dollars. He put it into his savings account.

→ _____

14. Can you show me a photograph of the girl? You said you wanted to introduce her to me.

→ _____

15. My brother has gone on an expedition up the river. You have met him before.

→ _____

16. The dog was killed by a truck. The truck was traveling at a great speed.

→ _____

17. The doctor has given me some medicine. I must take the medicine when I feel dizzy.

→ _____

18. You will have your reward on the day. You capture the murderer. He has killed a number of people.

→ _____

PART 4

請利用形容詞子句將下列句子合併為一句。請注意 that 僅限用於一定要使用的情況，同時也避免用非正式的 who 來取代正式的 whom。

1. I remember the day. The transport workers were on strike that day.

   → _____

2. Where is the key? I left it in the keyhole.

   → _____

3. I know the reason. I know why he went home early.

   → _____

4. She forgave the boy. He had placed a live lizard on her desk.

   → _____

5. Have you fixed the time? We are supposed to meet at that time.

   → _____

6. She helped the old man across the road. It was very kind of her.

   → _____

7. They know the place. They know where the smugglers hid the contraband goods.

   → _____

8. The man found a wallet. The wallet contained a lot of money.

   → _____

9. That student has failed in the exam again. He never studies or does his homework.

   → _____

10. My brother, Jim, is studying in that school. He was sixteen last week.

    → _____

11. My mother likes to travel. You met her yesterday.

    → _____

12. George Bernard Shaw died in 1950. He wrote *Pygmalion*.

    → _____

13. Do you know the time? Do you know when the conference will begin?

    → _____

14. These are the questions. You are to answer them as best as you can.

→ _____

15. My uncle missed the last train to Claxton. That annoyed him very much.

→ _____

16. We gave a farewell party for Miss Porter. She had been our English teacher for two years.

→ _____

17. The port is growing at a tremendous rate. It is situated in a very strategic position.

→ _____

18. Show me the spot. You hid the box there.

→ _____

PART 5

請在空格中填入適當的連接詞（不限一字）以形成副詞子句。

1. The child fell asleep _____ the show was still on.

2. He could not remember _____ he had put the key.

3. The sky looked _____ it would rain any minute.

4. _____ it proceeds, the typhoon causes damage to life and property.

5. _____ the old woman was recovering, the child always came to sit by her side in the evenings.

6. She felt _____ a sharp knife was stabbing at her heart.

7. _____ the teacher was strict, the boys weren't afraid of him.

8. We will meet you _____ the path turns toward the river.

9. _____ he was getting on the bus, he remembered he had left the bathroom faucet on.

10. She hid her face _____ we would not see that she had been crying.

11. They came across the map _____ they were searching for the book.

12. "Do _____ I say and don't argue!" he said.

13. Please arrange the chairs _____ I had told you.

14. _____ the telephone rings, please answer it for me.

15. I switched on the lamp _____ I could see the time.

16. He talked very softly, _____ only a few of us could hear him.

17. _____ he failed to win a prize, he did rather well in the sports competition.

18. _____ nobody was at home, we left a message by the door.

19. It was such an amazing sight _____ everybody stood in awe, gazing at it.

20. "_____ good you are, there is always somebody who is better," she said.

PART 6

請在空格中填入適當的連接詞（不限一字）以形成副詞子句。

1. The woman had _____ a great shock _____ she fainted.

2. She goes around collecting donations _____ she has the time.

3. _____ you don't tell him that, he may not get so angry.

4. The teacher told them to study harder _____ they would pass the exams.

5. Every Sunday, he goes to the beach _____ he can get a little peace and quiet.

6. The manager scolded the worker _____ he was an irresponsible person.

7. Make hay _____ the sun shines.

8. The doctor said that I could leave the hospital _____ the cast was taken off.

9. She has not come to see me _____ she went to her aunt's place.

10. All salesmen must be prepared to go _____ the manager sends them.

11. I left as early as possible _____ I had a lot of work to do at home.

12. _____ he is given some expert help, he can't lead a normal life.

13. I shut the door _____ the cat would not be able to come in.

14. Mickey is _____ afraid to show his report card to his father _____ he doesn't want to go home at all.

15. They could not find it _____ they had searched the house from top to bottom.

16. I must remember to give him the information _____ he can pass it on to his brother.

17. It was _____ a sad story _____ they cried on hearing it.

18. I will place this chair _____ you tell me.

PART 7

請在空格中填入適當的連接詞（不限一字）以形成副詞子句。

1. The soldiers were at a great disadvantage _____ they were hopelessly outnumbered.

2. We will pay you _____ the goods are delivered.

3. The kitten lapped up the milk _____ it was very hungry.

4. "There will be discipline on this ship _____ I am commanding it," he said.

5. The terrorists were captured _____ they came out into the open for food.

6. Write the word down _____ you may forget all about it.

7. I will speak the truth _____ I am threatened or not.

8. He thinks that he can buy off everyone _____ he is rich.

9. What would you answer _____ I put such a question to you?

10. _____ the result may be, I will not accept it.

11. You have to dust the room _____ the guests arrive.

12. You may finish the piece of handiwork _____ you like.

13. She studies hard _____ she may do well in her exam.

14. He sold the car _____ it always gave him a lot of trouble.

15. She wasn't happy with the results of the draw _____ she won a prize.

16. _____ he is old, he is able to do as much work _____ a younger man.

17. She bought a present for him _____ she didn't have much money.

18. He was _____ weak _____ he could hardly speak. His companion could not hear what he was saying _____ his voice was barely audible.

19. They were commanded to wait _____ the signal was given. They neither flinched nor moved back _____ the enemy approached.

20. No one knew exactly _____ the prisoner was kept. They only knew that the soldiers guarded him closely _____ he should escape.

PART 8

請在空格中填入適當的連接詞（不限一字）以形成副詞子句。

1. I will visit that place _____ I go to Italy.

2. We will leave _____ you are ready.

3. He received his salary yesterday, _____ he can now pay his rent.

4. This assignment is not so easy _____ you think it is.

5. She arrived late _____ her taxi broke down on the way.

6. He looked _____ sorry _____ his mother forgave him.

7. We were not depressed _____ we had lost the match.

8. He looks _____ he had seen a ghost.

9. _____ this pair of brown shoes is not so good _____ that black pair, I like to wear the brown ones _____ they are more comfortable.

10. He is working late tonight _____ he might finish the work. I have never seen a person more hardworking _____ he is.

11. " _____ he asks you to go to the match with him, will you go?" "I'm going _____ he asks me or not."

12. We did the work _____ it should have been done, but our supervisor was not pleased _____ we showed it to him.

13. _____ he was not feeling well, he went to school. He refused to go home _____ his teacher urged him to.

14. We will have a picnic on the beach _____ it doesn't rain.

15. I will pay you _____ you deliver the parcel to me. My house is on the left _____ you turn into the lane.

16. We should remember this moment for _____ we live.

Chapter 21　基本書寫概念

21-1　大寫字母

(a) 句首第一個字母須大寫。

USAGE PRACTICE

▶ **I**t was dark. **T**he sun had set.　天黑了。太陽下山了。

▶ **T**he boys came home in the rain.　男孩們冒雨回家。

▶ **M**y sister is ill. **S**he can't go to school today.　我妹妹生病了。她今天不能上學。

(b) 專有名詞（例如人、地方、河流、城鎮、國家、種族、星期和月份的名稱等）第一個字母都必須大寫。

USAGE PRACTICE

Mary 瑪莉	**T**om 湯姆	**A**nthony 安東尼
Smith 史密斯	**F**rancis 法蘭西斯	**U**ncle **W**illiam 威廉叔叔
Prince **C**harles 查爾斯王子	**M**ajor **C**ooper 古柏少校	**C**hinese 中國人
Italian 義大利人	**M**onday 星期一	**J**uly 七月
December 十二月	**L**ondon 倫敦	**T**aiwan 台灣
Africa 非洲	**S**outh **A**merica 南美洲	**E**urope 歐洲
Mississippi **R**iver 密西西比河		

---

 aunt、father、captain、doctor 等作普通名詞時，不特別使用大寫字母，除非指涉特定的人。

▶ **D**octor, may I go home tomorrow?　醫生，明天我可以回家嗎？

▶ **M**other and I are going to the market.　媽媽和我正要去市場。

▶ "You have to ask **F**ather for permission," **M**other said.　「你必須請求父親准許。」母親說。

(c) 書名、詩歌名、電影名或劇作名等名稱，所有字的首字母都必須大寫，但介系詞和冠詞除外，除非是該名稱的第一個字。

USAGE PRACTICE

Lawrence of **A**rabia （電影名）阿拉伯的勞倫斯

Under the **G**reenwood **T**ree （電影名）綠林蔭下

The **M**erchant of **V**enice （劇名）威尼斯商人

Fiddler on the **R**oof （音樂劇名）屋頂上的提琴手

Toward **B**etter **E**nglish （書名）增進英文能力

The **D**affodils （詩名）水仙花

Of **H**uman **B**ondage （書名）人性的枷鎖

▶ **C**aptain **L**ight enjoyed reading the book *The Jungle Is Neutral*.

　　萊特上尉喜歡讀《叢林中立》這本書。

(d) 首字母縮略字多屬專有名詞，通常全部大寫。

USAGE PRACTICE		
U.S.A./USA 美國	**U.K./UK** 英國	**EU** 歐盟
WHO 世界衛生組織	**CNN** 美國有線電視新聞網	**M.P.** 憲兵
AIDS 愛滋病	**R.S.P.C.A.** （英國）皇家防止虐待動物協會	

(e) 直接引句的首字母須大寫。

USAGE PRACTICE
▶ "**W**ait!" she said. "**T**here's something here." 「等等！」她說。「這裡有東西。」
▶ "**W**ait for me at the junction tonight," he said. 「今晚在交叉口等我。」他說。
▶ "**W**e are all going to the circus," I told him. 「我們全都要去看馬戲表演。」我告訴他。
▶ I said, "**C**ome as soon as possible." 我說：「盡快來這裡。」
▶ "**H**ave you seen Mr. Baker?" I asked. "**H**e seems to have disappeared."   　「你有看到貝克先生嗎？」我問道。「他好像消失了。」

小練習

請將必要處改成大寫，使句子的書寫正確無誤。

1. what are you waiting for, mary?

2. please buy me a comb, an exercise book, and a ruler, nicholas.

3. my mother wanted me to tell you that lunch is ready.

4. i wonder what time it is. i must be home by 9 p.m.

5. it was late. we were still several kilometers away from the nearest village.

6. they were hungry, tired, and sleepy. they had been walking without food for two days.

7. we left for the airport at four o'clock. halfway there, the car broke down.

8. he squeezed some lemon into the glass, added a spoonful of sugar and some water. then, he stirred the mixture vigorously.

9. christmas day fell on saturday last year.

10. mr. lea is going to paris on october 5th.

11. on new year's day, many families go visiting their friends and relatives. everyone dresses up on this day.

12. his uncle lives in north province. it takes him four days to travel to his uncle's farm.

13. by the end of july, they will have finished their primary school leaving examination.

14. they visited mr. and mrs. jolly when they were in rainbow valley. they met derek, jimmy, mary, and helen, too.

15. miss white said we were to learn by heart either "the village blacksmith" or "the highwayman."

16. the class will be doing shakespeare's *merchant of venice* next year.

17. "earthquake"and "jaws" are two very exciting movies. I have seen both of the movies.

18. my brothers were watching "mission in space." my father was reading the *evening post*.

19. when the third act of *swan lake* ended, everybody applauded loudly.

20. "have you read *in the alpine mountains* written by a geologist who risked his life doing research there?" asked brenda.

☞ 更多相關習題請見本章應用練習 Part 1。

21-2 句點

(a) 句點用來標示一個完整句子的結束。

USAGE PRACTICE

▶ Tony is already home. 東尼已經在家了。

▶ A fish swims. 一條魚在游動。

▶ Come here, Johnny. 過來，強尼。

▶ Please shut the door. 請把門關上。

▶ Please come here. 請到這裡來。

(b) 句點也用於簡寫字、首字母縮略字或人名之中。此處的句點一般通稱為「縮寫點」。

USAGE PRACTICE

President = Pres. 董事長　　　　　　　Captain = Capt. 機長

Bachelor of Arts = B.A. 文學士　　　　General Headquarters = G.H.Q. 總司令部

Dr. Pamela Caroline Davis = Dr. P. C. Davis 潘蜜拉‧卡洛琳‧戴維斯博士

 首字母縮略字原本大部分都會加上縮寫點，但現在的書寫趨勢傾向於不加，直接將字母連寫即可。不過一般簡寫字和人名還是不能省略縮寫點。

North Atlantic Treaty Organization → **N.A.T.O.** → **NATO** 北大西洋公約組織

Féderation Internationale de Football Association → **F.I.F.A.** → **FIFA** 國際足球協會

小練習

請寫出下列詞彙的簡寫字或首字母縮略字。

1. department _____　　　　2. Captain _____

3. September _____　　　　4. et cetera _____

5. example _____　　　　6. that is _____

7. standard _____　　　　8. kilograms _____

9. latitude _____　　　　10. Bachelor of Arts _____

11. General Post Office _____　　12. Saturday _____

13. prisoner of war _____　　14. United Kingdom _____

15. Greenwich Mean Time _____　　16. United Nations _____

17. Mount _____　　　　18. Before Christ _____

19. limited _____　　　　20. President _____

21. Friday _____　　　　22. company _____

23. Assistant _____　　　　24. World Health Organization _____

☞ 更多相關習題請見本章應用練習 Part 2～Part 3。

21-3 逗點

(a) 逗點用來分隔一連串的物品、事件或動作。

USAGE PRACTICE

▶ She piled cakes, cookies, sandwiches, and candies on the tray.

她把蛋糕、餅乾、三明治和糖果都堆在托盤上。

▶ We bought a lot of apples, oranges, pears, and bananas.

我們買了許多蘋果、橘子、梨和香蕉。

▶ He thinks there isn't much difference between moths and butterflies, ants and termites, and bees and wasps. 他認為蛾和蝴蝶、螞蟻和白蟻、以及蜜蜂和黃蜂之間沒有多大的區別。

▶ He walked into the house, through the hall, and up the stairs.

他走進房子、穿過大廳並上樓去。

▶ Please run upstairs, go into my bedroom, and get me my bag.

請你跑上樓、走進我的臥室並替我拿我的手提袋。

▶ I signed my name, folded the letter, put it into the envelope, and sealed it.

我簽了名、摺好信、把它放進信封並把它封了起來。

▶ He passed the ball to Edward, and Edward passed it to me.

他傳球給愛德華,愛德華再把它傳給我。

(b) 逗點用在被稱呼者名字的前面或後面。

USAGE PRACTICE

▶ You look pretty tonight, Alice. 今晚你看起來很漂亮,愛麗絲。

▶ Molly, are you ready to go now? 茉莉,你現在準備好要走了嗎?

(c) 逗點用在同位語的前後。

USAGE PRACTICE

▶ Mr. Howard, our personnel manager, will interview you.

霍華先生,我們的人事經理,將要面試你。

▶ The new science teacher, Mr. Watson, will arrive on Monday.

新的科學老師,華森先生,將在星期一到達。

▶ The captain, Mr. John Smith, was generally liked by all the members of the crew.

機長,約翰・史密斯先生,受到所有機組人員普遍的愛戴。

▶ My brother, a member of the students association, had to go to the meeting, too.

我的哥哥，學生會的一員，也必須去開會。

(d) 逗點用來分隔主要子句與 however、indeed、without doubt、of course、after all、therefore 等副詞或副詞片語。

USAGE PRACTICE

▶ It was, however, too thick for our purposes. 然而，它太厚不合我們使用。

▶ This, indeed, is news to me! 這對我來說的確是新聞！

▶ Indeed, this was exactly what he had feared would happen.

的確，這正是他所害怕會發生的事。

▶ There is, without doubt, a good chance of recovery for him.

無疑地，他有很大的機會可以康復。

▶ They had, therefore, to take the test again. 因此，他們必須再考一次。

▶ On the other hand, there will be trouble if we don't sign the agreement.

另外一方面，如果我們不簽同意書，就會有麻煩。

 如果放在句首的副詞或副詞片語很短，逗點常常被省略。

▶ One day(,) a stranger came to the house. 有一天，一個陌生人來到這間房子。

▶ After dinner(,) they went to a show. 晚飯後，他們去看表演。

▶ For two days(,) he had not eaten anything. 他已經兩天沒有吃任何東西了。

(e) 逗點用來引導或結束直接引句。

USAGE PRACTICE

▶ Mrs. White said, "Sally, please set the table for dinner."

懷特太太說：「莎利，請擺好晚餐要用的餐具。」

▶ Mary said, "I have lost my book." 瑪麗說：「我遺失了我的書。」

▶ "Come with me, John," he said. 「跟我來，約翰。」他說。

▶ "If you are interested, Agnes, you may come along," he said.

「如果你有興趣，阿格尼絲，你可以一起來。」他說。

▶ The man said, "I wish to speak to Mr. Anderson."

那個男人説：「我希望和安德森先生講話。」

▶ The signboard read, "Trespassers Will Be Prosecuted." 告示牌寫著：「侵入者將被起訴。」

(f) 逗點用來分隔主要子句和從屬子句。

USAGE PRACTICE

▶ If you must do it, do it quickly. 如果你必須做這件事，就快點去做。

▶ If it rains, we will stay indoors. 如果下雨，我們將留在室內。

▶ If you are hungry, eat the piece of cake on the table. 如果你餓了，就吃桌上的那塊蛋糕。

▶ Although it was raining quite heavily, many spectators came to watch the match.
雖然雨下得很大，但很多觀眾來看比賽。

▶ Although they were tired, they continued working. 雖然他們很累，他們還是繼續工作。

▶ When the bell rang, all the children went home. 當鈴聲響時，所有的小孩都回家了。

▶ After she had written the letter, she went to bed. 寫好信之後，她就去睡覺了。

(g) 逗點用來分隔主要子句和非限定關係子句。

USAGE PRACTICE

▶ My brother, who is in Australia, is getting married. 我哥哥住在澳洲，他快要結婚了。

▶ Jennifer, whom you met last week, is inviting you to her party.
你上禮拜遇見的那個珍妮佛正想邀請你參加她的派對。

▶ The house, which is between two shops, will be renovated.
這間房子介於兩家店之間，將重新整修。

▶ The hens have laid some eggs. I saw seven, three of which were broken.
母雞生了一些蛋。我看到七個，其中有三個破了。

(h) 逗點用來分隔主要子句和分詞片語或分詞構句。

USAGE PRACTICE

▶ Closing the door softly, she tiptoed into the room. 輕輕地關上門，她躡手躡腳地走入房間。

▶ Seeing his plight, I went forward to help him. 看到他的困境，我走上前幫助他。

▶ Betty, after having finished her homework, went for a walk. 貝蒂完成功課之後，出去散步。

▶ The man, not knowing the horse's temper, jerked at the reins.

那個人不知道馬的性情，猛拉韁繩。

▶ The rain having stopped, we made our way home. 雨已停了，我們踏上回家的路。

▶ The price being right, we bought the new car. 價格適當，我們買了這部新車。

(i) 逗點用來分隔 "the more..., the more..." 此類比較級的句型。

<table><tr><td>USAGE PRACTICE</td></tr></table>

▶ The more he thought about it, the more determined he was to find out the reason.

他對這件事想得越多，越是堅決要找出原因來。

▶ The longer she waited, the more nervous she felt. 她等得越久，就覺得越緊張。

▶ The higher we climbed, the steeper it became. 我們爬得越高，路變得越陡。

(j) 逗點用來分隔不合語言習慣的字組。

<table><tr><td>USAGE PRACTICE</td></tr></table>

▶ I went in, in answer to his call. 我進去，接他的電話。

(k) 逗點用來分隔插入語與主要子句。

<table><tr><td>USAGE PRACTICE</td></tr></table>

▶ We discovered that we were further away from, rather than nearer to, our destination.

我們發現我們離目的地不是更近，而是更遠。

▶ She hopes to, and undoubtedly will, succeed in persuading her parents.

她希望能成功地說服她的父母，而這點是毫無疑問的。

▶ The most exciting, if not the most important, part of the show was saved until the end.

這場表演中，若不是最重要的，就是最刺激的部分被保留到後面。

小練習

請在必要處加上逗點，使句子的書寫正確無誤。

1. A good breakfast will give a man energy alertness and vitality.

2. Mary put a cutting board a knife some carrots and meat on the kitchen table.

3. Please let me have some paint a brush a bottle and a piece of paper.

基礎文法寶典❺
Essential English Usage & Grammar

4. Paul collects stamps shells and even matchbox labels.

5. The mixture contains flour butter sugar eggs some baking powder and a pinch of salt.

6. She was carrying an umbrella two books a parcel and her handbag.

7. There were all kinds of animals in the zoo: lions tigers elephants giraffes monkeys birds and snakes.

8. Mary Rita Jeremy and Stephen please go to the principal's office.

9. To make the bookcase you will need a hammer some nails four planks and a saw.

10. After taking these pills you will be strong healthy energetic and alert.

11. I threw open the door stood there for a moment and marched into the room.

12. Paint the sky blue the trees grass and leaves green and the flowers yellow or red.

13. Belinda ran up the stairs went into her room shut the door and leaned against it.

14. The doctor took the patient's pulse examined his eyes and throat asked him a few questions and finally wrote out a prescription.

15. She woke up rubbed her eyes and stretched herself lazily before getting out of bed.

16. Nancy Susan and their two brothers got off the train held their tickets and followed the rest of the passengers toward the exit.

17. He walked to the park sat on a bench opened his newspaper and began to read it.

18. Mrs. Hill said "My daughter hasn't been home the whole day."

☞ 更多相關習題請見本章應用練習 Part 4～Part 8。

21-4 引號

(a) 雙引號可以用來引導直接引句。

USAGE PRACTICE

▶ "Hello, John," I said. 「哈囉，約翰。」我說。

▶ "I want to go home," the boy cried. 「我想回家。」男孩哭著說。

▶ "Hey! Wait for me," I shouted. 「嘿！等等我。」我大聲喊叫。

▶ "Alan, where are you?" I shouted. 「艾倫，你在哪裡？」我大聲喊叫。

▶ "Alice, how is your mother?" I asked. 「愛麗絲，你的母親近來可好？」我問道。

▶ The tailor said, "You can try on the dress now." 裁縫師說：「你現在可以試穿那件洋裝了。」

(b) 雙引號可以用來引導名言或格言。

USAGE PRACTICE

▶ Disraeli said: "The secret of success is constancy to purpose."

迪斯雷利說：「成功的奧秘在於堅持不懈地朝目標前進」。

▶ Carlyle said, "Literature is the thought of thinking souls."

卡萊爾說：「文學是有思想靈魂的見解」。

(c) 雙引號可以用來標示論文標題、船名、電影名等。

USAGE PRACTICE

▶ I went to see "Lawrence of Arabia." 我想看「阿拉伯的勞倫斯」。

(d) 單引號常用於引用句中的引用句。

USAGE PRACTICE

▶ "Did you hear her say 'I can't be bothered' when I told her?" I asked.

「當我告訴她時，你有聽到她說『別吵我』嗎？」我問道。

▶ "Sarah and I are going to see the movie 'The Horsemen'," he said.

「莎拉和我要去看『騎士』這部電影。」他說。（請注意逗點是在單引號之外）

(e) 雙引號可以用來標示外來字之類的特殊用字。

USAGE PRACTICE

▶ We wished him "bon voyage" before he set sail. 在他航行前，我們祝他「一路順風」。

▶ His "laissez-faire" attitude irritated his colleagues. 他的「放任」態度激怒了他的同事。

小練習

請在必要處加上引號，使句子的書寫正確無誤。

1. Come, Helen. Here's an interesting book for you to read, her uncle said.

2. Mr. Norton is giving us a dinner treat tonight, she told us. He has just been promoted to assistant manager.

3. You can't refuse to come, Mona said. It'll spoil all our plans.

4. John, meet me at the Federal Coffee House at eight-fifteen a.m., he said. I want to discuss with you how to get the trip organized. Please be punctual.

5. The policeman instructed us, Follow this road until you come to the bridge where there is an intersection. Then, take the turning on your left. Drive straight on till you see the traffic lights.

6. The book gives a comprehensive account of the various types of fish found in tropical waters, he said. It ought to interest you.

7. Never mind, said David. I expect we will be able to get tickets for My Fair Lady tomorrow night."

8. Maria, take this note to Miss White tell her that I'm waiting for her reply, Aunt Sally said.

9. The Sea Queen was berthed somewhere away from the dock.

10. Mr. Bright said, Boys, divide yourselves into two groups. We'll play a game called King's Camp.

11. Let's go now, Nick said. We can get better seats if we go earlier.

12. Do visit us when you're free, Mrs. Smith told us.

13. The Happy Wanderer and Let's Get Together are two of his favorite songs.

14. Please come in. I've just finished writing a letter, Raymond told me.

15. Have you seen The Sound of Music? he asked Charles.

16. Sit down, the manager said. What can I do for you?

17. Why don't you see whether The Empress of India is still in the harbor? the sailor suggested.

18. The sign on the board read, Beware of Dogs.

☞ 更多相關習題請見本章應用練習 Part 9～Part 10。

21-5 問號

(a) 問號用在疑問句（即直接問句）的句尾。

USAGE PRACTICE

▶ How are you? 你好嗎？

▶ Are you there, Mary? 瑪麗，你在嗎？

▶ Where are you going, John? 約翰，你要去哪裡？

▶ Do you know where John is going? 你知道約翰要去哪裡嗎？

▶ She asked, "What are you doing?" 她問說：「你在做什麼？」

▶ She said, "Do you know how I can get there?" 她説：「你知道我該如何到那裡嗎？」

(b) 問接問句的句尾不用問號，而是句點。

▶ Tell me where you found that book. 告訴我你在哪裡找到那本書。

▶ I didn't know what you were doing there. 我不知道你在那裡做什麼。

▶ I asked him where he had been the whole morning. 我問他一整個早上在哪裡。

▶ I asked her why she hadn't called me. 我問她為什麼沒打電話給我。

▶ Paul asked me whether I knew where he had left the bag.

保羅問我是否知道他把手提袋放在哪。

注意 表示「禮貌的請求」時，句尾也不用問號。

▶ "Will you please wait here," the receptionist said. 「請你在這裡等一等。」接待員説。

▶ "Could I have your name, madam," the clerk said. 「女士，請告訴我您的大名。」店員説。

 小練習

請在必要處加上問號，使句子的書寫正確無誤。

1. "Where are you going, Danny" his father asked. "It is late. Are you going to town again"

2. Mark called out to his friend, "We're going to watch a badminton match. Care to come along, Henry"

3. Charles asked us whether we were going to the picnic. "Have you given him your answer" Janet asked me.

4. I asked him, "Henry, are you going to the post office today Could you mail a letter for me, please"

5. Nancy asked me whether I knew her brother. She said, "Haven't you met him before"

6. "What's happening" he inquired. No one answered him. "What's wrong" he asked again.

7. "Hello, Miss Davis. How are you" John asked. "You look tanned. Have you been to the beach"

8. "Did you find the book" Jill's father asked. "I might have put it on the top shelf. Have you searched for it there"

☞ 更多相關習題請見本章應用練習 Part 11～Part 12。

21-6 驚嘆號

(a) 驚歎號用於表示「恐懼、驚訝、快樂、憤怒」等情緒或讚嘆的句子之後。

USAGE PRACTICE

▶ Happy birthday! 生日快樂！

▶ Here she comes! 她來了！

▶ That's good news! 那真是好消息！

▶ No! I will not allow it! 不！我不答應！

▶ Ouch! You've hurt me! 唉喲！你弄痛我了！

▶ "I'm so worried!" Mrs. Grey said. 「我好擔心！」葛雷太太說。

▶ "I've lost my ring!" she cried. 「我遺失了我的戒指！」她大喊。

▶ "Oh, there you are!" she exclaimed. 「噢，你在那裡！」她驚呼。

▶ How nice to see you here! 在這裡見到你真是太好了！

▶ "I do hope that nothing will go wrong!" he said fervently.

　　「我真希望一切不會出錯！」他熱烈地說。

▶ "What a beautiful sunset!" I exclaimed. 「多麼美麗的夕陽啊！」我驚嘆道。

(b) 驚歎號用在突然、匆忙或緊張的狀態下，脫口而出的命令句之後。

USAGE PRACTICE

▶ Help! Help! 救命！救命！　　▶ Shut up! 閉嘴！

▶ Come here! 過來！　　　　　▶ Get out! 出去！

▶ Go away! 走開！

(c) 驚歎號用在擬聲字之後。

USAGE PRACTICE

▶ Crash! The thunder sounded overhead. 轟隆！頭頂上響起雷聲。

▶ We heard the ducks calling, "Quack! Quack!" 我們聽到鴨子叫：「呱！呱！」

請在必要處加上驚嘆號，使句子的書寫正確無誤。

1. "Hurrah We're going to the zoo" the children exclaimed.

2. "Get out of there" he shouted angrily.

3. The men cried, "Quick, run The branch is falling"

4. "Here comes the bus" she said. "Let's run for it, Eddie"

5. "Ha-ha I've tricked you, haven't I?" the man exclaimed with excitement.

6. "No I won't go" Wendy said. "Please, please, don't make me go" she pleaded.

7. "Fire Help" the woman screamed. "Oh, my child is trapped in there Please save him"

8. She remarked, "What a beautiful dress"

9. "Merry Christmas to you" Mary said. "And a Happy New Year, too"

10. "Go away, and don't disturb me" I said in irritation. "I have a lot of homework to do"

☞ 更多相關習題請見本章應用練習 Part 13～Part 16。

21-7 省略號和所有格符號

(a) 省略號用在縮寫時，表示省略的字母。

USAGE PRACTICE		
will not = won't	do not = don't	must not = mustn't
are not = aren't	I would = I'd	they are = they're
they will = they'll	it is/it has = it's	we have = we've
there is = there's		

(b) 所有格符號用在名詞之後，表示「擁有」。

USAGE PRACTICE		
Susie's cat 蘇西的貓	James' uncle 詹姆士的叔叔	the boys' bags 男孩們的袋子
women's talk 女人們的談話	birds' nests 鳥的巢	

注意 有關所有格符號的使用規則，請參考 2-1。

請加上正確的所有格型式。

1. women laughter _____
2. a policeman uniform _____
3. my father opinion _____
4. the judge decision _____
5. Nicholas watch _____
6. those guards footsteps _____
7. a minute rest _____
8. wolves howling _____
9. a businessman responsibility _____
10. the headman son _____
11. her mother-in-law words _____
12. the princess horses _____
13. two hours delay _____
14. someone elses voice _____
15. ladies dresses _____
16. Francis racket _____
17. brother-in-law car _____
18. Aunt Polly cakes _____
19. the committee decision _____
20. Mrs. Smiths report _____
21. workers salaries _____
22. Henry the Eighth reign _____
23. father-in-law present _____
24. New Year Eve _____
25. today paper _____
26. a month notice _____
27. the people aim _____
28. for old time sake _____
29. her heart desire _____
30. no one else business _____

☞ 更多相關習題請見本章應用練習 Part 17～Part 21。

21-8 連字號

(a) 連字號可用來形成複合形容詞。

USAGE PRACTICE

eighty-five 八十五	twenty-one 二十一	forty-four 四十四
long-winded 冗長的	short-sighted 近視的	upside-down 顛倒的
self-supporting 自給的	self-appointed 自己任命的	happy-go-lucky 逍遙自在的

 注意 複合形容詞可以用來修飾名詞。

a coal-black face 一張漆黑的臉　　　　　a two-hour delay 兩小時的延遲
a two-meter-long pole 一根兩公尺長的柱子　a three-year-old boy 一個三歲的男孩

(b) 連字號可用來分開一個字的音節，這種標號在印刷時文字換行處經常可見。

USAGE PRACTICE
---

ac-com-mo-da-tion 住處	con-temp-tu-ous 瞧不起的
in-flam-ma-tion 燃燒	or-na-men-tal 裝飾的

▶ Doing business around the world is not just about attending meetings and visiting different countries. It is also about understanding and following different patterns of **communication**. Do you know more than 70 percent of our daily communication is conducted **non-verbally**?

(c) 連字號可用來分隔字首和單字本身。

USAGE PRACTICE

re-enact 重新制定	re-elect 重選	re-entry 再進入
semi-literate 半文盲	co-operate 合作	

注意 拼法一樣的字，含連字號和不含連字號所表示的意思可能完全不同。

▶ The prisoner was **released** yesterday. 這個犯人昨天被釋放了。(release → 釋放)

▶ The man **re-leased** his apartment for another year.
這個男人再出租這層公寓一年。(re-lease → 再出租)

▶ He could not **recollect** when the incident had occurred.
他無法想起事件是何時發生的。(recollect → 回想)

▶ It is difficult to **re-collect** all the feathers that have been blown away.
要再收好已經被吹走的羽毛很困難。(re-collect → 重新集合)

 小練習

請在必要處加上連字號，使句子的書寫正確無誤。

1. The man, self appointed as head of the department, had no regard for other people's opinions.

2. The woman was so narrow minded that she could not believe the girls had not done anything wrong.

3. He was so self conscious that he refused to take part in the play.

4. Mr. Hill, the President of the Chess Players Association, was already fifty five years old.

5. With your co operation, we should be able to finish the work by the end of the month.

6. There was first rate service at the hotel and we enjoyed our two week stay here.

7. Having lived with her grandparents for twenty two years, Sally had acquired some of their old

fashioned ideas.

8. He always boasts of the fact that though he is only semi literate, he is a self made man.

9. He counted the money in his wallet. It was still thirty five dollars and seventy five cents.

10. When the president of the club resigned, they had to re elect another person to take over.

11. At the end of the three hour long play, the audience got up to stretch their legs.

12. The laboratory was fitted with up to date equipment.

13. At the age of twenty three, she had already established herself in the business world.

14. Charles works in his father in law's firm as a sub accountant.

15. The sound of music came from a pocket size transistor radio by the window.

16. His son in law was taking a ten minute break when he spotted a child in trouble.

17. The teacher in charge wanted us to re act the scene, but this time showing improvement.

18. The good tempered housekeeper nodded obligingly and promised the three year old girl some jam tarts.

19. As she entered the smoke filled room, she nearly choked.

20. We will have to re elect a president for our club as John's three year term will soon be over.

21. The young mother to be bought a book on childcare and began reading it.

22. The man of war slipped into the harbor unnoticed by the enemy.

23. The well known surgeon operated on him when he was in a semi conscious state.

24. The ranger and his chief assistant set out to hunt for the man eating lion.

☞ 更多相關習題請見本章應用練習 Part 22～Part 24。

21-9 破折號

(a) 破折號可用來強調、重覆或解釋某件事。

USAGE PRACTICE

▶ He looked at the sight——a sight which made him tremble.

他看著這個景像——一個使他發抖的景象。

▶ She heard a terrible scream——a scream which she shivered to recall.

她聽到一陣可怕的尖叫聲——一陣令她回憶時忍不住顫抖的尖叫聲。

▶ I heard a mournful sound——a sound which sent a shiver down my spine.

我聽到一個悽慘的聲音——一個令我背脊發涼的聲音。

(b) 破折號可用來表示在講話時的猶豫、受到阻礙或中斷。

USAGE PRACTICE

▶ "I—I—I will do it at once, sir!" he said. 「先生，我——我——我會立刻去做！」，他說。

▶ "He—He isn't at home. He is—oh, there he is!" she exclaimed with relief.

　「他——他不在家。他是在——噢，他在那裡！」她鬆了一口氣，大聲喊著。

▶ What I'm telling you is true—no, don't laugh—it really did happen!

　我告訴你的都是真的——不，別笑——它的的確確發生過！

▶ "Well," he said, "I'll—oh, here's my bus! I'll tell you about it some other time."

　「嗯，」他說，「我會——噢，我的公車來了！我改天再告訴你這件事。」

▶ "He—he said that he'd kill me!" I stammered.

　「他——他說他會殺了我！」我結結巴巴地說。

(c) 破折號可用來代替冒號，針對句子的前面或後面部份舉出實例、加以說明。

USAGE PRACTICE

▶ We searched everywhere—in the house, in the garden, and in the backyard—but he was nowhere around.

　我們到處搜過了——房子裡、花園裡還有後院——但哪也找不到他。

▶ His father, his teacher, his eldest brother—these are the people he admires most.

　他的父親、他的老師、他的大哥——這些都是他最欽佩的人。

▶ He lost everything in the fire—his house, his money, his clothing, and his famous collection of paintings.

　他在大火中失去一切——他的房子、他的錢、他的衣服還有他著名的畫作收藏。

▶ There were cookstoves, mixing machines, huge ovens, refrigerators—all the kitchen equipment for the best cookery course.

　這裡有烹調用爐、攪拌機、大烤箱、電冰箱——全都是用來教授最佳烹飪課程的廚房設備。

▶ He has everything that a man prizes—wealth, power, influence, and respect.

　他有一切所有人都重視的東西——財富、權力、影響力和他人的尊敬。

▶ Lack of funds, lack of time, and inadequate manpower—all these are problems that he has to face. 缺乏資金、缺乏時間和不足的人力——這些都是他必須面對的問題。

(d) 破折號可用來標示句子中的停頓處，並插入另一完整的句子。

USAGE PRACTICE

▶ Something was swimming towards him——it was a shark!

有東西正向他游過來——是一隻鯊魚！

▶ I have some important information for her——perhaps it should wait until she has

recovered. 我有一些重要的消息要告訴她——也許要等到她康復的時候再說。

▶ It was reported that forty people——it could be more——had died in the fire.

據報導，四十人——可能更多——已經在火場裡喪生。

小練習

請在必要處加上破折號，使句子的書寫正確無誤。

1. "Look over there no, not there on this side. Look!" he exclaimed.

2. She had beautiful clothes, a car, a house, servants in fact, everything a woman could wish for,

but she was not happy.

3. "Where is oh, there you are, Henry," his mother said.

4. "Would you like to come out to dinner tonight perhaps you would prefer to come tomorrow?"

5. Money, power, fame none of these things is important without health.

6. There were a stale cookie, a banana, a piece of cake and a can of milk all I had to last me until

rescue came.

7. Mr. Fraser he must have stayed up last night thinking of a solution came down for breakfast,

looking tired and worn-out.

8. "My glasses where did you put them?" the angry, old man cried.

9. I did not know what to do yes, I was desperate as there was so little time left.

10. For the past two years and he was now twelve Jeremy had lived with his mother in the old

castle.

☞ 更多相關習題請見本章應用練習 Part 25～Part 27。

21-10 冒號

(a) 冒號可用來表示兩個陳述句之間的停頓，其中第二個陳述句是第一句的實例或說
明。

▶ We stood dumbfounded: it happened so quickly. 我們目瞪口呆地站著：它發生得那麼快。

▶ It was useless to shout for help: nobody ever passed by the place.

大聲求救是沒有用的：沒人會經過那個地方。

▶ He had no way of contacting them: his telephone was out of order.

他沒有辦法與他們聯繫：他的電話壞了。

(b) 冒號可用來引導前述名詞所包含的項目。

▶ The ingredients are as follows: eggs, sugar, flour, butter, salt, and milk.

成份如下：雞蛋、糖、麵粉、奶油、鹽和牛奶。

▶ These are the things required: a strong piece of rope, a flashlight, a large bag, and a pocket knife. 這些是必要的東西：一條堅固的繩索、一個手電筒、一個大袋子和一把小摺刀。

▶ All that you need are these: a length of rope, some planks, some nails, and a hammer.

你需要的所有東西如下：一節繩子、一些厚板、一些釘子和一把鐵錘。

(c) 冒號可用來引導直接引句或名言。

▶ He announced his decision: "I will fight them to the end."

他宣布了他的決定：「我會和他們奮戰到最後。」

▶ He thought for a while, and then said: "All right, I'll do it, but on one condition."

他想了一會兒，然後說：「好吧，我來做，但是有一個條件。」

▶ Oscar Wilde once said: "Experience is the name everyone gives to his mistakes."

王爾德曾經說過：「人人都把自己的錯誤美其名為經驗。」

 小練習

請在必要處加上冒號，使句子的書寫正確無誤。

1. Her reason for not going to the party was she was too tired after the expedition.

2. My brother collects almost everything stamps, coins, matchboxes, badges, and postcards.

3. The director finally announced his decision "Let the workers go on strike if they dare to."

4. The cause of their unrest was not difficult to determine they were dissatisfied with their working conditions.

5. There are only two ways by which you can get there by the path along the hillside and by boat across the lake.

6. To make a bookcase, you need these things three planks, some nails, a hammer, and a saw.

7. The scouts were stationed at several points at the main gate, near the porch, and along the corridor.

8. I know what his motto is "Live and let live."

9. Tickets can be obtained at these places United Supermarket, Speedy Limited Trading, and Macdonald Company.

10. The subject of his talk will be "Careers for Young People."

11. There are two reasons why I can't go lack of money and lack of time.

12. Explain the meaning of these words vouch, protrude, taunt, and replenish.

13. The machine has only one big fault it needs constant oiling.

14. Fuller once said "Knowledge is a treasure, but practice is the key to it."

15. The tourists visited all the places of interest the Memorial Park, Pirates' Cove, the Museum, the Art Gallery, and the Cool Springs.

16. The reason for their behavior was plain they were envious of each other.

17. It was very difficult for them to make up their minds both applicants seemed equally good.

18. These were the repairs to the bicycle the front tire was changed, the handle bars repainted, and the saddle fixed.

19. What really occurred was this the parrot had learned the captain's words and repeated them, thus revealing his secret.

☞ 更多相關習題請見本章應用練習 Part 28～Part 31。

21-11 分號

(a) 分號可用來連接兩個獨立的子句。

USAGE PRACTICE

▶ The portrait was removed from the hall; in its place was hung a landscape.

畫像被移出大廳；它的位置改掛了一幅風景畫。

> ▶ Five men must come to the storeroom immediately; without them, the work cannot be completed. 五個人必須立刻到倉庫；沒有他們的話，這項工作無法完成。
>
> ▶ The village can be reached only by this path; there is no other way.
>
> 這村莊只能由這條小徑抵達；沒有其他的路。
>
> ▶ They had an early dinner; then, they set off on their journey.
>
> 他們很早吃了晚餐；然後，他們就出發去旅行。

(b) 分號可用來分隔長句中的子句。

USAGE PRACTICE

> ▶ According to the latest news, he has just reached Parkland; now, he is preparing to go to Black City. 根據最新消息，他剛到達帕克蘭；現在，他正準備要去布萊克市。

請在必要處加上分號，使句子的書寫正確無誤。

1. They were afraid that the lifeboats would sink nevertheless, the captain refused to let them use the life jackets.

2. The journey back to our village would be a difficult one however, with a little luck, we might be able to make it.

3. The framework of the airplane is made of aluminum therefore, it is very light.

4. The repairs will be expensive for example, the cost of replacing those windowpanes will come to close to a hundred dollars.

5. Not all their attempts were unsuccessful occasionally they managed to produce good results.

6. If the weather was fine, the men would go out to sea if not, they would stay at home.

7. Their lives follow a fixed pattern in the day time they sleep, and at night they hunt for food.

8. The earthquake shook the whole city even where we lived, the earth trembled.

9. Bit by bit, he pieced the evidence together there was no doubt then who the victim was.

10. From indistinguishable sounds, men developed a system of language today, there exist more than 3,000 different languages.

11. Some people contract the sickness fairly frequently others rarely experience it.

12. We were lucky to catch the bus otherwise, we would have had to walk home.

13. The castle could be approached only by the bridge there was no other way.

14. The road forks here—one leads to the town the other, a steep winding road, runs along the coast.

15. He looked at the thermometer carefully he had to record the slightest change.

16. Sometimes the prisoners react with hysterical laughter sometimes they break down and cry.

17. The work was a dull routine we checked the figures until lunch time and then started again till the end of the day.

18. We had to get away as quickly as possible they would be after us the moment that they discovered the loss.

19. It was impossible for the island to be self-supporting it had to get supplies from outside.

20. Even at night, the temperature remained much the same there was not a breath of wind to cool the atmosphere.

☞ 更多相關習題請見本章應用練習 Part 32～Part 36。

21-12 括弧

(a) 括弧在較不正式的寫法中可用來補充說明（通常會用逗號或破折號代替）。

USAGE PRACTICE

▶ When you see him (probably at the dinner party), please give him my best wishes.
當你看見他（可能在晚宴時），請轉達我對他的祝福。

▶ She told me (and you can rely on her) that the others are planning a surprise attack.
她告訴我（你可以相信她）其他人正在計畫一次突襲。

(b) 括弧在書面中可用來補充更進一步的訊息。

USAGE PRACTICE

▶ I left school (1997) and started working as an editor.
我離開學校（1997 年）並且開始擔任編輯人員。

 小練習

請在必要處加上括弧，使句子的書寫正確無誤。

1. When you get your results probably in March, be sure to write to let me know.

2. I was present on both occasions: the day he was enrolled June 5th, 1974 and the day he graduated July 4th, 1975 with flying colors.

3. My friend Susan she has great determination says that she wants to be a commercial pilot.

4. You must take a jeep it is the only form of transportation to the hilltop.

5. Cindy and Joe they are already engaged will be getting married sometime this year.

6. He led the donkeys into the garden a most foolish thing to do and left them there while he set off for the market.

7. He has a great deal of work to do, but he does not or will not sit down to do it.

8. What does the word "posse" Line 23 mean?

9. She enclosed her photograph postcard-size and colored in her letter.

10. The truth is that many students perhaps the majority simply do not know how to use this punctuation mark.

21-13 商業書信的基本格式

(a) 在商業書信中，對方公司的地址或部門必須放在左邊、寄信者地址的下方。除非知道收信者的性別或姓名，不然都應該以 Dear Sir/Madam 或 Dear Sir or Madam 起頭。 如果有必要寫標題的話， 可以加底線來做強調。 正式信件必須以 Yours faithfully 或 Yours truly 結尾，注意 faithfully 或 truly 都要用小寫，且後面要加上逗點。

USAGE PRACTICE

84 Oak Street,
Seattle, WA 98101

The Manager,
Orange Computer, Inc.,
12 Finn Road,
San Jose, CA 95160

August 23rd, 2008

Dear Sir/Madam,

Application for Sales Manager

（書信內容）

Yours faithfully,

（署名）

(b) 寫書信地址時，在公司名、路名、街名等後要加上逗點，門牌號碼後則不用；整個地址寫完後才加上句點（常被省略）。郵遞區號是地址的重要部分，不可隨意省略。

USAGE PRACTICE	
The White House,（機構名稱） 1600 Pennsylvania Avenue, （門牌號碼，路名） NW Washington, DC 20500 （城鎮名，州名和郵遞區號） USA.（國名）	The British Museum,（機構名稱） 1 Great Russell Street,（門牌號碼，路名） London WC1B 3DG（城鎮名和郵遞區號） UK.（國名）

 小練習

請在以下信件內容中加上完整的標點符號，並使用正確的大小寫。

23 ocean road

sea park

sinalay 207

the advertiser

daily times press

p o box 1450

sinalay 208

july 17th, 2000

dear sir or madam

application for the post of junior clerk

with reference to your advertisement in todays *daily times* i wish to apply for the above post until the end of last year i was studying in the good hope girls school i took and passed my examination with a second grade i enclose certified copies of my results

at the moment I am studying shorthand and typing as i intend to take up a secretarial course in addition i am also studying accounting and bookkeeping i enclose testimonials from the head of my school and from my instructor in the commercial school

i hope you will kindly consider my application

yours faithfully

ann lawson

☞ 更多相關習題請見本章應用練習 Part 37。

Chapter 21　應用練習

PART 1

請將必要處改成大寫，使句子的書寫正確無誤。

1. she finished *tales of the uninvited*, switched off the lights, and went to bed.

2. the opening night for *a midsummer night's dream* will be on september 16th. tickets are available at thrifty supermarket and oriental department store.

3. the river has its source in the north. it flows into the pacific ocean.

4. the people of south province are mainly fruit farmers and fishermen. the people in north province are more industrialized.

5. "father, will you read *the children's bedside stories* to me?" betty asked.

6. the sailors came back with wonderful tales of the mysterious east. as a child, christopher columbus used to go down to the harbor to listen to them.

7. "can we go too, uncle joe?" little danny asked, looking at him with beseeching eyes.

8. since the second world war, the usefulness of the port has been seriously affected. vessels from the west by-pass it and so do ships from the east.

9. the school is putting up the play *romeo and juliet*. the drama society will be selecting students to take part.

10. mr. white is the manager in the jetline plastic industry company.

11. we went to see mr. s.t. evans off at the peyton airport. charles brown drove us there.

12. a mr. brown asked to see our sales manager. Mr. brown said he was from the a.i.a.

13. during the heavy rain, part of maxwell bridge was washed away. drivers were advised to use the route via happy village to reach golden beach resort.

14. the eskimos use blocks of ice to build their homes. sometimes they freeze arctic plants into the ice to increase the strength.

15. the idea was proposed to the british, the canadians and the americans. the u.s.a. rejected it and so did canada. however, britain was for the idea.

16. "tomorrow afternoon we will visit the botanical gardens and the national park. by friday, we will have finished visiting all the places of interest," the guide told us.

17. "we can write directly to north korea, can't we?" monica asked.

18. on new year's day, belinda and i were very excited. mother had promised to take us to the zoo.

PART 2

請使用必要的大寫和標點符號，使下列句子的書寫正確無誤。

1. Please send me the girls who are taking part in this game

2. My mother said that she was too busy to watch television she wanted to finish the ironing

3. By nine o'clock, we had finished our test we decided to leave

4. Mr and Mrs F L Norton will be attending the meeting tomorrow at 10 am

5. The sun went behind a dark cloud it was going to rain

6. The clock struck ten Dr West was still in his office

7. By 8 pm, most of the guests had arrived mother wanted to serve dinner then

8. Capt White looked up he smiled at me

9. We were traveling at nearly eighty kph, for we intended to reach the city before seven o'clock

10. His father is a money lender he lends out money at ten percent pa

11. Lieut Wilson had to report to the GHQ on the first of July

12. San Francisco is in the USA it has a temperate climate

13. They were expecting some VIP's for dinner among the guests was the MD, Mr Taylor

14. Prof Hopkins was in the lab, doing some research work

15. the three members of the committee are mr ronald e anderson of paper ware products, mrs helen smith of manual publishing and mr thomas brown of get-about transport

16. my sister, rosemary, was reading a book called *the war of the worlds* by h g wells she said that

it was very interesting

17. about one third of the people of coniland are eskimos originally, they lived in the southern part of greenland

18. general napoleon bonaparte was a popular figure with his soldiers he had a knack of remembering the names of everyone in his army

19. sir isaac newton was born in england at the age of nineteen, he went to study at cambridge university

20. on february 15th 1942, the japanese commander, major general yamashita, accepted the surrender of the colony from the british commander

PART 3

請使用必要的大寫和標點符號，使下列句子的書寫正確無誤。

1. the international committee of the red cross was formed in geneva by a swiss named henri dunant

2. every year, hindus celebrate one of their great festivals, deepavali or "the festival of lights" it commemorates the victory of lord krishna over a demon king

3. at the airport, we watched a boeing 737 coming in to land nearby, another plane was warming up for departure

4. "have you read *she stoops to conquer*?" mrs grey asked

5. aunt emily came to invite mother to see the show "from russia with love" they have both left already

6. sir percy livingston attended the charity premiere of the film *star wars*

7. prof bright was explaining something to the students suddenly, insp bond walked in

8. madam a l mason is a retired teacher she used to teach english in the central high school.

9. alice couldn't pass her gmat exam her uncle advised her to take up a commercial course instead

10. inspector sharp went to the high street boys' school to give a talk on traffic rules during "safety week"

11. the school choir is going to take part in the festival of songs it will be held in the cultural hall on saturday

12. henry's mind worked fast he had to warn david of the impending danger

13. nurse susan woke up the patient it was time for him to take his medicine

14. capt anderson didn't know what to say he was stunned by martin's retort

15. he is a technician at the brightlite electrical company mr brown is his manager

16. a series of books called *toward better english* has recently been published the ministry has approved of its use in the schools

17. it was late when they left seagull bay and there was a slight drizzle however mr and mrs wilson were confident of reaching their destination before midnight

18. the regional marine biological center was set up in january 1975 its aim is to improve the efficiency of fishermen in this region

19. the ship "marianne" lay at anchor off port sunset it was renewing its fuel supplies before sailing off to pearl isle

20. "i've got to go now father will be waiting anxiously for me see you later," she said as she hurried off

21. it was still early when inspector henderson left graystone avenue he had had a good night's sleep and felt very fresh

22. sarah said, "i have the book *sons and lovers* by d h lawrence would you like to read it?"

PART 4

請在必要處加上逗點，使句子的書寫正確無誤。

1. "It is going to rain" Tony said.

2. "Walk straight until you come to the intersection. Turn left and you'll see the sign over the building" the man told us.

3. The teacher instructed them "Write your names in the top right-hand corner put the date beneath and draw a line after that."

4. Susan bought a pretty blue polka-dot dress a pair of shoes and a handbag to match.

5. "Peter go with Harry to get the pail from Aunt Polly" she told him.

6. "London" said Miss White "is the capital city of England."

7. Because of the heavy rain the streets were flooded.

8. Without air none of us would survive.

9. Unless you pay the money you cannot take the parcel away.

10. After a short rest they continued on their journey.

11. If my brother were here he would know what to do.

12. After he had completed his work he left.

13. Before they had time to answer she asked them another question.

14. "Stella if I were you I wouldn't do that" she said.

15. "When you are ready John come to my office" the manager said.

16. Although the farmer was poor he often helped his neighbors.

17. "Unless you promise me that Jimmy I won't give it to you " she said.

18. Samuel Charles Gary all three of you come here.

19. The ship was modern high-powered armored and expensive.

20. Up and down in and out around and around the children ran.

PART 5

請在必要處加上逗點，使句子的書寫正確無誤。

1. The first runner staggered fell got up and still managed to reach the tape before the others.

2. The cave contained as a rule no more than one meter of water.

3. The landslide as far as we could see had completely cut off the entrance to the cave.

4. Aidan the best boy in the class was also a champion athlete.

5. I will always remember Miss Bright my favorite teacher.

6. Shall we take a bus to town have lunch there go to a show and then return home in the evening?

7. Every now and then a truck would pass by.

8. Houdini one of the greatest magicians in the world died in 1926.

9. Hoping my sister-in-law was at home I knocked on the door.

10. "If there is an emergency break open the glass here and pull down the lever" he instructed.

11. He called me and said "Molly take this note to Mr. Smith wait for him to reply and bring back his note to me."

12. "Unless you clean up your room by this evening Susan you will get no dinner" her mother said.

13. "Should you need anything sir just ring this bell" the maid told him.

14. I walked past the house and saw a sign that read "To Let."

15. Having cooked the dinner Mother called us to eat.

16. Mrs. Green said "Unless you arrive early you won't be able to find a seat."

17. Books magazines and pieces of paper were strewn all over the floor.

18. "However difficult the task is Allen you must at least try to do it" his father advised.

19. Taking up his pen Robert started to write the letter.

20. "In fact cats are cleaner animals than dogs" Mr. Fraser our science teacher explained.

PART 6

請修正以下各句子的標點符號及大小寫方式，使其書寫正確無誤。

1. Walking home one day. I met Nora carrying a kitten in a basket.

2. I remember seeing the key; it was behind a pile of books, on the table.

3. Susan and Anna were late for school. Because they played on the way.

4. When the time came for them to leave. Everyone said goodbye, some even shed tears.

5. Although it was early. The movie theater was crowded with people, there was a long line at the box office.

6. David ran down the stairs, to answer the phone it was his father calling from the office.

7. We went for a walk. Because it was a cool evening, the sun was setting.

8. Opening the umbrella she stepped off the bus. Right into a puddle.

9. The man walked up to the door he knocked twice, there was no answer.

10. They were early. So they went for a cup of coffee. At a nearby café.

11. In order to get a good seat. You must book your ticket in advance.

12. The doctors couldn't find out. What was wrong with him? Knowing his illness could be contagious. They put him in the isolation ward.

13. "I think" he said "it is going to rain"

14. "You're right" she said "I should not have come"

15. Helen the nurse put her finger to her lips and said "Don't make any noise or she'll wake up"

PART 7

請在下列各句子中加上必要的標點符號，使其書寫正確無誤。

1. I saw the movie "Born Free" It is one of the best movies I have seen

2. The ball reached Andy our captain He kicked it hard and directed it into a corner of the net "Goal!"

3. "Good boy" Mary told the dog "you deserve a bone"

4. He travels from place to place on business He has been to London New York Tokyo Paris Berlin and many other major cities

5. We brought sandwiches cakes and a bottle of tea We couldn't find any eggs

6. "You're quite right Jeffrey The show is really interesting" Alex said

7. The captain took us around the ship We visited the bridge the cabins and the lounge

8. David here's your book Edward asked me to give it to you

9. There were brooches rings necklaces bangles and earrings in the box

10. As soon as the last spectator had left the stadium at ten am the painters started their work

11. It was a bright sunny morning in the garden you could see bees and butterflies flying among the flowers

12. As Jane walked home it began to get dark looking at her watch she saw that it was nearly eight

13. I can't come at 4:30 pm because I will be working I'll meet you at 5

14. If you are afraid you'd better stay at home I can go by myself

15. "Sit down for a while" Mr Taylor said. "You need a rest and a good meal after that we will discuss the problem"

16. "Have you read *gone with the wind* Richard? It is an interesting book" I said

17. "Mary Paul Agnes and David please go to the principal's office He has something to say to all of you" the teacher said

18. He finished reading *kidnapped* switched off the light and went to bed

PART 8

請在下列各句子中加上必要的標點符號，並修正大小寫方式，使其書寫正確無誤。

1. the sooner you come to your senses the better for all of us

2. the water having flooded the fields the farmers began their plowing

3. nick hopes to and probably will complete his homework by five oclock

4. many students attended the seminar out of every ten five were from our school

5. the tramp who walked with a limp came up to the house and asked for a glass of water

6. they were all eager to and soon they will meet the king

7. it being a cold night we went to bed early

8. the angrier she was the redder her face became

9. if you must speak speak now or remain silent forever

10. "think it over and let me know your answer" she said "the earlier you tell me the better"

11. "this plan though not foolproof is still the safest" he assured them

12. billy being a shy boy sat in a corner and watched the others play

13. "don't try to stop him the more you persuade him the more stubborn he becomes" she warned

14. having found the leak in the tube he then proceeded to mend it

15. "if you find it hard to do do try again" aunt maria urged "don't give up so easily"

16. the news which spread like fire soon reached the ears of the mayor himself

PART 9

請在必要處加上引號，使句子的書寫正確無誤。

1. Some of his early poems like Autumn Wind, Blossoms in May, and The Golden Buttercups depict the beauty of nature.

2. Look! she pointed. Isn't that the Seagull beside the ocean liner Queen Elizabeth?

3. When are Kenneth and Joseph coming? he asked.

4. Quick, Sammy, he called. Throw the ball over here!

5. He will only reply I don't know, if you ask him.

6. The ship Sea Princess was berthed at the harbor.

7. Would you like to see Song of Norway tonight? Peter asked.

8. Don't you know that he who laughs last, laughs longest? Nancy asked Paul.

9. Mr. Takahashi said sayonara to me before he left.

10. What is the meaning of the word post as given in the passage?

11. How long do you think that we'll have to wait? Martin asked.

12. When the Sea Queen docked at the harbor, the captain and his crew went ashore.

13. Absence makes the heart grow fonder and Out of sight, out of mind are two sayings that have opposite meanings.

14. Please pass me the *Daily Times*, Mr. White said to his son.

15. Did I say I won't when you asked me to do it? my brother replied.

16. The movie The Good Earth is based on the novel written by Pearl S. Buck, isn't it? he asked.

17. Yes, that's a lovely place for a picnic, Mary agreed.

18. The Stranger and The Cottage on the Hill are two of his favorite poems.

PART 10

請在下列各句子中加上必要的標點符號，並修正大小寫方式，使其書寫正確無誤。

1. and now said the announcer we come to the last item on tonight's program

2. what time did you come home last night desmond his mother asked i was too sleepy to wait up for you

3. no replied sandra i havent read *all's well that ends well* will you lend it to me please

4. where are you going he asked that isn't the way to the manager's office

5. make hay while the sun shines and strike while the iron is hot are proverbs with similar meanings

6. slow down toby laughed jeffrey haven't you heard the proverb more haste less speed

7. i can't find the binoculars father george said where did you put them

8. my fair lady is one of the most entertaining movies I've ever seen said mary

9. now eric take out your book turn to page fourteen and start reading the passage the teacher said

10. come along boys the teacher said we must get on with our lesson

11. what's that you're making? the child asked is it a kite?

12. the horsemen is a movie in which omar sharif and jack palance play the leading roles jack read

13. mallet according to the dictionary means a hammer with a wooden head

14. she thought i can't let him go alone i must follow him secretly

15. how do you spell the word succeed? joan asked her brother

16. he asked me are you sure? many times before he finally believed me

PART 11

請在下列各句子中加上必要的標點符號，並修正大小寫方式，使其書寫正確無誤。

1. What is meant by "the survival of the fittest"

2. "Did you hear the explosion, David" my father asked

3. "Answer me; do you hear I want to know how you failed the test," the angry father shouted

4. "What do you mean by that" I asked

5. Do you know where we can get some postcards

6. She asked me how much of the book *Mill on the Floss* I had read

7. The principal said, "Would you like to have a few words with the staff They are all in the next room"

8. "Is this the International Hotel" he asked "Can you please connect me to Room 401"

9. The question is whether we will be allowed to go to camp with them or not

10. Did the sailors stop at the port on their way to the East Indies

11. We asked him if his father could drive us to the station

12. The man has certainly been friendly, but can we trust him

13. I'm very sorry for my unreasonable behavior last night Andrew said Will you forgive me

14. A play will be staged by the students to raise funds for the new school library It is entitled the dream.

15. May I have a piece of cake mother Betty asked

16. uncle harry has promised to take us to the seaside this weekend isn't that wonderful!

17. Come on it's time to get ready for the show lucy said We'll be late if we delay any longer

18. He walked into the room switched on the television set settled into his favorite armchair and lit a cigarette

19. Tony please do not sit on the bench, mr white said I painted it this morning and the paint is still wet

20. The movie *the mummy 3* has been showing at the federal cinema for several weeks

PART 12

請在下列各句子中加上必要的標點符號，並修正大小寫方式，使其書寫正確無誤。

1. are you free dora i wonder if you can do something for me

2. when is the meeting robin asked ben i couldn't hear the announcement properly just now

3. the question is whether the rain will stop in time for us to get back

4. do you know when mr biggs will be back the lady asked the secretary

5. alice find out what time the train comes in you know the telephone number don't you my sister asked

6. i asked him how he was he replied i'm fine how is your business getting along

7. nelson said when is the match due to start it's already half past four now

8. can you tell me whether this is the road to the zoo the stranger inquired

9. she asked them whether they would like to have tea or coffee for breakfast the next morning

10. i'm not sure whether my father is at home now can you wait while i find out

11. the problem is: how can we let them know we are here mary doesn't have a telephone in her

house

12. he said do you know where he went i wonder if he left a message behind will you please look around to see if there is a note anywhere

PART 13

請在下列各句子中加上必要的標點符號，使其書寫正確無誤。

1. "Get out of here" she cried "I don't want to see you again"

2. "What a lovely surprise Thank you so much," I said to Doris

3. "No I won't apologize" the little boy screamed

4. "Mew Mew" the kitten purred, rubbing itself against her legs

5. "What" he exclaimed "Have you spoiled it again?"

6. As he was walking home, he heard someone shout, "Help I've been robbed Stop, thief"

7. Cupping his hands to his mouth, William shouted, "Turn back The bridge is broken"

8. "Stop" the guard ordered "You can't go in there"

9. Crash The bicycle hit the cart and all the fruit fell onto the road

10. "Fire Fire" Peter shouted"Quick, Jane Call the fire department," he said excitedly

11. "Congratulations" she said, shaking my hand

12. Twang The arrow shot forth and hit the target right in the center

13. "Oh dear Do you have to bang the door" the old lady asked

14. "Where have I left the key" he muttered to himself scratching his head

15. "Hurrah We're going to the circus" Betty said clapping her hands

16. "Put that down at once" Thomas shouted to Lucy "Don't you know it's poisonous"

17. He strode angrily into the room and shouted "Peter Are you responsible for this"

18. "Father Come quickly! There's a snake in the garden" Danny shouted

19. "Can't you walk faster Billy" he asked irritably "Look There goes our bus"

20. "Mother Mother" she called "Where are you"

21. "Stop laughing What's so funny" she said

22. "Where did you find this" the boy asked "Give it to me"

PART 14

請在下列各句子中加上必要的標點符號，使其書寫正確無誤。

1. She said, "Go away Why don't you leave me alone"

2. "Help"he shouted. "The kitchen's on fire"

3. "I can't" Liza cried out. "How can you expect me to finish it within two days"

4. Eagerly she opened the envelope. Inside was a blank sheet of paper

5. The whole room is in a mess Who has been in there

6. "Stop" the guard called. "Do you know you are trespassing"

7. Does anybody know what has happened to Francis

8. "What a beauty" I exclaimed. "Where did you find it"

9. "I've won the first prize" she exclaimed. "Isn't that wonderful"

10. "Peter" Mr. Wilson called. "Are you there"

11. "Where did you put it Tell me" he commanded.

12. "Wait" Tom said. "What can you see here"

13. Toot Toot The man behind sounded his horn at me In a panic I tried to start the car again

14. He wants to know when Andrew and his sister are coming

15. Don't you know where your mother is

16. Would you like to go with us, Paul

17. They can't force us to do it, can they

18. She called, "Wait for me"

19. John couldn't decide whether to go or not

20. "I'm so worried" Mrs Brown said

PART 15

請在下列各句子中加上必要的標點符號，並修正大小寫方式，使其書寫正確無誤。

1. tell me she shouted why did you do it

2. be quiet the masked man ordered the whimpering child stop that at once or ill gag you

3. oh sandra what a lovely dress you have on cried jill where did you buy it

4. you won't tell father will you the naughty boy pleaded

5. andy don't touch that tony shouted to his younger brother its' a cactus; its thorns will hurt you

6. what exclaimed carol did he really say that

7. ssh please dont make so much noise mrs brown whispered the baby's asleep

8. why didn't you report the incident at once the corporal asked the sentry

9. i won't do it the child screamed you can't make me do it

10. how's your uncle joe has he recovered from his operation yet

11. goal mark shouted almost knocking colin off the bench in his excitement

12. has any one of you read *the call of the wild* by jack london it's an excellent book

13. magnificent andy cried as he was watching an acrobatic act on stage

14. silence please the teacher shouted immediately the class became quiet

15. tony struggled in the water gasping with effort grab the rope mark shouted to him

16. what a pity she exclaimed i wish you were coming with us instead of going to school

17. this time he said angrily you must not fail

18. never the manager shouted such a thing will never happen

PART 16

請在下列各句子中加上必要的標點符號,並修正大小寫方式,使其書寫正確無誤。

1. whether you like it or not you have to do it boys the principal said

2. last sunday my father drove us to a seaside restaurant to eat crabs The trip was long but we enjoyed the ride

3. in spite of the heavy rain we went out to search for sooty the cat

4. on reaching the open sea the fishermen cast their nets over the side of their boat hoping to have a big catch

5. *the moon and us* was an interesting unusual and exciting movie We saw it at the odeon cinema last friday

6. the king tried to sleep but he could not seeing this the ladies-in-waiting said to the queen as the king cannot sleep why dont you tell him a story

7. by the time mona and her sister had gotten to the top of the slope rain had begun to fall It became heavier and heavier

8. on christmas day the children visited their aunt and uncle merry christmas they said

9. according to the regulations we have to take you back for questioning the police officer said but as you are evidently well-known to the sergeant we will only take down your name and address

10. when everything was packed and ready mrs robinson came down and said goodbye to the servants goodbye arthur she said addressing the gardener first

11. clean up the mess before you go home mrs brown said

12. waiter he called can you please bring me a menu

13. ready pull francis shouted from below we tugged at the rope pulling with all our might

14. suddenly i heard someone call out catch him catch him he's a thief

15. she couldn't even spell a simple word like their

16. the officer asked did you bring your registration card

17. what did you say speak louder the old man said

18. we went to see *romeo and juliet* at the central cinema

PART 17

請在下列各句子中加上必要的標點符號，使其書寫正確無誤。

1. I dont know why theyve changed their minds. Perhaps its because they cant afford the trip.

2. Cant Jane make the sandwiches for us? Isnt she willing to make them?

3. "Whos that?" the commander-in-chief asked. "Why dont you identify yourself?"

4. Its four oclock now. Why arent they back yet?

5. "I hope you didnt tell anyone about it yet. Thatll give me few more days to think it over," Henry said.

6. "Tell me whats wrong. Ill do my best to help you," she said.

7. The shop doesnt sell these brushes. Weve got to buy them somewhere else.

8. Hes worried about the dog's paw. It doesnt seem to be healing.

9. We couldnt all get into one car, so Mary had to make two trips instead.

10. "Arent you going to bed yet?" Christopher asked. "Its nearly eleven oclock."

11. "Ann is a great cook," he said. "You shouldve tasted her curry yesterday."

12. "Dont disturb me! Cant you see Ive got work to do?" she said irritably.

13. Shed never met James before. Thats why she didnt recognize him.

14. "You mustnt take anyone else's things. You shouldnt hide them, either," I told the child.

15. Wed better hurry The bus comes around eight oclock Tina said Oh there it is

16. Were going to school in Uncle Bens car Terry said Oh there he is

PART 18

請在下列各句子中加上必要的標點符號，使其書寫正確無誤。

1. Stop the little girl shouted Don't you know its cruel to pull the cats tail

2. A stranger came yesterday to ask where Karen had gone I told him that shed gone to her brother-in-laws house

3. Get out of bed you lazy girl the woman shouted Dont you know theres the washing and ironing to be done

4. Run run she panted The creatures just behind us

5. Four years savings all gone in a blaze he exclaimed Then he buried his head in his hands and cried

6. Quiet the teacher said She waited before she said I want you all to behave yourselves

7. Dont be rude child Aunt Agnes told Maggie Speak up when others talk to you now go to apologize to your uncle

8. Dont talk so loudly Marys mother told her

9. Wheres my book Whos taken it I asked puzzled

10. We cant talk here Come lets go into my study

11. Ive been waiting here since three oclock Couldnt you have come earlier

12. You arent angry with me are you I didnt know it was so late already

13. Isnt Henry coming to pick you up Janets brother asked her

14. "They wouldnt have gotten into trouble if theyd listened to me he said

15. If they arent here by eight oclock we wont wait for them

16. Theres been an accident at the traffic lights Michaels car couldnt move because of the jam

17. Its my dog Brownie Look Its paw is hurt

18. Isnt this book yours it cant be Alisons because hers has her name written in it

PART 19

請在下列各句子中加上必要的標點符號，並修正大小寫方式，使其書寫正確無誤。

1. this is neither peters bicycle nor davids it is bens

2. my friends brother told me joan asked me to say she cant play tennis tomorrow shes got a bad cold

3. i saw simons dog running all around the childrens playground

4. these shoes belong to me; yours are over there by the boys bicycles

5. if he isnt here by four oclock i wont wait a minute longer she grumbled

6. he promised that he would pass james book to me when hed finished reading it; however hes passed it to edward tom complained

7. youd have done the same thing if youd been in my place wouldnt you francis sister asked

8. tomorrows the day of the big walk the principal reminded the students dont forget to come in shorts and rubber shoes

9. mother theyve come cried nellie as she ran downstairs to meet her cousins

10. its no good; it wont work he said well have to think of something else

11. dont give up so easily boys mr white encouraged its not as difficult as you think

12. welcome my dear james aunt greeted him did you have a pleasant journey? you must be thirsty come well have tea now

13. perhaps youre right i admitted we wouldnt have escaped if it werent for him

14. i cant come now I have a lot of work to do ill meet you at six oclock my sister said

15. you mustnt cry rosie here wipe your tears thats a good girl miss davis said giving her a handkerchief

16. i was tired cold hungry and also desperately longing for home

17. dont panic the police and firemen are coming theyll help us he said

18. allen my eldest brother is the school captain my father mother and sister are just as proud of him as i am

19. we went to the grocery store and bought flour eggs cherries sugar butter and milk

20. besides nora two others also had a high score on the test They were tony and john

PART 20

請在以下段落加上必要的標點符號，並修正大小寫方式，使其書寫正確無誤。

karen put the telephone receiver down and turned to her younger sister that was mother amy she said the car broke down and she cant get back in this storm so shes staying the night in town with granny

did you tell her about father asked amy

no that would only worry her karen replied

their father was on a business trip and he was expected back that night however he had called to say that he would be one day late so now the two girls were left alone at home

come on amy lets go and have dinner said karen cheerfully trying to conceal her nervousness their house stood far off the main road among farms often karen had complained that it was too quiet and boring

but i hope that nothing happens tonight she thought

hardly had they sat down to eat when there was a rap at the front door quick as a flash amy was out of her chair ill answer it she cried

PART 21

請修正以下各句子的標點符號及大小寫方式，使其書寫正確無誤。

1. "Have you seen it too," I asked.

2. "Hurry, the bus is coming," Sandra called.

3. He was late, he had missed the bus.

4. My parents sisters and brothers, were not at home.

5. "Can you tell me where he is," Kenneth asked.

6. He couldn't decide whether he should go or not?

7. William took off his shoes unlocked the door, and went into the house.

8. We listened to Hotel California all night.

9. The furniture consisted only of a low table four chairs an icebox, and a stove.

10. Their lights are off, they must be asleep.

11. "Go away," she screamed at him.

12. I know he will come with me?

13. "When you are ready?" he said, "we'll go immediately."

14. They searched, among the flowers in between the rows of cabbages around the trees and, even in the fish pond.

15. "Yes Sir," the boy said loudly, as he saluted.

16. He walked quickly hurrying his footsteps over the cobbled footpath. Without turning around once.

17. I was worried, that he might lose his way in the strange, new town.

18. "Is it time to go home, Peter asked?"

PART 22

請在下列各句子中加上必要的標點符號（特別是連字號），並修正大小寫方式，使其書寫正確無誤。

1. my brother bought a second hand typewriter from an ex classmate of his

2. the project if well financed would have far reaching effects

3. her brother in law had a job doing house to house selling

4. the taxi driver agreed to take him on a four hour cruise around the island

5. the expectant mother bought an up to date book on childcare

6. the car he recently bought is high powered and has a self starting machine

7. at the end of the four month course he was promoted to editor in chief

8. after a careful re examination of the spider the naturalist said it was one of the rarest specimens in the world

9. the commander in chief of the army made a long distance call to headquarters to confirm the change of plans

10. his matter of fact attitude led her to think that he was a heartless man

11. he had copied the idea from one of the do it yourself books but he had designed the instrument himself

12. alice helped her mother re cover the cushions in preparation for christmas

13. daniel received a long distance call last night; it was from his pen pal in new zealand

14. if all of you co operate i think that we can get this done by four thirty said lawrence

15. the traveler demanded first class accommodation for the trip

16. the old man had such a tear provoking story to tell that at the end of it all of us were upset

17. edwards brother richard is twenty four years old and 1.8 meters tall

18. jill who is long legged and slim wants to be a model when she leaves school

PART 23

請在下列對話中加上必要的標點符號，並修正大小寫方式，使其書寫正確無誤。當不同的人發言時，請換行書寫。

1. excuse me is this the way to the post office he asked oh no sir the girl replied youre on the wrong road

    → _____

    → _____

2. mary was cutting the cucumber when she suddenly exclaimed oh ive cut my finger how could you be so careless her mother said come let me bandage it for you

$\rightarrow$ _____

$\rightarrow$ _____

3. look isnt that tony susan cried where i asked there she said pointing cant you see him hes in a blue striped shirt

$\rightarrow$ _____

$\rightarrow$ _____

$\rightarrow$ _____

4. will you be free tonight cindy asked her brother why do you want to know cindy well i was wondering if you would like to go to a show with me

$\rightarrow$ _____

$\rightarrow$ _____

$\rightarrow$ _____

5. youre wrong he declared uncle Peter isnt forty five years old yes he is tammy said emphatically how do you know her brother asked uncle Peter told me himself

$\rightarrow$ _____

$\rightarrow$ _____

$\rightarrow$ _____

$\rightarrow$ _____

6. dont worry mrs richards he said ill find andy for you he cant have gone far sobbing mrs richards said john youre such a good boy why cant my andy be like you

$\rightarrow$ _____

$\rightarrow$ _____

7. hurry up girls mr bill said its already half past two weve got to be there at three were coming papa they said as they ran down the stairs

$\rightarrow$ _____

$\rightarrow$ _____

8. somethings wrong with my car i told the mechanic it refuses to move well lets see he said lifting the hood he peered at the engine poking around with his fingers nothings wrong here could it be the fan belt i suggested helpfully

$\rightarrow$ _____

$\rightarrow$ _____

→ _____

9. we are going to see the wizard of oz tonight said larry want to come along the wizard of oz oh id love to see that exclaimed jill mike looked up from his picture book and asked can i come too well if you are a good boy ill take you along said larry

→ _____

→ _____

→ _____

→ _____

10. ice cream ice cream the man called oh stop please mr ice cream man said bobby may i have two ice cream cones the ice cream man stopped and proceeded to give bobby two ice cream cones here you are son thatll be twenty cents he said

→ _____

→ _____

→ _____

PART 24

請在以下段落加上必要的標點符號，並修正大小寫方式，使其書寫正確無誤。

in a short while mrs whites efficiency and doris eagerness had made the dust disappear the furniture shone the beds were re made with fresh sheets the bathroom was scrubbed and the dirty dishes were washed and stacked neatly away the women were so busy working that they did not notice mr browns absence until he returned carrying a few parcels with him you both must be hungry he said ive bought chicken fish and vegetables dare i ask both of you to stay for dinner oh mr brown how marvelous doris cried she quickly dried her hands and helped him carry the parcels into the kitchen wed love to stay for dinner but you really shouldnt have spent so much money

PART 25

請在下列各句子中加上必要的標點符號（特別是破折號），並修正大小寫方式，使其書寫正確無誤。

1. it was rumored that the enemy had a secret weapon a weapon against which there was no possible defense

2. he remembered that a lady he did not know what her name was had asked for the price of the vase

3. she dislikes everything about her shabby room the dirty walls the faded curtain and the old furniture

4. something moved in the tall bushes it was a tiger resting in the afternoon heat

5. quickly she ran to warn them and only just in time for they were about to cross the bridge

6. at last the hunters reached the clearing the place where the tiger was believed to have last been seen

7. i looked at the cage a moment ago the bird was there now it was gone

8. i can tell you only this much your daughter is safe the anonymous caller said and hung up

9. she opened her eyes, but everything was a blur the room the furniture and even the person sitting next to her

10. he looked horror-stricken at the scene in the room a scene which would haunt his dreams for many nights

11. david recalled that a stranger he couldnt remember his face had stopped him and asked him the way to the station

12. i i it didnt occur to me sir he stammered

13. no one has heard from him for nearly ten years she said

14. there is no doubt that children even very young ones have a certain degree of wisdom in them

15. he ran around the corner quickly but stopped short two policeman barred the way

16. many changes have taken place in that country since its independence changes for the better

17. jimmy said goodbye to everyone his teachers his classmates his neighbors and his relatives

18. the firefighter rushed out of the burning house and just in time, for the roof crashed immediately after him

PART 26

請在下列各句子中加上必要的標點符號，並修正大小寫方式，使其書寫正確無誤。

1. it was quite dark in the backyard i looked around adjusting my eyes to the darkness Then i saw it a long thin shape by the bushes It was the python

2. suddenly the silence of the night was shattered by a thin high pitched scream that died off abruptly I got out of bed quickly put on my robe switched on the light and looked out of the window It was dark and silent

3. this watch is no good it keeps stopping she complained giving the watch a vigorous shake look

an hour ago it was 10:35 a m now it is still 10:35 a m

4. its such a fine day lets go fishing eddie suggested we could pack some sandwiches some cakes and some fruit for a picnic well take our bicycles and ride to stillwater pond i hear that the fishing there is very good

5. after lunch the men started on their trip They checked their gear and supplies filled up their water bottles drove to the gas station to give their truck a last minute check and soon they were off

6. i need some more flour to bake the cakes mrs brown said margaret be a good girl run to the shop across the street and buy me a kilogram of flour heres the money

7. the car screeched to a halt beside the gate and the driver jumped out is mr taylor at home he asked the gardener ive got some urgent news for him i must see him at once

8. yes yes i remember the man you are referring to now He is hunchbacked and he walks with a limp He used to beg for a living around our neighborhood i said whats happened to him

9. go away i shouted in a trembling voice if you dont ill phone the police

10. ha phone the police go ahead the old man sneered i know you dont have a phone because i didnt see any wires around you didnt think i would check did you

11. i was furious with him for seeing through my bluff so quickly and kicked wildly at his leg with my steel shod boots

12. for a moment we stood staring at each other my legs were trembling so much that i thought they would give way licking my dry lips i forced myself to ask firmly what do you want

PART 27

請在以下段落加上必要的標點符號，並修正大小寫方式，使其書寫正確無誤。

crawling through a gap in the fence toby found a lovely apple tree laden with fruit he climbed it and was picking the ripe apples when a loud voice shouted hey you what do you think youre doing up there staring up at him was the farmer himself

why eating apples of course said toby cheekily would you like me to throw some down to you they are delicious

they are indeed snorted the angry farmer shaking his heavy cane at the boy thats my tree youre on you rascal so youd better come down at once

toby hesitated if you dont mind sir he said meekly id rather stay up here oh so you wont come down will you well i cant wait here all day but ill be back in the evening to deal with you then the farmer strode off toward the farmhouse

ha he thinks im going to sit here and wait for him till evening chuckled toby

but he soon found out that he had no choice for just then the farmer gave a shrill whistle and a large bulldog came trotting up from the farmhouse patting the animal the farmer said good dog rover then he pointed his cane at toby and said guard him rover guard him

PART 28

請在必要處加上冒號或破折號，使句子的書寫正確無誤。

1. Something cold hopped onto my leg it was a toad!
2. What really happened was this the elevator jammed while it was halfway down.
3. The stranger had a frightening look on his face a look which repelled most people.
4. Our chief clerk he has been working here for years has suddenly handed in his resignation.
5. There were five men in the car two in front and three in the back.
6. "Who who are you? What what do you want?" she stammered in fright.
7. We rushed out of the burning house and only just in time for the roof crashed down, sending sparks flying.
8. There was no hope left he had tried everything and failed.
9. While abroad, he witnessed an incident an incident that impressed him greatly.
10. She told him to buy these things a packet of salt, a bottle of tomato sauce, some pepper and a piece of ginger.
11. "Tell me this did you see his face or not?" the lawyer demanded.

PART 29

請在下列各句子中加上必要的標點符號，並修正大小寫方式，使其書寫正確無誤。

1. after much persuasion she told me her secret she is engaged to be married
2. on the desk you will find the following pens pencils erasers a ruler and a book
3. all applicants must possess certain qualifications the ability to read and write fluent English some knowledge of accounting and at least two years working experience
4. what really happened was this the baby pulled the dogs tail when nobody was looking so the animal bit him

5. bobby knew that he could not escape the kidnappers were watching him too closely

6. michael has one ambition to be a doctor

7. shakespeare wrote cowards die many times before their deaths

8. after a while mary said what i suggest is this each of us will take turns bringing flowers for the class

9. we need these things for our room new curtains a rug and some bookshelves

10. after a moments thought she gave her answer i will accept the post

11. the school holidays had just begun thirteen year old tony was very excited he was flying with his parents to europe

12. get out he shouted angrily i dont need your help

13. hello eric how are you now asked henry we were sorry that you were ill; all of us are glad that youre back in class again

14. the schools which participated in the debate were the following the star institution the holly avenue girls school and the first boys high school

15. judy is not sure when to use colons or semicolons commas or periods and brackets or dashes

16. peters father capt robinson likes to exercise to keep fit he takes an hours walk every evening

17. the stranger crept up the stairs entered the room closed the door softly behind him and started searching through the documents on the desk

18. havent you heard the saying pride goes before a fall the teacher asked the conceited student

PART 30

請在以下段落加上必要的標點符號，並修正大小寫方式，使其書寫正確無誤。

kevin made his way slowly to the school gym he opened the door and there were the familiar things the basketball nets the rope ladders and the mattresses less than a year ago they had been his world but now

hello there

kevin spun around almost dropping his crutches in his surprise a small cheerful looking boy was sitting on the horizontal bars hello said kevin

youre kevin brown arent you asked the boy

yes thats right i didn't think anyone would be here

i always come here said the boy by the way im danny from the primary school next door what are you doing here anyway kevin demanded dont you know that the gym is off limits

PART 31

請在下列各句子中加上必要的標點符號，並修正大小寫方式，使其書寫正確無誤。

1. we found him lying unconscious on the floor He had fainted from loss of blood
2. mary i want you to go to the grocery store to buy these things for me half a kilogram of butter half a kilogram of flour a packet of raisins and a can of baking powder
3. by the time it was evening the men had finished harvesting the wheat
4. if they arent at home just leave the parcel on the doorstep mother said
5. my brother who has come home for the holidays wants to invite you to his birthday party
6. although i wasnt free i had to do it because if i didnt who would
7. it was a pleasant evening I took my dog brownie for a walk
8. in a fright the lizard dropped its tail scurried up the wall and hid in a crevice
9. we discussed several topics one of which was marriage and its problems
10. i enjoyed reading the book *to kill a mockingbird* by harper lee It won a pulitzer prize
11. have you found what you wanted he asked here let me get it for you there you are
12. what a marvelous plan i exclaimed im sure itll succeed

PART 32

請在下列各句子中加上必要的標點符號（但不可使用破折號），並修正大小寫方式，使其書寫正確無誤。

1. He shook out the contents of the wallet a few coins a photograph and a crumpled ticket
2. Some passers by took pity on the child They stopped to drop some money into the outstretched palm
3. If you want to succeed in school John you must concentrate his father said
4. Its too late now she wailed
5. Be quiet How can I hear the news broadcast if all of you talk so loudly he said
6. The letter where is it? Quick tell me she urged
7. Huddled together for warmth we waited for dawn to come perhaps we would be able to find our way home when it was light
8. There was a long line of cars along the road somewhere ahead an accident had occurred thus

causing the traffic jam

9. That looks like uncle Ryans car It is his car isnt it she cried excitedly

10. Did you know that etcetera is actually a latin word

11. The walking stick was made of ebony it had an ivory handle

12. though deserts are hot and dry certain plants animals and even people manage to survive there

13. it spends most of its life underground the teacher told them thats why it has such small eyes

14. nobody knows exactly when the first olympic games were held Records show that they took place in olympia in greece

15. the following are some of the events running jumping swimming boxing and wrestling

16. get back he shouted to wendy the bridge is rotten It wont support your weight

17. i cant carry the bag its too heavy wont you help me carry it

18. we were reluctant to leave the final match was not over yet and the results of the contest not announced

19. william have you finished your homework his father asked if you have come and help me water the garden

20. ive been robbed call the police he cried all my money is gone

21. where did you get this eddie alice asked did you steal it come on tell me

PART 33

請在下列各句子中加上必要的標點符號（但不可使用破折號），並修正大小寫方式，使其書寫正確無誤。

1. at one time books were very expensive now with the modern methods of printing they are within everyones reach

2. the truth became obvious anna was not to blame for either of the mishaps

3. in the box you will find these things a pair of scissors a roll of bandages a bottle of iodine and some ointment

4. i know what his answer will be do as i say and not as i do

5. dictionaries are the most useful books they can be found in the library in the home in the office and sometimes in peoples pockets too

6. we knew there was no way of escape we had fallen into their trap

7. under the circumstances his only way out was to accept neither proposition in fact it was the

only possible way

8. one road runs parallel with the shore the other road more to the west leads to the lake

9. there was no escape from the dust it penetrated even through the slightest crack

10. some insects have wings others do not

11. there were many africans on the ship all of them were bound for tasmania

12. two scouts stood at the entrance the others lined the driveway

13. i doubt that they will turn up today theyve never been so late before

14. sometimes they go to work enthusiastically at other times they grumble and complain

15. to say it is easy to do it is an entirely different matter

16. the fire lighted up the whole countryside even from the road we could see it

17. seen from his point of view the situation was not hopeless it needed only some expert handling

18. if the earth is suitable they will grow corn if not they will plant yams

19. each of the contestants tries his best to be the first to spear the animal the one who does so wins the trophy

20. did you say television is an aid to education i dont agree with you my mother said

21. the rumor that the town had to be evacuated spread like fire It created panic and fear in homes and in the streets

22. hello peter when did you come back william asked why didnt you inform us of your arrival so that we could have met you at the railway station

PART 34

請在以下段落加上必要的標點符號，並修正大小寫方式，使其書寫正確無誤。

　　attention please attention came the captains voice over the loudspeaker im afraid we have to make an emergency landing please fasten your safety belts the passengers a party of thirty schoolboys and their history teacher did as they were told they were on a study trip to crete to explore some of the ancient temples and monuments mr biggs the history teacher stopped talking to the boys instead he peered out of the window through his spectacles and muttered what a nuisance i wonder where we are do you know jeffrey he asked the boy who sat beside him eighteen year old jeffrey walton was the class monitor no sir said jeffrey i cant make out a thing its very dark outside as the plane descended to earth the roar of the engines stopped further conversation after a series of bumps the plane screeched to a halt.

PART 35

請在以下段落加上必要的標點符號，並修正大小寫方式，使其書寫正確無誤。

around the hut was the river i had only to look out of the house to see it i could even see it through the spaces between the floorboards it was the home of fish crocodiles and strong currents

i was eleven years old then and i had grown up on the river i knew all about its secrets and powers for i heard my parents talk of it every day and yet i was very afraid of it

you should try not to think that way son my father advised the river gives us life fish to eat and water to drink without it how can the traders travel up and down how can we then get money to buy things remember son we fear only what we dont know

ill try to think as you do father i always replied but i retained my fear of the murky waters

often travelers on their way down the river would drop in at our house they always had many stories to relate and i would sit still for hours listening to them

PART 36

請修正以下各句子的標點符號及大小寫方式，使其書寫正確無誤。

1. Although the sky was dark. It did not rain, as we had feared it would.

2. The burglar put on his gloves. Switched on the flashlight and shone it on the lock of the safe.

3. Thinking it was late. I hurried through my breakfast and dashed off to school.

4. The question was not as easy to answer. As it seemed, it required a great deal of thought.

5. There were many interesting articles on display, some of them were my sister's handiwork.

6. Because of the floods. The examinations were postponed. Until further notice.

7. After a great deal of bargaining the shopkeeper agreed, to let us have both the vases for twenty dollars.

8. So far only, a few have managed to pass the test there are many reasons for this.

9. One of the largest ports in this region Port Deepwater enjoys a flourishing trade.

10. They left the windows open. Not knowing what damage the monkeys could do once they got into the house.

11. The police questioned the man and Philip, took down their conversation.

12. At the age of five Tim could read short stories. Do simple arithmetic problems. And converse fluently in English. in fact he was a remarkably intelligent child.

13. With a last great effort I climbed the hillside and stood at its summit the view was

breathtaking.

14. The contents of the case. When it was opened, came as a great surprise to us there was nothing inside but a pile of old newspapers!

15. During his stay here he had only one complaint. He could not bathe every day. Because of the insufficient water supply.

16. "Are you sure thats the right way to fix it," he asked, "Hadnt you better consult somebody first."

17. Vultures circled the area they were waiting for the man to die. In the desert heat.

18. Todays menu consists of the following. Soup fried chicken an omelet and fish curry.

19. Electricity serves many useful purposes. it works motors generates heat and provides light.

20. There is nothing much with her, the doctor said, "Most of her illnesses are imagined.

PART 37

請在以下信件內容中加上完整的標點符號，並使用正確的大寫。

---

145 hill road

green acres park

new castle W5G23

august 8th 2001

dear mrs brown,

i am extremely grateful to you for inviting me to spend the holidays with you at golden sand beach a holiday by the sea is just what i need after the long hours of study preparing for my end-of-the-term examination im glad thats all over now

im already looking forward to spending the week with you how are johnny tommy and betty im sure well have lots of fun together again at the beach

i will be seeing all of you on august 12th i will be coming to your house by train but you neednt meet me at the station as i know the place well enough already

until then bye-bye

yours lovingly

linda white

基礎文法寶典❺
Essential English Usage & Grammar
習題解答

Chapter 18 解答

18-1 小練習

1. "Where are you going?" he asked me.　2. "Please show me the way to the post office," she said. 3. "I would like to know what Mary is doing now," said the man.　4. "Father," the girl called, "there's someone here to see you."　5. "Samuel," the teacher said, "can you tell me where Brussels is?"　6. "I am a doctor," he said. "I can help you."　7. He said, "It is already eight o'clock."　8. "Do you want to go with us, Liza?" I asked.　9. "Thank goodness that you are safe!" she exclaimed. "I have been so worried about you!"　10. "Won't you give me a coin, sir?" the beggar pleaded. "I am so hungry."　11. He asked anxiously, "Are you sure that you're all right? You still look a bit shaken."　12. "Give me time to consider your proposition," I said. "I'll give you my answer tomorrow."　13. "When are you going to France?" she asked me. "Perhaps I'll go to the airport to see you off."　14. "My father said 'All right' when I asked him for permission," the little girl stated.　15. He scolded his younger brother, "What a careless boy you are! Now, you'll have to do your work all over again."　16. "Aren't you hungry?" she asked. "You haven't eaten anything all day!"　17. "Cease fire!" the major ordered. 18. "Alex, where have you been all this while?" his sister asked. "Your friends have been here for almost an hour."

18-2 小練習

1. Tell me what you have in the cupboard.　2. Do you know how she did it?　3. Does he know what the message is?　4. Ask him how he is.　5. Does she know when the concert is going to begin?　6. Ask John where the envelopes are.　7. Please tell me what the population of India is.　8. I don't know when the train from Reno arrives in Sacramento.　9. Tell me how long it usually takes you to walk to school.　10. Do you know why elephants don't eat meat?　11. Ask Professor Howard what the meaning of "euthanasia" is.　12. Do you know how long it will be before the mangoes ripen?　13. Tell me why you don't get more sleep.　14. I don't know where he usually parks his car.　15. Ask her which color she prefers, blue or green.　16. Do you know how many children he has?　17. Please tell me what is the matter with everyone in the house.　18. Ask him what the results of the experiment in the laboratory are.　19. Ask Danny who that girl over there is.　20. Do you know when you are going to visit your aunt?　21. I want to know how you operate this machine.　22. I'll ask the boys if/whether there are any letters for me.　23. He wants to know when they are going home.　24. I will ask them why they always quarrel.

136

基礎文法寶典 ❺
Essential English Usage & Grammar

18-3 小練習

1. He says that he is reading the newspapers.   2. He says that he will repair my bicycle for me.   3. He says that they are going to the fair on Saturday.   4. He says that Mary has lost the key to her room.   5. He says that he will help me to pack my clothes.   6. He says that his parents are going on a trip next month.   7. He says that she knows his uncle very well.   8. He says that he is cutting a slice of cake for me.   9. He says that he doesn't understand what I'm talking about.   10. He says that those fruit trees belong to them.   11. He says that he is looking for his watch.   12. He says that the meeting will start at four o'clock this afternoon.   13. He says that he will be looking forward to my next visit there.

18-4 小練習

1. My father told us not to open the can and to let him do it for us.   2. The doctor told him to try to get out in the sun as often as possible.   3. She ordered the girl to leave the books alone.   4. He told me not to cause so much trouble on his account.   5. The customer asked the waitress to bring him/her a glass of water.   6. I advised her not to be too confident of herself.   7. He told them to look after themselves while he was away.   8. She told them not to throw the trash on the road, or they might get fined.   9. She told him to bring her that jar from the shelf.   10. He told us to be early, or we wouldn't be able to get a place to sit.   11. I asked Karen to explain the meaning of that word to me.   12. They told us to wait there while they parked the car at the end of the road.   13. The motorist told us to look where we were going.   14. She told them to help themselves to the food.   15. He asked me not to wake him up before seven o'clock.   16. The teacher told us not to run along the hallways.   17. She told us to hurry up, or we would miss the bus.   18. She asked Julia to make sure that the gate was shut properly.   19. He told her not to show the letter to anyone.   20. They warned her not to spend all her money on clothes.   21. He ordered the little boy to drop that stick at once.   22. My sister exclaimed that she had forgotten to bring her books.

應用練習

PART 1

1. He remarked, "I heard her say to Harry, 'What a lazy boy you are!'"   2. "Tell me, young man," the woman said, "is your mother at home?"   3. "Tony, run down to the shop and get me some groceries," his mother said.   4. "Are you feeling all right?" he asked. "Let me get you a drink."   5. Molly asked, "Have you seen the movie *Star Wars*?"   6. The military officer shouted to his men, "Halt!"   7. "If you see Paul," she said, "send him to me."   8. I exclaimed, "You have lived here all your life and you don't even know your neighbors!"   9. "Do you have anything else to tell me, Raymond?" I asked.

10. "Look here, boys. This is the way to set up a tent," the young man said.　11. "Say 'Thank you,' Shirley," her mother told her.　12. He scolded his younger brother, "I have often told you not to play with fire!"　13. "Hurry up!" he shouted. "The ship 'Marianne' is going to sail soon!"　14. "Oh, dear! I am ruined!" the businessman cried.　15. "What time is it?" Robert asked. "I want to watch 'Mystery Movie' on television."　16. "Mother!" the boy called. "Where are you?"　17. "May I have the book *Detective Stories* for today? I want to read it," my little brother asked.　18. "Of the two poems 'The Rain' and 'Snow,' which one appeals more to you?" the teacher asked.

PART 2

1. I asked him why they were absent.　2. I don't know when they left the city.　3. I want to know what time it is.　4. Tell me how many people there are in the room.　5. I asked her what the price of that shirt is.　6. He wants to know where the railroad station is.　7. Tell us what they were arguing about.　8. I want to know how they go to work every day.　9. He asked me where I usually parked my car at night.　10. We don't know what kind of house he lives in.　11. I'm not sure what the date is today.　12. Nobody knows why there is a white line across the road.　13. Tell us how long it takes to go from your house to the school.　14. I asked him when electricity would be supplied to the new houses.　15. I want to know how much the oranges cost.　16. Tell me what she is doing in that corner.　17. Tell me whether you are going to the shop or to the market.　18. Do you know whom these strangers are looking for?　19. Ask your mother whether you should come back later to help me with my work.　20. He'll ask them where the bus stop is.　21. Tell me if/whether she has given you an answer yet.　22. They don't know when the game starts.　23. I'll ask the mechanic if/whether the car is in good condition.　24. Ask Marina if/whether the boys are coming along with us in this car.

PART 3

1. He asked me if/whether I knew that girl.　2. He wanted to know if/whether I was going to see "The Three Musketeers" the next day.　3. They wanted to know what I was doing with that piece of wood.　4. They asked us if/whether all of us were going to the picnic on Saturday.　5. I wanted to know why Uncle James and Aunt Alice couldn't come that week.　6. I asked her if/whether she had seen William or Alex when she went to the party.　7. The teacher asked which one of us had borrowed John's fountain pen during lunchtime.　8. The reporter asked the prisoners if/whether the guards let them walk around the compound.　9. Benny asked his mother if/whether it was time for them to get up.　10. The policeman asked the old lady why she couldn't tell them what the man looked like.　11. She wanted to know where I had hidden the money that she left on the dressing table.　12. The boy asked me

if/whether I would like to see some of the stamps he had collected.   13. I asked her if/whether she was all right then.   14. My mother asked me what was the matter with me.   15. I asked the boys where we should meet.   16. My sister asked me what I was staring at.   17. The teacher wanted to know how I had gotten that answer.   18. I asked her when she would be free the next/following day.   19. Mr. Richards asked his colleague if/whether they had been on holiday the previous month.   20. The boy asked the girl if/whether she dare go home alone.

PART 4

1. I asked him if/whether they were listening to the radio.   2. I don't know if/whether my mother has spoken to the shopkeeper yet.   3. We are not sure if/whether he likes to eat chocolate.   4. He asked us if/whether the car had skidded on the road.   5. I'll find out if/whether he is a medical student.   6. We are not sure if/whether they are making a clay model of the airplane.   7. He asked us if/whether he planted orchids in his garden.   8. I want to know if/whether your writing has improved since I last saw it.   9. He'll find out if/whether they can wade across the river.   10. I ask him if/whether I may use the telephone.   11. I want to know if/whether he has put the ointment on his feet.   12. She doesn't know if/whether there is anybody practicing on the piano.   13. I want to know if/whether you can look after my pet while I am away.   14. We are not sure if/whether they have been doing their homework lately. 15. He asked me if/whether I had looked through the history notes he had given me.   16. I don't know if/whether we should hold the meeting in the hall or in the classroom.   17. She asked me if/whether it was possible for a person of her size to defeat a person twice her size.   18. He asked me if/whether I wanted to go swimming with them in the river after they had had tea.   19. He wondered if/whether there was an empty room where he could stay for the night.   20. She asked me if/whether she should prepare a nice hot meal for me before I left.   21. I wondered if/whether they would help us solve that problem if we asked them to.   22. He asked her if/whether she was angry with him for ignoring her in front of the others the day before/the previous day.

PART 5

1. I told them that exercise makes our muscles strong.   2. She said that eggs contain a lot of protein. 3. We reported that she was painting a portrait.   4. He says that he is grateful to me for my help.   5. Mr. Brown said that he was trying to repair his watch.   6. I will tell her that she is making a terrible mistake.   7. He will say that he has more endurance than me.   8. They said that they were polishing their shoes.   9. Our Science teacher told us that light travels 300,000 kilometers in one second.   10. He said that he was leaving for Sunway Park on the three o'clock train.   11. My father said that success

is the fruit of hard work. 12. She is telling her friend that her sister is absent today because she has sprained her ankle. 13. The doctor says that his condition is getting worse. 14. He told us that that road leads to Holly Avenue. 15. Last week, his grandfather told him that he was making a will. 16. I thought that the truck would hit the cow. 17. He said that the boy hadn't had his anti-cholera injection yet.

PART 6

1. The shopkeeper said that I could settle my account at the end of that month. 2. Peter told me that he was writing an article for the school magazine. 3. I said that he would arrive by train that night. 4. The radio announcer said that the weather would be fine on that day. 5. The teacher said that everyone might leave the class then. 6. My mother warned me that I would be late for school if I didn't hurry. 7. The manager said that I would have to complete the work by three o'clock that afternoon. 8. He said that he had an appointment with the dentist at ten o'clock the next/following day. 9. She said that she had read all the newspapers in the house. 10. He told me that he had been playing chess at his uncle's house the night before. 11. His father told him that he might buy whatever he wished. 12. The doctor explained that having an X-ray taken is not painful. 13. The teacher told us that a diamond is a very valuable stone. 14. The teacher explained that intransitive verbs do not have objects. 15. He said that he would go there the next/following day. 16. I said to him that I would not take back what I had said. 17. She says that examinations will never be abolished. 18. They told her that she was lying.

PART 7

1. He said that he had lived in India for many years. 2. He will say that they do not know where Polly has gone. 3. I said that her brother had gone there the previous week/the week before. 4. She told me that she had finished her work days before. 5. I said that I must not be disrespectful to my elders. 6. He told me that his brother was not free then. He was writing letters. 7. The man said to the girl that he knew her father very well. 8. The gardener told her that she could pick as many flowers as she liked from that bed. 9. He says that he is not so foolish as to believe me. 10. She said that they had better start doing their work then as they had to hand it in the following week. 11. The supervisor told the girl that she mustn't be so slow with her work next time. 12. I wondered if/whether I would be able to beat them in the competition. 13. I asked the man if/whether he had seen the accident happen. 14. She asked her employee if/whether she/he had done the marketing yet. 15. The stranger inquired if/whether I knew where Mr. West had shifted to. 16. She asked her friend if/whether all his/her answers had been correct. 17. The children asked their mother when Uncle would come to visit them

again.　18. She asked where I was working then.

PART 8

1. The teacher questioned her why she had been hiding behind the door.　2. I wondered if/whether I had to apologize to her.　3. The doctor asked the mother if/whether the child had been vaccinated against smallpox.　4. The landlady asked him why he hadn't paid her the previous month's rent.　5. She asked if/whether I smelled something burning.　6. She asked me if/whether the lights had still been on when I had come home the previous night/the night before.　7. My father asked my sister where she had put his gardening tools.　8. She asked if/whether I was feeling thirsty after the long walk.　9. They said that they had their hair cut at the barber shop next door.　10. He says that he may be having a nap when I arrive at the house.　11. I will tell him that I am looking for my report card.　12. The doctor told us that he was out of danger then. We could probably take him home in a week.　13. My grandfather always says that the beaten road is the safest.　14. The doctor said that the soldiers had donated blood to the hospital that morning.　15. She said that hydrogen explodes when it is lighted.
16. The farmer said that the hens had laid some eggs. He would go to the market the following/next day to sell them.

PART 9

1. The teacher told them to sing louder.　2. She advised him to take an aspirin and to go to bed.　3. The teacher asked the students to pass in their books then.　4. He told us to be careful not to trespass while we were camping.　5. She advised him to sit down and to tell her the whole story.　6. My father told me not to be too discouraged with my results.　7. The doctor advised him not to strain himself and to try to get more rest.　8. The captain commanded them to stand at ease.　9. We asked them to let us do it by ourselves.　10. The teacher told his students not to read the sentence so fast, or nobody would understand what they were reading.　11. He warned me not to play with fire.　12. The nurse asked them to sit down and said that the doctor would see them in a few minutes.　13. My brother remarked that I was a fool.　14. He remarked angrily that my behavior was really stupid.　15. The old man asked his son to help him carry that load as it was too heavy for his shoulders.

PART 10 （下列引述動詞的使用並非唯一解答，僅供參考）

1. She ordered the children to go out to play and not to disturb her while she was cooking.　2. The receptionist invited him to go that way.　3. She greeted him and said that there was a letter for him.
4. The woman ordered the thief to stop.　5. She requested me to shut the door when I went out.　6. I asked my friend to wait for me as I would be back in a few minutes.　7. The lady advised the driver to

be careful as the road there was very slippery.　　8. I urged her to be quick as I really couldn't hold on much longer.　　9. Mr. Brown told Peter not to argue with his mother.　　10. She told Jane to put the cake into the oven and to turn the temperature to 150 degrees.　　11. He told me not to forget to lock all the windows and the door before I left the house.　　12. The secretary told me to go straight in and said that the manager was waiting for me.　　13. He greeted us and wanted us to open our books to Page 71 and to start reading to ourselves.　　14. The teacher ordered me to speak louder as no one could hear me if I murmured.　　15. He instructed his secretary not to open his mail while he was away and said that he would handle it when he returned.　　16. Peter told Sally to tell John to meet him at Mary's house in half an hour.　　17. He told me that it was the way to repair it and asked me to watch carefully while he was repairing it.　　18. She exclaimed that it was a beautiful painting and enquired who had painted it.

PART 11（下列引述動詞的使用並非唯一解答，僅供參考）

1. She apologized to me and said that her brother wouldn't be back until late that night.　　2. The guard reported that he had heard some shots and run out into the compound to investigate.　　3. Stella inquired when he would be back and said that she had something important to tell him.　　4. Jeffrey asked me if/whether I had gone to the circus that was performing there and added that it had been a wonderful show.　　5. She greeted me and asked after my health, adding that she had heard that I had been quite sick.　　6. He ordered the frightened boy to go to him at once and added that if he didn't, he would give him a beating.　　7. The doctor advised Mrs. Brown not to do too much heavy work but to get as much rest as possible.　　8. He invited me politely as he wanted to show me his new fish which his father had bought the day before.　　9. My mother asked me if/whether I was going out then and told me to be back by ten if I were.　　10. I told her to go ahead and added that I would wait there until she returned.　　11. He enquired where he could buy striped shirts like those and added that they seemed to be in fashion then.　　12. She told the little boy not to be afraid and assured him that the dog wouldn't hurt him as it only wanted to make friends with him.　　13. She asked John to shut the door properly on his way out as it kept banging away.　　14. The maid said that he was probably sleeping then and enquired if/whether she should call his sister to come down.

PART 12（下列並非唯一解答，僅供參考）

1. He ordered him, "Leave the house at once!"　　2. "We have waited an hour for you," they said to me.　　3. He said, "I have come against my will."　　4. "Come fishing with me, Paul," said Peter.　　5. "I'm not hungry," I said. "I don't want anything."　　6. My mother often tells me, "If you are good, everything will be all right."　　7. She replied, "I have seen the film before."　　8. He said, "What an

interesting novel it was!" 9. He commanded them, "Stand at attention!" 10. The teacher explained, "Temperature decreases with ascent." 11. He proposed, "Let's wait till the rain stops." 12. He said, "It gives me great pleasure to preside over the meeting." 13. She advised them, "Don't quarrel among yourselves." 14. Mrs. Lea shouted to her children, "Keep quiet!" 15. I explained, "The earth revolves around the sun." 16. I said, "Long ago, people believed that the earth was the center of the universe." 17. The traveler said, "I have come a long way." 18. She said to the visitors, "Please sit down."

PART 13（下列並非唯一解答，僅供參考）

1. "Will my husband get home safely?" the woman wondered anxiously. 2. The man asked them, "Should you hang around in such a place?" 3. "Have you collected the mail?" I asked my brother. 4. The policeman asked, "What has been going on in the casino?" 5. "Isn't the weather too rough for fishing?" she asked her husband. 6. I asked Jane, "Will you lend me a pencil?" 7. The teacher asks them, "Where have you put the books?" 8. They asked us, "Where did you go during the interval?" 9. She asked herself, "Did I do right?" 10. "Has the road been repaired yet?" he asks. 11. "What have you done so far to remedy the situation?" he demanded. 12. The lawyer asked him, "Why are you snooping around the house?" 13. "Mother, where did you put the jam tarts?" the child asked. 14. The little boy pestered his parents, "Buy me a toy train." 15. She asked, "Is your name Alfred?" 16. He wondered, "Why isn't anybody at home?" 17. Miss Hillman asked the fortuneteller, "What will my future be like?" 18. The boys asked their teacher, "Shall we leave now?" 19. The students exclaimed, "How can anyone get distinctions for all the subjects in the examination?"

Chapter 19 解答

19-3 小練習

1. can't you 2. has it 3. mustn't he 4. don't you 5. aren't they 6. can I 7. wouldn't she
8. has it 9. isn't he 10. won't he/she 11. does he 12. don't you 13. shouldn't he
14. doesn't she 15. weren't they 16. have they 17. didn't it 18. didn't they 19. won't he
20. will we 21. did they 22. are you 23. couldn't it

應用練習

PART 1

1. won't they 2. shouldn't he/she 3. can't they 4. do you 5. aren't they 6. hadn't he
7. did we 8. would you 9. doesn't it 10. hadn't they 11. do we 12. don't they
13. shouldn't I 14. does she 15. didn't it 16. didn't you 17. don't they 18. hasn't she

19. didn't they   20. can't he   21. did they   22. couldn't it   23. may it   24. aren't I/am I not

PART 2

1. won't he   2. couldn't you   3. aren't they   4. were there   5. isn't he   6. isn't it

7. shouldn't you   8. were they   9. won't we   10. don't they   11. aren't they   12. hasn't he/she

13. will you   14. dare they   15. wasn't it   16. don't they   17. mightn't they   18. didn't it

19. do they   20. isn't it   21. did it   22. couldn't they   23. isn't it   24. can it

PART 3

1. must   2. should   3. didn't   4. is   5. do   6. did   7. couldn't   8. hadn't   9. doesn't

10. did   11. haven't   12. hasn't   13. doesn't   14. can   15. isn't   16. did   17. doesn't   18. do

19. should   20. don't

PART 4

1. would they; they wouldn't   2. must; must they   3. was she; she wasn't   4. didn't they; they did

5. didn't you; I did   6. won't we; we will   7. didn't; did he   8. is there; there isn't

9. wouldn't you; I would   10. has; they have   11. dare; daren't we   12. doesn't she; she does

13. didn't they; they did   14. shouldn't they; they should   15. mustn't there; there must

16. couldn't; they couldn't   17. hadn't it; it had   18. don't you; I do   19. isn't; it is

20. haven't; they haven't   21. can't they; they can

PART 5

1. should you; I shouldn't   2. aren't I/am I not; you are   3. didn't she; she did

4. mightn't he; he might   5. do you; I don't   6. mightn't she; she might   7. could she; she couldn't

8. might they; they mightn't   9. hasn't he; he has   10. won't she; she will   11. have you; I haven't

12. don't you; I do   13. did she; she didn't   14. didn't he; he did   15. are they; they aren't

16. won't he; he will   17. have I; you haven't   18. doesn't she; she does   19. aren't they; they are

PART 6

1. did you; I didn't   2. wasn't he; he was   3. aren't there; there are   4. didn't she; she did

5. can she; she can't   6. isn't it; it is   7. has he; he hasn't   8. will they; they won't

9. haven't you; I have   10. doesn't he; he does   11. does she; she doesn't   12. isn't he; he is

13. doesn't he; he does   14. weren't they; they were   15. must they; they mustn't   16. doesn't it; it does

17. haven't they; they have   18. will he; he won't   19. mightn't he; he might

20. should we; we shouldn't

PART 7

1. can she; she can't   2. haven't they; they have   3. couldn't they; they could   4. won't I; you will

5. won't you; I will   6. doesn't she; she does   7. didn't you; we did   8. aren't I/am I not; you are

9. doesn't it; it does   10. haven't they; they have   11. will we; we won't   12. is there; there isn't

13. mustn't we; we must   14. won't he; he will   15. shouldn't he/she; he/she should

16. must she; she mustn't   17. had she; she hadn't   18. isn't there; there is   19. haven't they; they have

20. won't they; they will   21. have I; you haven't   22. doesn't it; it does

PART 8

1. will it; it won't   2. didn't she; she did   3. can't I; you can   4. can't they; they can

5. don't they; they do   6. didn't you; I did   7. doesn't he; he does   8. does he; he doesn't

9. didn't they; they did   10. do we; we don't   11. shouldn't she; she should   12. didn't they; they did

13. did he; he didn't   14. mustn't we; we must   15. will I; you won't   16. doesn't he; he does

PART 9

1. doesn't it; it does   2. don't we; we do   3. didn't she; she did   4. should I; you shouldn't

5. didn't you; I did   6. doesn't it; it does   7. didn't he/she; he/she did   8. will he; he won't

9. didn't they; they did   10. will we; we won't   11. was there; there wasn't   12. is it; it isn't

13. should they; they shouldn't   14. don't you; I do   15. couldn't they; they could

16. don't they; they do   17. isn't he; he is   18. shouldn't he; he should

PART 10

1. mustn't we; we must   2. would I; you wouldn't   3. can't they; they can   4. will she; she won't

5. would he; he wouldn't   6. can't they; they can   7. shouldn't I; you should

8. could he; he couldn't   9. mightn't he; he might   10. don't I; you do   11. must they; they mustn't

12. aren't we; we are   13. won't you; I will   14. wouldn't I; you would   15. has it; it hasn't

16. do you; I don't

PART 11

1. doesn't she; she does   2. didn't she; she did   3. doesn't it; it does   4. must they; they mustn't

5. are there; there aren't   6. should they; they shouldn't   7. mustn't they; they must

8. don't they; they do   9. didn't we; we did   10. weren't they; they were   11. isn't it; it is

12. weren't they; they were   13. can't they; they can   14. didn't it; it did   15. is there; there isn't

16. don't they; they do   17. did they; they didn't   18. doesn't it; it does   19. didn't it; it did

20. can they; they can

PART 12

1. can't you; I can   2. can it; it can't   3. haven't they; they have   4. should I; you shouldn't

5. isn't there; there is   6. mightn't it; it might   7. don't I; you do   8. dare you; I daren't

9. do they; they don't   10. wouldn't she; she would   11. can it; it can't   12. will you; I won't

13. aren't they; they are   14. did they; they didn't   15. doesn't it; it does   16. didn't it; it did

17. don't they; they do   18. didn't they; they did

Chapter 20　解答

20-1 小練習

1. I am very sure (that) he did not come to my house that evening.   2. I agree (that) none of them should have approached the principal in such a manner.   3. Please tell me how you managed to persuade that girl to come.   4. People believe (that) the treasure was hidden somewhere on the island. 5. I am very confident (that) he will break the old record and set a new one for the high jump.   6. It annoyed me that he kept on grumbling about it.   7. His mother is worried (that) he may be too ill to go to school.   8. I found out (that) the man had been returning home very late every night.   9. That she was feeling homesick and longing to go home was apparent.   10. The fact is that no one except Mr. Smith will be able to solve such a difficult problem.   11. What I want to discuss with him is not important.   12. It is certain (that) no one else could have had the chance to go into the room.   13. I am afraid (that) he isn't going to like this at all.   14. Why they did such a foolish thing is certainly incredible.   15. They told me (that) I was going to be put in charge of the whole operation.   16. Where else they could have gone in such stormy weather was the question.

20-2 小練習（本大題無唯一標準答案，以下所列僅供參考）

1. Did you watch the procession which passed by here just now?   2. There is a girl who looks like you working in that shop.   3. The insect (which) you killed just now is a cicada.   4. We spoke to the lady whose cat you had rescued from the tree last night.   5. The roof where a few tiles have been displaced needs repairing.   6. You should take the elevator which goes to all the floors.   7. Bring me the scissors which are in the topmost drawer.   8. He is the most conceited person (that) I have ever met. 9. They postponed the match which was supposed to take place tomorrow evening.   10. The thief must have climbed in through that window where he left fingerprints.   11. Have you seen the movie which was shown at the Grand Cinema last week?   12. Did you tell the news to the man whose daughter you are very friendly with?   13. One day he will meet someone who means a lot to him.   14. The article which was written by Andrew was printed in the school's newsletter.   15. The person who is waiting in

the lounge says that he is the former chief clerk here.   16. The boy who fell from the top of the tree broke both legs.   17. My mother, who is a great storyteller, told us an amusing story.   18. The friend who helps you in time of need is a real friend.   19. The child died from a disease which was unknown to the doctors at that time.   20. Did you read the notice which was pinned onto the board two days ago?

20-3 小練習（本大題無唯一標準答案，以下所列僅供參考）

1. until   2. before   3. while   4. If   5. as if   6. where   7. If   8. However   9. after

10. as soon as   11. Though   12. unless   13. where   14. as if   15. if   16. unless   17. while   18. as

19. so that   20. such; that

應用練習

PART 1（本大題無唯一標準答案，以下所列僅供參考）

1. The tree which has lost all its leaves is beginning to die.   2. Do you know the time when he came home last night?   3. The commander who gave the order himself didn't know what to do.   4. I can't remember the exact place where I have seen these books on display.   5. His father gave him everything (that) he asked for.   6. The experiment which was tried on various kinds of fish proved that fish respond to light.   7. Success which does not come easily to people is the result of hard work.   8. The bridge which was destroyed during last night's storm is being repaired.   9. He put the straw near the fireplace, which was a dangerous thing to do.   10. They planned to have the meeting on Sunday, when most of the adults were not at home.   11. Their house which is surrounded by a tall hedge has a big garden.   12. The noise which had disturbed him had been made merely by some mice scratching against a floorboard.   13. The person who wrote that essay has a unique style.   14. He was given the Victoria Cross, which any person would feel honored to receive.   15. The plan which one of the boys proposed is quite a sensible one.   16. No one knew the reason why he left so hurriedly.   17. Shakespeare was buried in the place where he was born.   18. My father, whom you met at the station once, has invited you to stay with us during the holidays.   19. I wonder if you still remember the day when we were discussing how farmers forecast the weather.   20. In the cave where Andy had sheltered the previous night was a huge lion.

PART 2（本大題無唯一標準答案，以下所列僅供參考）

1. I have finished doing the homework (which) the teacher gave to us this morning.   2. He wants to go to the place (which) his grandmother had bought a few years ago.   3. The student who was caught smoking in school will be severely punished.   4. We saw the old lady whose son had been seriously injured in an accident.   5. The accident which happened at the crossroads near the market was a very

serious one.　6. Can you describe the girl (whom) you say was the one who stole your pen?　7. Did you recognize the man who was biking past us with a basket on the handlebars?　8. I told her the time when he would be returning from the office.　9. John, whose cousin is your neighbor, is going off to South Africa this week.　10. Those children who are playing in the garden are my nieces and nephews. 11. The dog which was chasing the neighbor's cat just now has already been tied up.　12. Any person in the village (whom) you ask can tell you the story.　13. The reason (which) she gave for being late was unsatisfactory.　14. The poem which was written by Lord Byron is a very beautiful one.　15. Stella, whom you met in my house last week, has sent an invitation card to you.　16. This boy, whose brother is in my class, has been waiting to see me for half an hour.　17. The students who are all twelve years old have applied for their identity cards.　18. We went to inspect the house (which) we wanted to buy.

PART 3（本大題無唯一標準答案，以下所列僅供參考）

1. The boy who climbs too high up the tree is sure to fall.　2. Where is the book (which) he left there for me?　3. Any person (that) you ask will show you the place.　4. I have received the message (which) you sent to me.　5. No one stopped at the grave where a wartime hero was buried.　6. He remembers the days of his childhood when he used to fish in the river which is near his home.　7. He cannot reach the encyclopedia which is on the topmost shelf.　8. The new manager who was appointed by the board of directors called a staff meeting.　9. The children who are strong and healthy have no need for a doctor.　10. The CD (which) you bought recently has a few scratches on it.　11. You proposed a plan which I think is an excellent one.　12. He can't wear any shoes on his foot which has swollen to twice its size.　13. His father gave him ten dollars (which) he put into his savings account. 14. Can you show me a photograph of the girl (whom) you said you wanted to introduce to me?　15. My brother (who) you have met before has gone on an expedition up the river.　16. The dog was killed by a truck which was traveling at a great speed.　17. The doctor has given me some medicine (which) I must take when I feel dizzy.　18. You will have your reward on the day when you capture the murderer who has killed a number of people.

PART 4（本大題無唯一標準答案，以下所列僅供參考）

1. I remember the day when the transport workers were on strike.　2. Where is the key (which) I left in the keyhole?　3. I know the reason why he went home early.　4. She forgave the boy who had placed a live lizard on her desk.　5. Have you fixed the time when we are supposed to meet?　6. She helped the old man across the road, which was very kind of her.　7. They know the place where the smugglers hid the contraband goods.　8. The man found the wallet which contained a lot of money.　9. That

student who never studies or does his homework has failed in the exam again.   10. My brother, Jim, who was sixteen last week, is studying in that school.   11. My mother, whom you met yesterday, likes to travel.   12. George Bernard Shaw, who wrote *Pygmalion*, died in 1950.   13. Do you know the time when the conference will begin?   14. These are the questions (which) you are to answer as best as you can.   15. My uncle missed the last train to Claxton, which annoyed him very much.   16. We gave a farewell party for Miss Porter, who had been our English teacher for two years.   17. The port which is situated in a very strategic position is growing at a tremendous rate.   18. Show me the spot where you hid the box.

PART 5（本大題無唯一標準答案，以下所列僅供參考）

1. while   2. where   3. as if   4. As   5. Because   6. as if   7. Though   8. where

9. As soon as   10. so that   11. while   12. as   13. as   14. If   15. so that   16. so that   17. Though

18. Since   19. that   20. However

PART 6（本大題無唯一標準答案，以下所列僅供參考）

1. such; that   2. as long as   3. If   4. so that   5. where   6. because   7. while   8. after

9. because   10. wherever   11. because   12. Though   13. so that   14. so; that   15. even though

16. so that   17. such; that   18. as

PART 7（本大題無唯一標準答案，以下所列僅供參考）

1. because   2. after   3. because   4. as long as   5. when   6. in case   7. whether

8. as long as   9. if   10. Whatever   11. before   12. if   13. so that   14. because   15. even though

16. Though; as   17. even though   18. so; that; as   19. until; as   20. where; in case

PART 8（本大題無唯一標準答案，以下所列僅供參考）

1. when   2. as soon as   3. so   4. as   5. because   6. so; that   7. although   8. as if

9. Even though; as; since   10. so that; than   11. If; whether   12. as; when

13. Although; even though   14. if   15. after; after   16. as long as

Chapter 21   解答

21–1 小練習

1. What are you waiting for, Mary?   2. Please buy me a comb, an exercise book, and a ruler, Nicholas.

3. My mother wanted me to tell you that lunch is ready.   4. I wonder what time it is. I must be home by 9 p.m.   5. It was late. We were still several kilometers away from the nearest village.   6. They were hungry, tired, and sleepy. They had been walking without food for two days.   7. We left for the

airport at four o'clock. Halfway there, the car broke down.   8. He squeezed some lemon into the glass, added a spoonful of sugar and some water. Then, he stirred the mixture vigorously.   9. Christmas Day fell on Saturday last year.   10. Mr. Lea is going to Paris on October 5th.   11. On New Year's Day, many families go visiting their friends and relatives. Everyone dresses up on this day.   12. His uncle lives in North Province. It takes him four days to travel to his uncle's farm.   13. By the end of July, they will have finished their Primary School Leaving Examination.   14. They visited Mr. and Mrs. Jolly when they were in Rainbow Valley. They met Derek, Jimmy, Mary, and Helen, too.   15. Miss White said we were to learn by heart either "The Village Blacksmith" or "The Highwayman."   16. The class will be doing Shakespeare's *Merchant of Venice* next year.   17. "Earthquake" and "Jaws" are two very exciting movies. I have seen both of the movies.   18. My brothers were watching "Mission in Space." My father was reading the *Evening Post*.   19. When the third act of *Swan Lake* ended, everybody applauded loudly.   20. "Have you read *In the Alpine Mountains* written by a geologist who risked his life doing research there?" asked Brenda.

21-2 小練習

1. dept.   2. Capt.   3. Sept.   4. etc.   5. e.g.   6. i.e.   7. std.   8. kg.   9. lat.   10. B.A.
11. G.P.O.   12. Sat.   13. P.O.W.   14. U.K.   15. G.M.T.   16. U.N.   17. Mt.   18. B.C.   19. Ltd.
20. Pres.   21. Fri.   22. Co.   23. Asst.   24. W.H.O.

21-3 小練習

1. A good breakfast will give a man energy, alertness, and vitality.   2. Mary put a cutting board, a knife, some carrots, and meat on the kitchen table.   3. Please let me have some paint, a brush, a bottle, and a piece of paper.   4. Paul collects stamps, shells, and even matchbox labels.   5. The mixture contains flour, butter, sugar, eggs, some baking powder, and a pinch of salt.   6. She was carrying an umbrella, two books, a parcel, and her handbag.   7. There were all kinds of animals in the zoo: lions, tigers, elephants, giraffes, monkeys, birds, and snakes.   8. Mary, Rita, Jeremy, and Stephen, please go to the principal's office.   9. To make the bookcase, you will need a hammer, some nails, four planks, and a saw.   10. After taking these pills, you will be strong, healthy, energetic, and alert.   11. I threw open the door, stood there for a moment, and marched into the room.   12. Paint the sky blue, the trees, grass and leaves green, and the flowers yellow or red.   13. Belinda ran up the stairs, went into her room, shut the door, and leaned against it.   14. The doctor took the patient's pulse, examined his eyes and throat, asked him a few questions, and finally wrote out a prescription.   15. She woke up, rubbed her eyes, and stretched herself lazily before getting out of bed.   16. Nancy, Susan, and their two brothers got

基礎文法寶典 **❺**
Essential English Usage & Grammar

off the train, held their tickets, and followed the rest of the passengers toward the exit.　17. He walked to the park, sat on a bench, opened his newspaper, and began to read it.　18. Mrs. Hill said, "My daughter hasn't been home the whole day."

21-4 小練習

1. "Come, Helen. Here's an interesting book for you to read," her uncle said.　2. "Mr. Norton is giving us a dinner treat tonight," she told us. "He has just been promoted to assistant manager."　3. "You can't refuse to come," Mona said. "It'll spoil all our plans."　4. "John, meet me at the Federal Coffee House at eight-fifteen a.m.," he said. "I want to discuss with you how to get the trip organized. Please be punctual."　5. The policeman instructed us, "Follow this road until you come to the bridge where there is an intersection. Then, take the turning on your left. Drive straight on till you see the traffic lights."　6. "The book gives a comprehensive account of the various types of fish found in tropical waters," he said. "It ought to interest you."　7. "Never mind," said David. "I expect we will be able to get tickets for My Fair Lady tomorrow night."　8. "Maria, take this note to Miss White. Tell her that I'm waiting for her reply," Aunt Sally said.　9. The "Sea Queen" was berthed somewhere away from the dock.　10. Mr. Bright said, "Boys, divide yourselves into two groups. We'll play a game called 'King's Camp'."　11. "Let's go now," Nick said. "We can get better seats if we go earlier."　12. "Do visit us when you're free," Mrs. Smith told us.　13. "The Happy Wanderer" and "Let's Get Together" are two of his favorite songs.　14. "Please come in. I've just finished writing a letter," Raymond told me.　15. "Have you seen The Sound of Music?" he asked Charles.　16. "Sit down," the manager said. "What can I do for you?"　17. "Why don't you see whether 'The Empress of India' is still in the harbor?" the sailor suggested.　18. The sign on the board read, "Beware of Dogs."

21-5 小練習

1. "Where are you going, Danny?" his father asked. "It is late. Are you going to town again?"　2. Mark called out to his friend, "We're going to watch a badminton match. Care to come along, Henry?"　3. Charles asked us whether we were going to the picnic. "Have you given him your answer?" Janet asked me.　4. I asked him, "Henry, are you going to the post office today? Could you mail a letter for me, please?"　5. Nancy asked me whether I knew her brother. She said, "Haven't you met him before?"　6. "What's happening?" he inquired. No one answered him. "What's wrong?" he asked again.　7. "Hello, Miss Davis. How are you?" John asked. "You look tanned. Have you been to the beach?"　8. "Did you find the book?" Jill's father asked. "I might have put it on the top shelf. Have you searched for it there?"

21-6 小練習

1. "Hurrah! We're going to the zoo!" the children exclaimed.   2. "Get out of there!" he shouted angrily.   3. The men cried, "Quick, run! The branch is falling!"   4. "Here comes the bus!" she said. "Let's run for it, Eddie!"   5. "Ha-ha! I've tricked you, haven't I?" the man exclaimed with excitement.   6. "No! I won't go!" Wendy said. "Please, please, don't make me go!" she pleaded.   7. "Fire! Help!" the woman screamed. "Oh, my child is trapped in there! Please save him!"   8. She remarked, "What a beautiful dress!"   9. "Merry Christmas to you!" Mary said. "And a Happy New Year, too!"   10. "Go away, and don't disturb me!" I said in irritation. "I have a lot of homework to do!"

21-7 小練習

1. women's laughter   2. a policeman's uniform   3. my father's opinion   4. the judge's decision   5. Nicholas' watch   6. those guards' footsteps   7. a minute's rest   8. wolves' howling   9. a businessman's responsibility   10. the headman's son   11. her mother-in-law's words   12. the princess' horses   13. two hours' delay   14. someone else's voice   15. ladies' dresses   16. Francis' racket   17. brother-in-law's car   18. Aunt Polly's cakes   19. the committee's decision   20. Mrs. Smith's report   21. workers' salaries   22. Henry the Eighth's reign   23. father-in-law's present   24. New Year's Eve   25. today's paper   26. a month's notice   27. the people's aim   28. for old time's sake   29. her heart's desire   30. no one else's business

21-8 小練習

1. The man, self-appointed as head of the department, had no regard for other people's opinions.   2. The woman was so narrow-minded that she could not believe the girls had not done anything wrong.   3. He was so self-conscious that he refused to take part in the play.   4. Mr. Hill, the President of the Chess Players Association, was already fifty-five years old.   5. With your co-operation, we should be able to finish the work by the end of the month.   6. There was first-rate service at the hotel and we enjoyed our two-week stay here.   7. Having lived with her grandparents for twenty-two years, Sally had acquired some of their old-fashioned ideas.   8. He always boasts of the fact that though he is only semi-literate, he is a self-made man.   9. He counted the money in his wallet. It was still thirty-five dollars and seventy-five cents.   10. When the president of the club resigned, they had to re-elect another person to take over.   11. At the end of the three-hour-long play, the audience got up to stretch their legs.   12. The laboratory was fitted with up-to-date equipment.   13. At the age of twenty-three, she had already established herself in the business world.   14. Charles works in his father-in-law's firm as a sub-accountant.   15. The sound of music came from a pocket-size transistor radio by the window.   16.

His son-in-law was taking a ten-minute break when he spotted a child in trouble. 17. The teacher-in-charge wanted us to re-act the scene, but this time showing improvement. 18. The good-tempered housekeeper nodded obligingly and promised the three-year-old girl some jam tarts. 19. As she entered the smoke-filled room, she nearly choked. 20. We will have to re-elect a president for our club as John's three-year term will soon be over. 21. The young mother-to-be bought a book on childcare and began reading it. 22. The man-of-war slipped into the harbor unnoticed by the enemy. 23. The well-known surgeon operated on him when he was in a semi-conscious state. 24. The ranger and his chief assistant set out to hunt for the man-eating lion.

21-9 小練習

1. "Look over there—no, not there—on this side. Look!" he exclaimed. 2. She had beautiful clothes, a car, a house, servants—in fact, everything a woman could wish for, but she was not happy. 3. "Where is—oh, there you are, Henry," his mother said. 4. "Would you like to come out to dinner tonight—perhaps you would prefer to come tomorrow?" 5. Money, power, fame—none of these things is important without health. 6. There were a stale cookie, a banana, a piece of cake and a can of milk—all I had to last me until rescue came. 7. Mr. Fraser—he must have stayed up last night thinking of a solution—came down for breakfast, looking tired and worn out. 8. "My glasses— where did you put them?" the angry, old man cried. 9. I did not know what to do—yes, I was desperate—as there was so little time left. 10. For the past two years—and he was now twelve— Jeremy had lived with his mother in the old castle.

21-10 小練習

1. Her reason for not going to the party was: she was too tired after the expedition. 2. My brother collects almost everything: stamps, coins, matchboxes, badges, and postcards. 3. The director finally announced his decision: "Let the workers go on strike if they dare to." 4. The cause of their unrest was not difficult to determine: they were dissatisfied with their working conditions. 5. There are only two ways by which you can get there: by the path along the hillside and by boat across the lake. 6. To make a bookcase, you need these things: three planks, some nails, a hammer, and a saw. 7. The scouts were stationed at several points: at the main gate, near the porch, and along the corridor. 8. I know what his motto is: "Live and let live." 9. Tickets can be obtained at these places: United Supermarket, Speedy Limited Trading and Macdonald Company. 10. The subject of his talk will be: "Careers for Young People." 11. There are two reasons why I can't go: lack of money and lack of time. 12. Explain the meaning of these words: vouch, protrude, taunt, and replenish. 13. The machine has only

one big fault: it needs constant oiling.　14. Fuller once said: "Knowledge is a treasure, but practice is the key to it."　15. The tourists visited all the places of interest: the Memorial Park, Pirates' Cove, the Museum, the Art Gallery and the Cool Springs.　16. The reason for their behavior was plain: they were envious of each other.　17. It was very difficult for them to make up their minds: both applicants seemed equally good.　18. These were the repairs to the bicycle: the front tire was changed, the handle bars repainted and the saddle fixed.　19. What really occurred was this: the parrot had learned the captain's words and repeated them, thus revealing his secret.

21-11 小練習

1. They were afraid that the lifeboats would sink; nevertheless, the captain refused to let them use the life jackets.　2. The journey back to our village would be a difficult one; however, with a little luck, we might be able to make it.　3. The framework of the airplane is made of aluminum; therefore, it is very light.　4. The repairs will be expensive; for example, the cost of replacing those windowpanes will come to close to a hundred dollars.　5. Not all their attempts were unsuccessful; occasionally they managed to produce good results.　6. If the weather was fine, the men would go out to sea; if not, they would stay at home.　7. Their lives follow a fixed pattern; in the day time they sleep, and at night they hunt for food.　8. The earthquake shook the whole city; even where we lived, the earth trembled.　9. Bit by bit, he pieced the evidence together; there was no doubt then who the victim was.　10. From indistinguishable sounds, men developed a system of language; today, there exist more than 3,000 different languages.　11. Some people contract the sickness fairly frequently; others rarely experience it. 12. We were lucky to catch the bus; otherwise, we would have had to walk home.　13. The castle could be approached only by the bridge; there was no other way.　14. The road forks here—one leads to the town; the other, a steep winding road, runs along the coast.　15. He looked at the thermometer carefully; he had to record the slightest change.　16. Sometimes the prisoners react with hysterical laughter; sometimes they break down and cry.　17. The work was a dull routine; we checked the figures until lunch time and then started again till the end of the day.　18. We had to get away as quickly as possible; they would be after us the moment that they discovered the loss.　19. It was impossible for the island to be self-supporting; it had to get supplies from outside.　20. Even at night, the temperature remained much the same; there was not a breath of wind to cool the atmosphere.

21-12 小練習

1. When you get your results (probably in March), be sure to write to let me know.　2. I was present on both occasions: the day he was enrolled (June 5th, 1974) and the day he graduated (July 4th, 1975) with

基礎文法寶典 ❺
Essential English Usage & Grammar

flying colors.   3. My friend Susan (she has great determination) says that she wants to be a commercial pilot.   4. You must take a jeep (it is the only form of transportation) to the hilltop.   5. Cindy and Joe (they are already engaged) will be getting married sometime this year.   6. He led the donkeys into the garden (a most foolish thing to do) and left them there while he set off for the market.   7. He has a great deal of work to do, but he does not (or will not) sit down to do it.   8. What does the word "posse" (Line 23) mean?   9. She enclosed her photograph (postcard-size and colored) in her letter.   10. The truth is that many students (perhaps the majority) simply do not know how to use this punctuation mark.

21–13 小練習

23 Ocean Road,

Sea Park,

Sinalay 207.

The Advertiser,

Daily Times Press,

P.O. Box 1450,

Sinalay 208.

July 17th, 2000

Dear Sir or Madam,

Application for the Post of Junior Clerk

With reference to your advertisement in today's *Daily Times*, I wish to apply for the above post.

Until the end of last year, I was studying in the Good Hope Girls' School. I took and passed my examination with a second grade. I enclose certified copies of my results.

At the moment, I am studying shorthand and typing as I intend to take up a secretarial course. In addition, I am also studying accounting and bookkeeping. I enclose testimonials from the head of my school and from my instructor in the commercial school.

I hope you will kindly consider my application.

Yours faithfully,

Ann Lawson

應用練習

PART 1

1. She finished *Tales of the Uninvited*, switched off the lights, and went to bed.   2. The opening night

for *A Midsummer Night's Dream* will be on September 16th. Tickets are available at Thrifty Supermarket and Oriental Department Store.   3. The river has its source in the north. It flows into the Pacific Ocean.   4. The people of South Province are mainly fruit farmers and fishermen. The people in North Province are more industrialized.   5. "Father, will you read *The Children's Bedside Stories* to me?" Betty asked.   6. The sailors came back with wonderful tales of the mysterious East. As a child, Christopher Columbus used to go down to the harbor to listen to them.   7. "Can we go too, Uncle Joe?" little Danny asked, looking at him with beseeching eyes.   8. Since the Second World War, the usefulness of the port has been seriously affected. Vessels from the West by-pass it and so do ships from the East.   9. The school is putting up the play *Romeo and Juliet*. The Drama Society will be selecting students to take part.   10. Mr. White is the manager in the Jetline Plastic Industry Company.   11. We went to see Mr. S.T. Evans off at the Peyton Airport. Charles Brown drove us there.   12. A Mr. Brown asked to see our sales manager. Mr. Brown said he was from the A.I.A.   13. During the heavy rain, part of Maxwell Bridge was washed away. Drivers were advised to use the route via Happy Village to reach Golden Beach Resort.   14. The Eskimos use blocks of ice to build their homes. Sometimes they freeze Arctic plants into the ice to increase the strength.   15. The idea was proposed to the British, the Canadians and the Americans. The U.S.A. rejected it and so did Canada. However, Britain was for the idea.   16. "Tomorrow afternoon we will visit the Botanical Gardens and the National Park. By Friday, we will have finished visiting all the places of interest," the guide told us.   17. "We can write directly to North Korea, can't we?" Monica asked.   18. On New Year's Day, Belinda and I were very excited. Mother had promised to take us to the zoo.

PART 2

1. Please send me the girls who are taking part in this game.   2. My mother said that she was too busy to watch television. She wanted to finish the ironing.   3. By nine o'clock, we had finished our test. We decided to leave.   4. Mr. and Mrs. F. L. Norton will be attending the meeting tomorrow at 10 a.m.   5. The sun went behind a dark cloud. It was going to rain.   6. The clock struck ten. Dr. West was still in his office.   7. By 8 p.m., most of the guests had arrived. Mother wanted to serve dinner then.   8. Capt. White looked up. He smiled at me.   9. We were traveling at nearly eighty k.p.h., for we intended to reach the city before seven o'clock.   10. His father is a money lender. He lends out money at ten percent p.a.   11. Lieut. Wilson had to report to the G.H.Q. on the first of July.   12. San Francisco is in the U.S.A. It has a temperate climate.   13. They were expecting some V.I.P.'s for dinner. Among the guests was the M.D., Mr. Taylor.   14. Prof. Hopkins was in the lab., doing some research work.   15.

The three members of the committee are Mr. Ronald E. Anderson of Paper Ware Products, Mrs. Helen Smith of Manual Publishing and Mr. Thomas Brown of Get-About Transport.   16. My sister, Rosemary, was reading a book called *The War of the Worlds* by H. G. Wells. She said that it was very interesting.   17. About one third of the people of Coniland are Eskimos. Originally, they lived in the southern part of Greenland.   18. General Napoleon Bonaparte was a popular figure with his soldiers. He had a knack of remembering the names of everyone in his army.   19. Sir Isaac Newton was born in England. At the age of nineteen, he went to study at Cambridge University.   20. On February 15th, 1942, the Japanese commander, Major General Yamashita, accepted the surrender of the colony from the British commander.

PART 3

1. The International Committee of the Red Cross was formed in Geneva by a Swiss named Henri Dunant.   2. Every year, Hindus celebrate one of their great festivals, Deepavali or "The Festival of Lights." It commemorates the victory of Lord Krishna over a demon king.   3. At the airport, we watched a Boeing 737 coming in to land. Nearby, another plane was warming up for departure.   4. "Have you read *She Stoops to Conquer*?" Mrs. Grey asked.   5. Aunt Emily came to invite Mother to see the show *From Russia With Love*. They have both left already.   6. Sir Percy Livingston attended the charity premiere of the film *Star Wars*.   7. Prof. Bright was explaining something to the students. Suddenly, Insp. Bond walked in.   8. Madam A. L. Mason is a retired teacher. She used to teach English in the Central High School.   9. Alice couldn't pass her GMAT exam. Her uncle advised her to take up a commercial course instead.   10. Inspector Sharp went to the High Street Boys' School to give a talk on traffic rules during "Safety Week."   11. The school choir is going to take part in the "Festival of Songs." It will be held in the Cultural Hall on Saturday.   12. Henry's mind worked fast. He had to warn David of the impending danger.   13. Nurse Susan woke up the patient. It was time for him to take his medicine.   14. Capt. Anderson didn't know what to say. He was stunned by Martin's retort.   15. He is a technician at the Brightlite Electrical Company. Mr. Brown is his manager.   16. A series of books called *Toward Better English* has recently been published. The ministry has approved of its use in the schools.   17. It was late when they left Seagull Bay and there was a slight drizzle. However, Mr. and Mrs. Wilson were confident of reaching their destination before midnight.   18. The Regional Marine Biological Center was set up in January 1975. Its aim is to improve the efficiency of fishermen in this region.   19 The ship "Marianne" lay at anchor off Port Sunset. It was renewing its fuel supplies before sailing off to Pearl Isle.   20. "I've got to go now. Father will be waiting anxiously for me. See you later," she said as

she hurried off.　21. It was still early when Inspector Henderson left Graystone Avenue. He had had a good night's sleep and felt very fresh.　22. Sarah said, "I have the book *Sons and Lovers* by D. H. Lawrence. Would you like to read it?"

PART 4

1. "It is going to rain," Tony said.　2. "Walk straight until you come to the intersection. Turn left and you'll see the sign over the building," the man told us.　3. The teacher instructed them, "Write your names in the top right-hand corner, put the date beneath, and draw a line after that."　4. Susan bought a pretty, blue, polka-dot dress, a pair of shoes, and a handbag to match.　5. "Peter, go with Harry to get the pail from Aunt Polly," she told him.　6. "London," said Miss White, "is the capital city of England."　7. Because of the heavy rain, the streets were flooded.　8. Without air, none of us would survive.　9. Unless you pay the money, you cannot take the parcel away.　10. After a short rest, they continued on their journey.　11. If my brother were here, he would know what to do.　12. After he had completed his work, he left.　13. Before they had time to answer, she asked them another question.　14. "Stella, if I were you, I wouldn't do that," she said.　15. "When you are ready, John, come to my office," the manager said.　16. Although the farmer was poor, he often helped his neighbors.　17. "Unless you promise me that, Jimmy, I won't give it to you," she said.　18. Samuel, Charles, Gary, all three of you come here.　19. The ship was modern, high-powered, armored, and expensive.　20. Up and down, in and out, around and around, the children ran.

PART 5

1. The first runner staggered, fell, got up, and still managed to reach the tape before the others.　2. The cave contained, as a rule, no more than one meter of water.　3. The landslide, as far as we could see, had completely cut off the entrance to the cave.　4. Aidan, the best boy in the class, was also a champion athlete.　5. I will always remember Miss Bright, my favorite teacher.　6. Shall we take a bus to town, have lunch there, go to a show, and then return home in the evening?　7. Every now and then, a truck would pass by.　8. Houdini, one of the greatest magicians in the world, died in 1926.　9. Hoping my sister-in-law was at home, I knocked on the door.　10. "If there is an emergency, break open the glass here and pull down the lever," he instructed.　11. He called me and said, "Molly, take this note to Mr. Smith, wait for him to reply, and bring back his note to me."　12. "Unless you clean up your room by this evening, Susan, you will get no dinner," her mother said.　13. "Should you need anything, sir, just ring this bell," the maid told him.　14. I walked past the house and saw a sign that read, "To Let."　15. Having cooked the dinner, Mother called us to eat.　16. Mrs. Green said, "Unless you arrive

early, you won't be able to find a seat." 17. Books, magazines, and pieces of paper were strewn all over the floor. 18. "However difficult the task is, Allen, you must at least try to do it," his father advised. 19. Taking up his pen, Robert started to write the letter. 20. "In fact, cats are cleaner animals than dogs," Mr. Fraser, our science teacher, explained.

PART 6

1. Walking home one day, I met Nora carrying a kitten in a basket. 2. I remember seeing the key; it was behind a pile of books on the table. 3. Susan and Anna were late for school because they played on the way. 4. When the time came for them to leave, everyone said goodbye. Some even shed tears. 5. Although it was early, the movie theater was crowded with people. There was a long line at the box office. 6. David ran down the stairs to answer the phone. It was his father calling from the office. 7. We went for a walk because it was a cool evening. The sun was setting. 8. Opening the umbrella, she stepped off the bus, right into a puddle. 9. The man walked up to the door. He knocked twice. There was no answer. 10. They were early, so they went for a cup of coffee at a nearby café. 11. In order to get a good seat, you must book your ticket in advance. 12. The doctors couldn't find out what was wrong with him. Knowing his illness could be contagious, they put him in the isolation ward. 13. "I think," he said, "it is going to rain." 14. "You're right," she said. "I should not have come." 15. Helen, the nurse, put her finger to her lips and said, "Don't make any noise, or she'll wake up."

PART 7

1. I saw the movie "Born Free". It is one of the best movies I have seen. 2. The ball reached Andy, our captain. He kicked it hard and directed it into a corner of the net. "Goal!" 3. "Good boy," Mary told the dog," you deserve a bone." 4. He travels from place to place on business. He has been to London, New York, Tokyo, Paris, Berlin, and many other major cities. 5. We brought sandwiches, cakes and a bottle of tea. We couldn't find any eggs. 6. "You're quite right, Jeffrey. The show is really interesting," Alex said. 7. The captain took us around the ship. We visited the bridge, the cabins, and the lounge. 8. David, here's your book. Edward asked me to give it to you. 9. There were brooches, rings, necklaces, bangles, and earrings in the box. 10. As soon as the last spectator had left the stadium at ten a.m., the painters started their work. 11. It was a bright, sunny morning. In the garden, you could see bees and butterflies flying among the flowers. 12. As Jane walked home, it began to get dark. Looking at her watch, she saw that it was nearly eight. 13. I can't come at four-thirty p.m. because I will be working. I'll meet you at five. 14. If you are afraid, you'd better stay at home. I can go by myself. 15. "Sit down for a while," Mr. Taylor said. "You need a rest and a good meal. After that, we

will discuss the problem." 16. "Have you read *Gone with the Wind*, Richard? It is an interesting book," I said. 17. "Mary, Paul, Agnes, and David, please go to the principal's office. He has something to say to all of you," the teacher said. 18. He finished reading *Kidnapped*, switched off the light, and went to bed.

PART 8

1. The sooner you come to your senses, the better for all of us. 2. The water having flooded the fields, the farmers began their plowing. 3. Nick hopes to, and probably will, complete his homework by five o'clock. 4. Many students attended the seminar. Out of every ten, five were from our school. 5. The tramp, who walked with a limp, came up to the house and asked for a glass of water. 6. They were all eager to, and soon they will, meet the king. 7. It being a cold night, we went to bed early. 8. The angrier she was, the redder her face became. 9. If you must speak, speak now, or remain silent forever. 10. "Think it over and let me know your answer," she said. "The earlier you tell me, the better." 11. "This plan, though not foolproof, is still the safest," he assured them. 12. Billy, being a shy boy, sat in a corner and watched the others play. 13. "Don't try to stop him. The more you persuade him, the more stubborn he becomes," she warned. 14. Having found the leak in the tube, he then proceeded to mend it. 15. "If you find it hard to do, do try again," Aunt Maria urged. "Don't give up so easily." 16. The news, which spread like fire, soon reached the ears of the mayor himself.

PART 9

1. Some of his early poems like "Autumn Wind," "Blossoms in May," and "The Golden Buttercups" depict the beauty of nature. 2. "Look!" she pointed. "Isn't that the 'Seagull' beside the ocean liner 'Queen Elizabeth'?" 3. "When are Kenneth and Joseph coming?" he asked. 4. "Quick, Sammy," he called. "Throw the ball over here!" 5. He will only reply "I don't know," if you ask him. 6. The ship "Sea Princess" was berthed at the harbor. 7. "Would you like to see 'Song of Norway' tonight?" Peter asked. 8. "Don't you know that 'he who laughs last, laughs longest'?" Nancy asked Paul. 9. Mr. Takahashi said "sayonara" to me before he left. 10. What is the meaning of the word "post" as given in the passage? 11. "How long do you think that we'll have to wait?" Martin asked. 12. When the "Sea Queen" docked at the harbor, the captain and his crew went ashore. 13. "Absence makes the heart grow fonder" and "Out of sight, out of mind" are two sayings that have opposite meanings. 14. "Please pass me the *Daily Times*," Mr. White said to his son. 15. "Did I say I won't when you asked me to do it?" my brother replied. 16. "The movie *The Good Earth* is based on the novel written by Pearl S. Buck, isn't it?" he asked. 17. "Yes, that's a lovely place for a picnic, " Mary agreed. 18.

"The Stranger" and "The Cottage on the Hill" are two of his favorite poems.

PART 10

1. "And now," said the announcer, "we come to the last item on tonight's program."　2. "What time did you come home last night, Desmond?" his mother asked. "I was too sleepy to wait up for you."　3. "No," replied Sandra, "I haven't read *All's Well That Ends Well*. Will you lend it to me, please?"　4. "Where are you going?" he asked. "That isn't the way to the manager's office."　5. "Make hay while the sun shines" and "Strike while the iron is hot" are proverbs with similar meanings.　6. "Slow down, Toby," laughed Jeffrey. "Haven't you heard the proverb 'More haste, less speed'?"　7. "I can't find the binoculars, Father," George said. "Where did you put them?"　8. "'My Fair Lady' is one of the most entertaining movies I've ever seen," said Mary.　9. "Now, Eric, take out your book, turn to page fourteen and start reading the passage," the teacher said.　10. "Come along, boys," the teacher said, "we must get on with our lesson."　11. "What's that you're making?" the child asked. "Is it a kite?"　12. "'The Horsemen' is a movie in which Omar Sharif and Jack Palance play the leading roles," Jack read.　13. "Mallet," according to the dictionary, means "a hammer with a wooden head."　14. She thought, "I can't let him go alone. I must follow him secretly."　15. "How do you spell the word 'succeed'?" Joan asked her brother.　16. He asked me "Are you sure?" many times before he finally believed me.

PART 11

1. What is meant by "the survival of the fittest"?　2. "Did you hear the explosion, David?" my father asked.　3. "Answer me; do you hear? I want to know how you failed the test," the angry father shouted.　4. "What do you mean by that?" I asked.　5. Do you know where we can get some postcards?　6. She asked me how much of the book *Mill on the Floss* I had read.　7. The principal said, "Would you like to have a few words with the staff? They are all in the next room."　8. "Is this the International Hotel?" he asked. "Can you please connect me to Room 401?"　9. The question is whether we will be allowed to go to camp with them or not.　10. Did the sailors stop at the port on their way to the East Indies?　11. We asked him if his father could drive us to the station.　12. The man has certainly been friendly, but can we trust him?　13. "I'm very sorry for my unreasonable behavior last night," Andrew said. "Will you forgive me?"　14. A play will be staged by the students to raise funds for the new school library. It is entitled "The Dream."　15. "May I have a piece of cake, Mother?" Betty asked.　16. Uncle Harry has promised to take us to the seaside this weekend. Isn't that wonderful!　17. "Come on. It's time to get ready for the show," Lucy said. "We'll be late if we delay any longer."　18. He walked into the room, switched on the television set, settled into his favorite armchair and lit a

cigarette. 19. "Tony, please do not sit on the bench," Mr. White said. "I painted it this morning and the paint is still wet." 20. The movie *The Mummy 3* has been showing at the Federal Cinema for several weeks.

PART 12

1. Are you free, Dora? I wonder if you can do something for me. 2. "When is the meeting, Robin?" asked Ben. "I couldn't hear the announcement properly just now." 3. The question is whether the rain will stop in time for us to get back. 4. "Do you know when Mr. Biggs will be back?" the lady asked the secretary. 5. "Alice, find out what time the train comes in. You know the telephone number, don't you?" my sister asked. 6. I asked him how he was. He replied, "I'm fine. How is your business getting along?" 7. Nelson said, "When is the match due to start? It's already half past four now." 8. "Can you tell me whether this is the road to the zoo?" the stranger inquired. 9. She asked them whether they would like to have tea or coffee for breakfast the next morning. 10. I'm not sure whether my father is at home now. Can you wait while I find out? 11. The problem is: How can we let them know we are here? Mary doesn't have a telephone in her house. 12. He said, "Do you know where he went? I wonder if he left a message behind. Will you please look around to see if there is a note anywhere?"

PART 13

1. "Get out of here!" she cried. "I don't want to see you again!" 2. "What a lovely surprise! Thank you so much," I said to Doris. 3. "No! I won't apologize!" the little boy screamed. 4. "Mew! Mew!" the kitten purred, rubbing itself against her legs. 5. "What!" he exclaimed. "Have you spoiled it again?" 6. As he was walking home, he heard someone shout, "Help! I've been robbed! Stop, thief!" 7. Cupping his hands to his mouth, William shouted, "Turn back! The bridge is broken!" 8. "Stop!" the guard ordered. "You can't go in there!" 9. Crash! The bicycle hit the cart and all the fruit fell onto the road. 10. "Fire! Fire!" Peter shouted. "Quick, Jane! Call the fire department," he said excitedly. 11. "Congratulations!" she said, shaking my hand. 12. Twang! The arrow shot forth and hit the target right in the center. 13. "Oh dear! Do you have to bang the door?" the old lady asked. 14. "Where have I left the key?" he muttered to himself, scratching his head. 15. "Hurrah! We're going to the circus, "Betty said, clapping her hands. 16. "Put that down at once!" Thomas shouted to Lucy. "Don't you know it's poisonous?" 17. He strode angrily into the room and shouted, "Peter! Are you responsible for this?" 18. "Father! Come quickly! There's a snake in the garden," Danny shouted. 19. "Can't you walk faster, Billy?" he asked irritably. "Look! There goes our bus!" 20. "Mother! Mother!" she called. "Where are you?" 21. "Stop laughing! What's so funny?" she said. 22. "Where did you

find this?" the boy asked. "Give it to me!"

PART 14

1. She said, "Go away! Why don't you leave me alone?"   2. "Help!" he shouted. "The kitchen's on fire!"   3. "I can't!" Liza cried out. "How can you expect me to finish it within two days?"   4. Eagerly she opened the envelope. Inside was a blank sheet of paper!   5. The whole room was in a mess! Who has been in there?   6. "Stop!" the guard called. "Do you know you are trespassing?"   7. Does anybody know what has happened to Francis?   8. "What a beauty!" I exclaimed. "Where did you find it?"   9. "I've won the first prize!" she exclaimed. "Isn't that wonderful?"   10. "Peter!" Mr. Wilson called. "Are you there?"   11. "Where did you put it? Tell me!" he commanded.   12. "Wait!" Tom said. "What can you see here?"   13. Toot! Toot! The man behind sounded his horn at me. In a panic, I tried to start the car again.   14. He wants to know when Andrew and his sister are coming.   15. Don't you know where your mother is?   16. Would you like to go with us, Paul?   17. They can't force us to do it, can they?   18. She called, "Wait for me!"   19. John couldn't decide whether to go or not. 20. "I'm so worried!" Mrs. Brown said.

PART 15

1. "Tell me!" she shouted. "Why did you do it?"   2. "Be quiet!" the masked man ordered the whimpering child. "Stop that at once, or I'll gag you!"   3. "Oh, Sandra! What a lovely dress you have on!" cried Jill. "Where did you buy it?"   4. "You won't tell Father, will you?" the naughty boy pleaded.   5. "Andy! Don't touch that!" Tony shouted to his younger brother. "It's a cactus; its thorns will hurt you."   6. "What!" exclaimed Carol. "Did he really say that?"   7. "Shh! Please don't make so much noise," Mrs. Brown whispered. " The baby's asleep."   8. "Why didn't you report the incident at once?" the corporal asked the sentry.   9. "I won't do it!" the child screamed. "You can't make me do it!"   10. How's your uncle, Joe? Has he recovered from his operation yet?   11. "Goal!" Mark shouted, almost knocking Colin off the bench in his excitement.   12. Has any one of you read *The Call of the Wild* by Jack London? It's an excellent book.   13. "Magnificent!" Andy cried as he was watching an acrobatic act on stage.   14. "Silence, please!" the teacher shouted. Immediately the class became quiet.   15. Tony struggled in the water, gasping with effort. "Grab the rope!" Mark shouted to him. 16. "What a pity!" she exclaimed. "I wish you were coming with us instead of going to school."   17. "This time," he said angrily, "you must not fail!"   18. "Never!" the manager shouted. "Such a thing will never happen!"

PART 16

1. "Whether you like it or not, you have to do it, boys," the principal said.   2. Last Sunday, my father drove us to a seaside restaurant to eat crabs. The trip was long, but we enjoyed the ride.   3. In spite of the heavy rain, we went out to search for Sooty, the cat.   4. On reaching the open sea, the fishermen cast their nets over the side of their boat, hoping to have a big catch.   5. *The Moon and Us* was an interesting, unusual and exciting movie. We saw it at the Odeon Cinema last Friday.   6. The king tried to sleep, but he could not. Seeing this, the ladies-in-waiting said to the queen, "As the king cannot sleep, why don't you tell him a story?"   7. By the time Mona and her sister had gotten to the top of the slope, rain had begun to fall. It became heavier and heavier.   8. On Christmas Day, the children visited their aunt and uncle. "Merry Christmas!" they said.   9. "According to the regulations, we have to take you back for questioning," the police officer said, "but as you are evidently well-known to the sergeant, we will only take down your name and address."   10. When everything was packed and ready, Mrs. Robinson came down and said goodbye to the servants. "Goodbye, Arthur!" she said, addressing the gardener first.   11. "Clean up the mess before you go home," Mrs. Brown said.   12. "Waiter!" he called. "Can you please bring me a menu?"   13. "Ready? Pull!" Francis shouted from below. We tugged at the rope, pulling with all our might.   14. Suddenly, I heard someone call out, "Catch him! Catch him! He's a thief!"   15. She couldn't even spell a simple word like "their."   16. The officer asked, "Did you bring your registration card?"   17. "What did you say? Speak louder!" the old man said.   18. We went to see *Romeo and Juliet* at the Central Cinema.

PART 17

1. I don't know why they've changed their minds. Perhaps it's because they can't afford the trip.   2. Can't Jane make the sandwiches for us? Isn't she willing to make them?   3. "Who's that?" the commander-in-chief asked. "Why don't you identify yourself?"   4. It's four o'clock now. Why aren't they back yet?   5. "I hope you didn't tell anyone about it yet. That'll give me few more days to think it over," Henry said.   6. "Tell me what's wrong. I'll do my best to help you," she said.   7. The shop doesn't sell these brushes. We've got to buy them somewhere else.   8. He's worried about the dog's paw. It doesn't seem to be healing.   9. We couldn't all get into one car, so Mary had to make two trips instead.   10. "Aren't you going to bed yet?" Christopher asked. "It's nearly eleven o'clock."   11. "Ann is a great cook," he said. "You should've tasted her curry yesterday."   12. "Don't disturb me! Can't you see I've got work to do?" she said irritably.   13. She'd never met James before. That's why she didn't recognize him.   14. "You mustn't take anyone else's things. You shouldn't hide them either," I told the child.   15. "We'd better hurry. The bus comes around eight o'clock," Tina said. "Oh, there it is!"   16.

"We're going to school in Uncle Ben's car," Terry said. "Oh, there he is!"

PART 18

1. "Stop!" the little girl shouted. "Don't you know it's cruel to pull the cat's tail?"   2. A stranger came yesterday to ask where Karen had gone. I told him that she'd gone to her brother-in-law's house.   3. "Get out of bed, you lazy girl!" the woman shouted. "Don't you know there's the washing and ironing to be done?"   4. "Run! Run!" she panted. "The creature's just behind us!"   5. "Four years' savings all gone in a blaze!" he exclaimed. Then, he buried his head in his hands and cried.   6. "Quiet!" the teacher said. She waited before she said, "I want you all to behave yourselves."   7. "Don't be rude, child," Aunt Agnes told Maggie. "Speak up when others talk to you. Now, go to apologize to your uncle."   8. "Don't talk so loudly," Mary's mother told her.   9. "Where's my book? Who's taken it?" I asked, puzzled.   10. We can't talk here. Come! Let's go into my study.   11. I've been waiting here since three o'clock. Couldn't you have come earlier?   12. You aren't angry with me, are you? I didn't know it was so late already.   13. "Isn't Henry coming to pick you up?" Janet's brother asked her.   14. "They wouldn't have gotten into trouble if they'd listened to me," he said.   15. If they aren't here by eight o'clock, we won't wait for them.   16. There's been an accident at the traffic lights. Michael's car couldn't move because of the jam.   17. It's my dog, Brownie. Look, its paw is hurt!   18. Isn't this book yours? It can't be Alison's because hers has her name written in it.

PART 19

1. This is neither Peter's bicycle nor David's. It is Ben's.   2. My friend's brother told me, "Joan asked me to say she can't play tennis tomorrow. She's got a bad cold."   3. I saw Simon's dog running all around the children's playground.   4. These shoes belong to me; yours are over there by the boys' bicycles.   5. "If he isn't here by four o'clock, I won't wait a minute longer," she grumbled.   6. "He promised that he would pass James' book to me when he'd finished reading it; However, he's passed it to Edward," Tom complained.   7. "You'd have done the same thing if you'd been in my place, wouldn't you?" Francis' sister asked.   8. "Tomorrow's the day of the Big Walk," the principal reminded the students. "Don't forget to come in shorts and rubber shoes."   9. "Mother! They've come!" cried Nellie as she ran downstairs to meet her cousins.   10. "It's no good; it won't work," he said. "We'll have to think of something else."   11. "Don't give up so easily, boys," Mr. White encouraged. "It's not as difficult as you think."   12. "Welcome, my dear," James' aunt greeted him. "Did you have a pleasant journey? You must be thirsty. Come! We'll have tea now."   13. "Perhaps you're right," I admitted. "We wouldn't have escaped if it weren't for him."   14. "I can't come now. I have a lot of work to do. I'll

meet you at six o'clock," my sister said.　15. "You mustn't cry, Rosie. Here, wipe your tears. That's a good girl," Miss Davis said, giving her a handkerchief.　16. I was tired, cold, hungry, and also desperately longing for home.　17. "Don't panic! The police and firemen are coming. They'll help us," he said.　18. Allen, my eldest brother, is the school captain. My father, mother, and sister are just as proud of him as I am.　19. We went to the grocery store and bought flour, eggs, cherries, sugar, butter, and milk.　20. Besides Nora, two others also had a high score on the test. They were Tony and John.

PART 20

Karen put the telephone receiver down and turned to her younger sister. "That was Mother, Amy," she said. "The car broke down and she can't get back in this storm, so she's staying the night in town with Granny."

"Did you tell her about Father?" asked Amy.

"No, that would only worry her," Karen replied.

Their father was on a business trip, and he was expected back that night. However, he had called to say that he would be one day late. So now, the two girls were left alone at home.

"Come on, Amy. Let's go and have dinner," said Karen cheerfully, trying to conceal her nervousness.

Their house stood far off the main road among farms. Often, Karen had complained that it was too quiet and boring.

"But I hope that nothing happens tonight!" she thought.

Hardly had they sat down to eat when there was a rap at the front door. Quick as a flash, Amy was out of her chair. "I'll answer it!" she cried.

PART 21

1. "Have you seen it, too?" I asked.　2. "Hurry! The bus is coming!" Sandra called.　3. He was late. He had missed the bus.　4. My parents, sisters and brothers were not at home.　5. "Can you tell me where he is?" Kenneth asked.　6. He couldn't decide whether he should go or not.　7. William took off his shoes, unlocked the door and went into the house.　8. We listened to "Hotel California" all night.　9. The furniture consisted only of a low table, four chairs, an icebox, and a stove.　10. Their lights are off. They must be asleep.　11. "Go away!" she screamed at him.　12. I know he will come with me.　13. "When you are ready," he said, "we'll go immediately."　14. They searched among the flowers, in between the rows of cabbages, around the trees, and even in the fish pond.　15. "Yes, Sir!" the boy said loudly as he saluted.　16. He walked quickly, hurrying his footsteps over the cobbled

footpath without turning around once.   17. I was worried that he might lose his way in the strange, new town.   18. "Is it time to go home?" Peter asked.

PART 22

1. My brother bought a second-hand typewriter from an ex-classmate of his.   2. The project, if well-financed, would have far-reaching effects.   3. Her brother-in-law had a job, doing house-to-house selling.   4. The taxi driver agreed to take him on a four-hour cruise around the island.   5. The expectant mother bought an up-to-date book on childcare.   6. The car he recently bought is high-powered and has a self-starting machine.   7. At the end of the four-month course, he was promoted to editor-in-chief.   8. After a careful re-examination of the spider, the naturalist said it was one of the rarest specimens in the world.   9. The commander-in-chief of the army made a long-distance call to headquarters to confirm the change of plans.   10. His matter-of-fact attitude led her to think that he was a heartless man.   11. He had copied the idea from one of the do-it-yourself books, but he had designed the instrument himself.   12. Alice helped her mother re-cover the cushions in preparation for Christmas.   13. Daniel received a long-distance call last night; it was from his pen pal in New Zealand.   14. "If all of you co-operate, I think that we can get this done by four-thirty," said Lawrence.   15. The traveler demanded first-class accommodation for the trip.   16. The old man had such a tear-provoking story to tell that at the end of it, all of us were upset.   17. Edward's brother, Richard, is twenty-four years old and 1.8 meters tall.   18. Jill, who is long-legged and slim, wants to be a model when she leaves school.

PART 23

1. "Excuse me, is this the way to the post office?" he asked.

   "Oh no, sir," the girl replied, "you're on the wrong road!"

2. Mary was cutting the cucumber when she suddenly exclaimed, "Oh! I've cut my finger!"

   "How could you be so careless?" her mother said. "Come, let me bandage it for you."

3. "Look, isn't that Tony?" Susan cried. "Where?" I asked."

   There!" she said, pointing. "Can't you see him? He's in a blue-striped shirt."

4. "Will you be free tonight?" Cindy asked her brother.

   "Why do you want to know, Cindy?"

   "Well, I was wondering if you would like to go to a show with me."

5. "You're wrong!" he declared. "Uncle Peter isn't forty-five years old."

   "Yes, he is!" Tammy said emphatically.

解 答
Chapter 21

167

"How do you know?" her brother asked.

"Uncle Peter told me himself!"

6. "Don't worry, Mrs. Richards," he said. "I'll find Andy for you. He can't have gone far."

Sobbing, Mrs. Richards said, "John, you're such a good boy. Why can't my Andy be like you?"

7. "Hurry up, girls!" Mr. Bill said. "It's already half past two. We've got to be there at three."

"We're coming, Papa!" they said, as they ran down the stairs.

8. "Something's wrong with my car," I told the mechanic. "It refuses to move!"

"Well, let's see," he said. Lifting the hood, he peered at the engine, poking around with his fingers.

"Nothing's wrong here."

"Could it be the fan belt?" I suggested helpfully.

9. "We are going to see *The Wizard of Oz* tonight," said Larry. "Want to come along?"

"*The Wizard of Oz*? Oh, I'd love to see that!" exclaimed Jill.

Mike looked up from his picture book and asked, "Can I come, too?"

"Well, if you are a good boy, I'll take you along," said Larry.

10. "Ice cream! Ice cream!" the man called.

"Oh, stop, please, Mr. Ice-Cream Man," said Bobby. "May I have two ice-cream cones?"

The ice-cream man stopped and proceeded to give Bobby two ice-cream cones. "Here you are, Son. That'll be twenty cents," he said.

PART 24

In a short while, Mrs. White's efficiency and Doris' eagerness had made the dust disappear. The furniture shone, the beds were re-made with fresh sheets, the bathroom was scrubbed, and the dirty dishes were washed and stacked neatly away. The women were so busy working that they did not notice Mr. Brown's absence until he returned, carrying a few parcels with him. "You both must be hungry," he said. "I've bought chicken, fish, and vegetables. Dare I ask both of you to stay for dinner?" "Oh, Mr. Brown! How marvelous!" Doris cried. She quickly dried her hands and helped him carry the parcels into the kitchen. "We'd love to stay for dinner, but you really shouldn't have spent so much money."

PART 25

1. It was rumored that the enemy had a secret weapon—a weapon against which there was no possible defense.   2. He remembered that a lady—he did not know what her name was—had asked for the price of the vase.   3. She dislikes everything about her shabby room—the dirty walls, the faded curtain and the old furniture.   4. Something moved in the tall bushes—it was a tiger resting in the

afternoon heat.　　5. Quickly, she ran to warn them—and only just in time, for they were about to cross the bridge.　　6. At last, the hunters reached the clearing—the place where the tiger was believed to have last been seen.　　7. I looked at the cage. A moment ago, the bird was there—now it was gone. 8. "I can tell you only this much—your daughter is safe," the anonymous caller said and hung up.　　9. She opened her eyes, but everything was a blur—the room, the furniture and even the person sitting next to her.　　10. He looked horror-stricken at the scene in the room—a scene which would haunt his dreams for many nights.　　11. David recalled that a stranger—he couldn't remember his face—had stopped him and asked him the way to the station.　　12. "I—I—It didn't occur to me, sir," he stammered.　　13. "No one has heard from him for nearly ten years," she said.　　14. There is no doubt that children—even very young ones—have a certain degree of wisdom in them.　　15. He ran around the corner quickly but stopped short—two policemen barred the way.　　16. Many changes have taken place in that country since its independence—changes for the better.　　17. Jimmy said goodbye to everyone—his teachers, his classmates, his neighbors and his relatives.　　18. The firefighter rushed out of the burning house— and just in time, for the roof crashed immediately after him.

PART 26

1. It was quite dark in the backyard. I looked around, adjusting my eyes to the darkness. Then, I saw it—a long, thin shape by the bushes. It was the python.　　2. Suddenly, the silence of the night was shattered by a thin, high-pitched scream that died off abruptly. I got out of bed quickly, put on my robe, switched on the light and looked out of the window. It was dark and silent.　　3. "This watch is no good—it keeps stopping," she complained, giving the watch a vigorous shake. "Look, an hour ago, it was 10:35 a.m. Now, it is still 10:35 a.m.!"　　4. "It's such a fine day. Let's go fishing," Eddie suggested. "We could pack some sandwiches, some cakes and some fruit for a picnic. We'll take our bicycles and ride to Stillwater Pond. I hear that the fishing there is very good."　　5. After lunch, the men started on their trip. They checked their gear and supplies, filled up their water bottles, drove to the gas station to give their truck a last-minute check, and soon they were off.　　6. "I need some more flour to bake the cakes," Mrs. Brown said. "Margaret, be a good girl. Run to the shop across the street and buy me a kilogram of flour. Here's the money."　　7. The car screeched to a halt beside the gate, and the driver jumped out. "Is Mr. Taylor at home?" he asked the gardener. "I've got some urgent news for him. I must see him at once!"　　8. "Yes! Yes! I remember the man you are referring to now. He is hunchbacked, and he walks with a limp. He used to beg for a living around our neighborhood," I said. "What's happened to him?"　　9. "Go away!" I shouted in a trembling voice. "If you don't, I'll phone

the police!"   10. "Ha, phone the police! Go ahead!" the old man sneered. "I know you don't have a phone because I didn't see any wires around. You didn't think I would check, did you?"   11. I was furious with him for seeing through my bluff so quickly, and kicked wildly at his leg with my steel-shod boots.   12. For a moment, we stood staring at each other. My legs were trembling so much that I thought they would give way. Licking my dry lips, I forced myself to ask firmly, "What do you want?"

PART 27

Crawling through a gap in the fence, Toby found a lovely apple tree laden with fruit. He climbed it and was picking the ripe apples when a loud voice shouted, "Hey you! What do you think you're doing up there?" Staring up at him was the farmer himself.

"Why, eating apples, of course!" said Toby, cheekily. "Would you like me to throw some down to you? They are delicious."

"They are, indeed!" snorted the angry farmer, shaking his heavy cane at the boy. "That's my tree you're on, you rascal, so you'd better come down at once."

Toby hesitated. "If you don't mind, sir," he said meekly, "I'd rather stay up here."

"Oh, so you won't come down, will you? Well, I can't wait here all day, but I'll be back in the evening to deal with you." Then, the farmer strode off toward the farmhouse.

"Ha! He thinks I'm going to sit here and wait for him till evening," chuckled Toby.

But he soon found out that he had no choice—for just then, the farmer gave a shrill whistle, and a large bulldog came trotting up from the farmhouse. Patting the animal, the farmer said, "Good dog, Rover." Then, he pointed his cane at Toby and said, "Guard him, Rover! Guard him!"

PART 28

1. Something cold hopped onto my leg—it was a toad!   2. What really happened was this: the elevator jammed while it was halfway down.   3. The stranger had a frightening look on his face—a look which repelled most people.   4. Our chief clerk—he has been working here for years—has suddenly handed in his resignation.   5. There were five men in the car: two in front and three in the back.   6. "Who—who are you? What—what do you want?" she stammered in fright.   7. We rushed out of the burning house—and only just in time—for the roof crashed down, sending sparks flying.   8. There was no hope left: he had tried everything and failed.   9. While abroad, he witnessed an incident—an incident that impressed him greatly.   10. She told him to buy these things: a packet of salt, a bottle of tomato sauce, some pepper and a piece of ginger.   11. "Tell me this: did you see his face or not?" the lawyer demanded.

PART 29

1. After much persuasion, she told me her secret: she is engaged to be married.   2. On the desk you will find the following: pens, pencils, erasers, a ruler, and a book.   3. All applicants must possess certain qualifications: the ability to read and write fluent English, some knowledge of accounting, and at least two years' working experience.   4. What really happened was this: the baby pulled the dog's tail when nobody was looking, so the animal bit him.   5. Bobby knew that he could not escape: the kidnappers were watching him too closely.   6. Michael has one ambition: to be a doctor.   7. Shakespeare wrote: "Cowards die many times before their deaths."   8. After a while, Mary said, "What I suggest is this: each of us will take turns bringing flowers for the class."   9. We need these things for our room: new curtains, a rug, and some bookshelves.   10. After a moment's thought, she gave her answer: "I accept the post."   11. The school holidays had just begun. Thirteen-year-old Tony was very excited: he was flying with his parents to Europe.   12. "Get out!" he shouted angrily. "I don't need your help!"   13. "Hello, Eric. How are you now?" asked Henry. "We were sorry that you were ill; all of us are glad that you're back in class again."   14. The schools which participated in the debate were the following: the Star Institution, the Holly Avenue Girls' School, and the First Boys' High School. 15. Judy is not sure when to use colons or semicolons, commas or periods, and brackets or dashes.   16. Peter's father, Capt. Robinson, likes to exercise to keep fit—he takes an hour's walk every evening. 17. The stranger crept up the stairs, entered the room, closed the door softly behind him, and started searching through the documents on the desk.   18. "Haven't you heard the saying 'Pride goes before a fall'?" the teacher asked the conceited student.

PART 30

Kevin made his way slowly to the school gym. He opened the door and there were the familiar things: the basketball nets, the rope ladders and the mattresses. Less than a year ago, they had been his world, but now—

"Hello, there!"

Kevin spun around, almost dropping his crutches in his surprise. A small, cheerful-looking boy was sitting on the horizontal bars. "Hello," said Kevin.

"You're Kevin Brown, aren't you?" asked the boy.

"Yes, that's right. I didn't think anyone would be here."

"I always come here," said the boy. "By the way, I'm Danny, from the primary school next door."

"What are you doing here, anyway?" Kevin demanded. "Don't you know that the gym is off limits?"

PART 31

1. We found him lying unconscious on the floor. He had fainted from loss of blood.   2. "Mary, I want you to go to the grocery store to buy these things for me: half a kilogram of butter, half a kilogram of flour, a packet of raisins, and a can of baking powder."   3. By the time it was evening, the men had finished harvesting the wheat.   4. "If they aren't at home, just leave the parcel on the doorstep," Mother said.   5. My brother, who has come home for the holidays, wants to invite you to his birthday party.   6. Although I wasn't free, I had to do it because if I didn't, who would?   7. It was a pleasant evening. I took my dog, Brownie, for a walk.   8. In a fright, the lizard dropped its tail, scurried up the wall, and hid in a crevice.   9. We discussed several topics, one of which was marriage and its problems.   10. I enjoyed reading the book *To Kill a Mockingbird* by Harper Lee. It won a Pulitzer Prize. 11. "Have you found what you wanted?" he asked. "Here, let me get it for you. There you are."   12. "What a marvelous plan!" I exclaimed. "I'm sure it'll succeed!"

PART 32

1. He shook out the contents of the wallet: a few coins, a photograph, and a crumpled ticket.   2. Some passers-by took pity on the child. They stopped to drop some money into the outstretched palm.   3. "If you want to succeed in school, John, you must concentrate," his father said.   4. "It's too late now!" she wailed.   5. "Be quiet! How can I hear the news broadcast if all of you talk so loudly?" he said.   6. "The letter, where is it? Quick, tell me!" she urged.   7. Huddled together for warmth, we waited for dawn to come. Perhaps we would be able to find our way home when it was light.   8. There was a long line of cars along the road: somewhere ahead, an accident had occurred, thus causing the traffic jam. 9. "That looks like Uncle Ryan's car! It is his car, isn't it?" she cried excitedly.   10. Did you know that "etcetera" is actually a Latin word?   11. The walking stick was made of ebony; it had an ivory handle. 12. Though deserts are hot and dry, certain plants, animals, and even people manage to survive there. 13. "It spends most of its life underground," the teacher told them. "That's why it has such small eyes." 14. Nobody knows exactly when the first Olympic Games were held. Records show that they took place in Olympia in Greece.   15. The following are some of the events: running, jumping, swimming, boxing, and wrestling.   16. "Get back!" he shouted to Wendy. "The bridge is rotten. It won't support your weight!"   17. I can't carry the bag; it's too heavy. Won't you help me carry it?   18. We were reluctant to leave; the final match was not over yet and the results of the contest not announced.   19. "William, have you finished your homework?" his father asked. "If you have, come and help me water the garden."

20. "I've been robbed! Call the police!" he cried. "All my money is gone!"   21. "Where did you get this, Eddie?" Alice asked. "Did you steal it? Come on, tell me!"

PART 33

1. At one time, books were very expensive; now, with the modern methods of printing, they are within everyone's reach.   2. The truth became obvious; Anna was not to blame for either of the mishaps.   3. In the box, you will find these things: a pair of scissors, a roll of bandages, a bottle of iodine, and some ointment.   4. I know what his answer will be: "Do as I say and not as I do."   5. Dictionaries are the most useful books; they can be found in the library, in the home, in the office, and sometimes in people's pockets, too.   6. We knew there was no way of escape; we had fallen into their trap.   7. Under the circumstances, his only way out was to accept neither proposition; in fact, it was the only possible way. 8. One road runs parallel with the shore; the other road, more to the west, leads to the lake.   9. There was no escape from the dust; it penetrated even through the slightest crack.   10. Some insects have wings; others do not.   11. There were many Africans on the ship; all of them were bound for Tasmania. 12. Two scouts stood at the entrance; the others lined the driveway.   13. I doubt that they will turn up today; they've never been so late before.   14. Sometimes, they go to work enthusiastically; at other times, they grumble and complain.   15. To say it is easy; to do it is an entirely different matter.   16. The fire lighted up the whole countryside; even from the road, we could see it.   17. Seen from his point of view, the situation was not hopeless; it needed only some expert handling.   18. If the earth is suitable, they will grow corn; if not, they will plant yams.   19. Each of the contestants tries his best to be the first to spear the animal; the one who does so wins the trophy.   20. "Did you say television is an aid to education? I don't agree with you," my mother said.   21. The rumor that the town had to be evacuated spread like fire. It created panic and fear in homes and in the streets.   22. "Hello, Peter! When did you come back?" William asked. "Why didn't you inform us of your arrival so that we could have met you at the railway station?"

PART 34

"Attention, please! Attention!" came the captain's voice over the loudspeaker. "I'm afraid we have to make an emergency landing—please fasten your safety belts." The passengers—a party of thirty schoolboys and their history teacher—did as they were told. They were on a study trip to Crete to explore some of the ancient temples and monuments. Mr. Biggs, the history teacher, stopped talking to the boys. Instead, he peered out of the window through his spectacles and muttered, "What a nuisance! I wonder where we are. Do you know, Jeffrey?" he asked the boy who sat beside him. Eighteen-year-old

Jeffrey Walton was the class monitor. "No, sir," said Jeffrey. "I can't make out a thing; it's very dark outside." As the plane descended to earth, the roar of the engines stopped further conversation. After a series of bumps and spins, the plane screeched to a halt.

PART 35

Around the hut was the river. I had only to look out of the house to see it; I could even see it through the spaces between the floorboards. It was the home of fish, crocodiles and strong currents.

I was eleven years old then, and I had grown up on the river. I know all about its secrets and powers for I heard my parents talk of it every day, and yet I was very afraid of it.

"You should try not to think that way, Son," my father advised. "The river gives us life: fish to eat and water to drink. Without it, how can the traders travel up and down? How can we then get money to buy things? Remember, Son: we fear only what we don't know."

"I'll try to think as you do, Father," I always replied, but I retained my fear of the murky waters.

Often, travelers on their way down the river would drop in at our house. They always had many stories to relate and I would sit for hours, listening to them.

PART 36

1. Although the sky was dark, it did not rain, as we had feared it would.   2. The burglar put on his gloves, switched on the flashlight, and shone it on the lock of the safe.   3. Thinking it was late, I hurried through my breakfast and dashed off to school.   4. The question was not as easy to answer as it seemed; it required a great deal of thought.   5. There were many interesting articles on display; some of them were my sister's handiwork.   6. Because of the floods, the examinations were postponed until further notice.   7. After a great deal of bargaining, the shopkeeper agreed to let us have both the vases for twenty dollars.   8. So far, only a few have managed to pass the test; there are many reasons for this.   9. One of the largest ports in this region, Port Deepwater, enjoys a flourishing trade.   10. They left the windows open, not knowing what damage the monkeys could do once they got into the house.   11. The police questioned the man and Philip took down their conversation.   12. At the age of five, Tim could read short stories, do simple arithmetic problems, and converse fluently in English; in fact, he was a remarkably intelligent child.   13. With a last great effort, I climbed the hillside and stood at its summit; the view was breathtaking.   14. The contents of the case, when it was opened, came as a great surprise to us: there was nothing inside but a pile of old newspapers!   15. During his stay here, he had only one complaint: he could not bathe every day because of the insufficient water supply.   16. "Are you sure that's the right way to fix it?" he asked. "Hadn't you better consult somebody first?"   17. Vultures

circled the area; they were waiting for the man to die in the desert heat.　18. Today's menu consists of the following: soup, fried chicken, an omelet, and fish curry.　19. Electricity serves many useful purposes; it works motors, generates heat, and provides light.　20. "There is nothing much with her," the doctor said. "Most of her illnesses are imagined."

PART 37

145 Hill Road,

Green Acres Park,

New Castle W5G23.

August 8th, 2001

Dear Mrs. Brown,

　　I am extremely grateful to you for inviting me to spend the holidays with you at Golden Sand Beach. A holiday by the sea is just what I need after the long hours of study, preparing for my end-of-the-term examination. I'm glad that's all over now.

　　I'm already looking forward to spending the week with you. How are Johnny, Tommy and Betty? I'm sure we'll have lots of fun together again at the beach.

　　I will be seeing all of you on August 12th. I will be coming to your house by train, but you needn't meet me at the station as I know the place well enough already.

　　Until then, bye-bye.

Yours lovingly,

Linda White

Vocabulary 隨身讀系列